THE
RECRUIT

FIONA PALMER

ABOUT THE AUTHOR

Fiona Palmer has been writing rural stories and women's fiction for years and is now indulging in her love of YA. It's not a big change considering she already writes about strong women who fight for what they want. She is a full-time writer and mum of two teens from rural Western Australia.

www.fionapalmer.com
@fiona_palmer

The Recruit
*The Mission
*The Deception
*The Crescendo

The Family Farm
Heart of Gold
The Road Home
The Sunburnt Country
The Outback Heart
The Sunnyvale Girls
The Saddler Boys
The Family Secret

Secrets Between Friends
*Sisters and Brothers

* - coming soon to print

For Jim Jim

ACKNOWLEDGEMENTS

This story wouldn't have come about without the help and guidance of a very important person. I can't thank you enough, Jim; for not only teaching me how to run fast as a child but for continuing to teach me new things later in life. You truly are an amazing person, and I'm blessed to have you in my life. Also to my friends and family who read my work and give support: my mum and dad, Tammy Stone, Lea Murray, Brodie Simmons, Jeni Wyatt and Jacinta Holmes, you girls are awesome. Thanks to Claire de Medici for another fabulous edit. To Rachael Johns, fellow author and friend who helps me out continually, thank you so much. A super big thanks goes to another author friend, Cathryn Hein! Cathryn, without you I don't think this book would be in print. Thank you so much for all your help and continued guidance with self publishing. You are a super star! And to all my dedicated readers, I hope you enjoy this series. Thank you for your support.

CHAPTER 1

'BLOODY HELL, I knew I shouldn't have come,' mumbled Jaz as the sweaty, skimpily clothed bodies danced around her.

For one, she was under-age and technically wasn't allowed in the night-club. Two, she couldn't find her best friend, Taylor; he'd gone to get drinks and probably got lost in the smoky, strobe-lit room. Three, she'd noticed a very drunk girl, one she knew but didn't like, being carted off towards the exit door by two creepy-looking blokes. And four, instead of all this, she could have been back at her other best friend Anna's house in her pjs eating popcorn, watching a movie and minding her own business. Anna, who lived two houses away from Jaz, was at home being her alibi so she could come to the club with Taylor.

If only she could mind her own business now. But Jasmine Thomas had a problem: she couldn't help but smell foul play. How she had the ability to sniff out trouble, she wasn't sure, though Anna would say it was because she created most of it herself. Sadly, Anna was probably right.

Jasmine put her hands on her hips and shifted her sore feet, her mind whirling. Sure, she could keep dancing, but the conspiratorial smirk those two guys had shared kept haunting her. She knew what they planned to do with that girl. At school Minka treated Jaz like scum while she pranced around with her dad's silver spoon in her mouth, but she still didn't deserve what she was about to get. No woman did.

With a shake of her head, Jaz pushed her way through the crowd in the direction she saw the guys take Minka. A few steps later she hit a hard chest and looked up ready to apologise, but her words caught in her mouth. A very tall, very sexy bouncer wearing a tight black T-shirt that showed every muscle had rendered her speechless. His eyes stayed on her; she couldn't tell their colour because of the lights in the club, but they seemed dark. He didn't smile, but she liked the way he studied her; it showed curiosity, not aggression. At least someone appreciated her slinky black dress, even if it wasn't the person she had worn it for. Hot bouncer guy drew his eyes away from her face and placed his strong hands on her arms, shuffling her to the side so he could continue past. He left a lasting imprint on her skin as he dissolved into the crowd. It wasn't that he'd been rough but more that she could feel his strength. Jaz shook her head slightly, remembering that she had been on a mission before the hot guy had stolen her thoughts.

She flexed her fingers and rolled her shoulders. Things were about to get ugly. 'I knew I should have worn my boots,' she mumbled. But Anna had insisted her commando boots didn't go with her little black dress. Jaz begged to differ; her boots went with everything and they were wonderfully durable and comfortable.

As she broke free of the dancing crowd, she pushed through the exit door. Another bouncer in a black shirt stood nearby. He didn't even glance at her; he was probably asleep with his eyes open. She couldn't blame him, there were blokes carrying girls out of this nightclub all the time, why would he suspect foul play in this case? It probably wasn't in his job description to care unless someone was punching someone inside the bar.

Outside was a narrow alleyway; the left led back to the main street, the right went deeper and darker. The light above the exit door illuminated the alleyway six metres either side.

Jaz shuddered as she thought of what might happen if she tried to stop this, and for half a second she wondered if she should go back and ask the bouncer to help.

Minka's whimpers caught her attention and she automatically followed the sound. 'Minka Schubach, you had better thank me,' she hissed to herself as she saw them just on the edge of the light.

Jaz could hear Minka's feet dragging along the pavement.

'Come on, sweetheart, we'll make your night,' said one of the guys as he held her face and began to kiss her.

Minka groaned again. She was hanging limply in their arms but trying to move her head away from him.

'You hold her first,' said the guy who had tried to kiss her. He sounded too excited and Jaz instantly felt shivers up her spine. Stepping towards them quickly, she spoke up.

'Hey, is she okay?' Jaz tried to sound like a concerned bystander.

She saw one of the guys panic, his eyes widening. But the other one turned to her and smiled. He was older, mid-twenties, which made preying on a seventeen-year-old much worse. He had barbed wire tattooed around his neck and was quite solid, but she was sure she could take him if she had to.

'Yeah, she's okay. Just too much to drink. We'll look after her,' said barbed-wire guy.

'Here, I'll help.' Jaz stepped closer, wondering how this was going to play out. Would she spook them enough to dump and run or would they fight for their prize?

'No. She's my girlfriend. I can handle it,' said barbed-wire, this time with more grit. There was something nasty in his eyes and his pupils like pin heads. It was time to try a new tact.

'I don't think she has a boyfriend. Minka, are you okay?' Jaz spoke to the drunk girl. Reaching out a hand, she touched her shoulder.

Minka mumbled something incoherent as her head hung loosely.

'What should we do?' asked barbed-wire's skittish mate. He had long, skinny arms like a monkey and looked ready to split.

'How about I take her home?' said Jaz.

'How about you piss off now before I get angry? Unless you want to join us?' Barbed-wire raked his eyes over Jasmine's body, his smile showing just how much he liked what he saw. Jaz instantly wanted to take a bath in disinfectant.

'That's it,' she said firmly. 'I've had enough. Just hand her over and be on your way.' Jaz held out her arm.

Barbed-wire grunted, pushed Minka into his mate and stepped towards Jaz. But Jaz didn't give him time to touch her. She knew surprise would be her best option. Reaching out she grabbed his wrist, spun him around, pulled his arm up his back, and pushed him face-first up against the wall. 'Did you not understand what I said?'

'Bitch!' he yelled. 'Do something,' he growled out to his mate as he tried to shake Jaz off. But she tightened her grip on his arm and yanked it higher.

'What the hell?'

Jaz almost laughed at his shock. 'Yeah, I bet you didn't expect that from little ol' me, now, did you?'

Behind them, his mate dropped Minka to the ground and stepped towards Jaz. She pushed forward on the guy she held so she could kick out behind with her foot, aiming for the approaching guy's crotch.

'Ooooh.' Clutching at his groin, monkey-arms went down like a sack of spuds.

'Huh, maybe these shoes aren't so bad after all,' she said admiring the points on Anna's black high heels.

While she was busy admiring her shoes her detainee managed to use his weight to pull from her grip, turning and ready to swing a hit at her face. But she blocked it and landed one on his jaw. And while he was getting over the shock of that, she gave him another one in the kidneys. Had he been a bit bigger she'd have to hit him in the groin too, but for now the kidneys would probably suffice.

'Do you want to stay and play some more with me? Huh? Like taking advantage of girls, do you?' She watched him think as she held her arms up ready and eager for a fight, hoping he'd take another swing. She was fired up now, she wanted to make this sicko hurt.

Instead, he backed away down the alley towards the main road, holding his bleeding nose and leaving his mate to hobble behind him. 'Crazy bitch,' he yelled as he went.

Jaz watched them until they had turned the corner before turning back to Minka.

Grabbing her arm, she helped Minka up off the ground. Her legs were dirty and she looked like a beggar, her gold dress smeared with dirt and stained with spilt drinks. Her hair was a tangled mess and she reeked of alcohol. What would Daddy think of his rich little girl now? Jaz felt only the slightest bit of pity.

'Are you okay?' she asked just as Minka bent over and hurled. Jaz stepped back. 'Ah, gross. Some thanks,' she said screwing up her nose.

After Minka finished, Jaz pulled her arm over her shoulder and guided her back to the main road. Minka's steps were shaky and she stumbled just as the hot bouncer opened the exit door to let two more girls out. He paused when he saw Jaz, his eyes flicking to Minka and then back to her, his eyebrow raised. Jaz gave him a smile to reassure him. Actually, the smile came naturally upon seeing his rippling arms. Man, he was fit.

The corner of his lips almost curved up as he shut the door, and Jaz had a feeling that if he'd smiled fully it would have softened that hard soldier-boy look he was rocking.

On the main street Jaz helped Minka sit against the nightclub wall. She was looking more with it, trying to push her blonde hair away from her face. She recognised Jaz, pulling a face she hissed like a cat stuck in a room with the dog she hates.

Jaz ignored her, but imagined knocking that expression from her face with her knuckles. With a sigh she pulled her phone from her bra and called for an Uber.

When it arrived she tried to help Minka into the car, but she shook her off, offering a glare instead of thanks. Yep, there was the Minka she knew.

'Jaz!' She turned to see Taylor jogging towards her, his long legs fluid with each step. 'Is everything okay?'

Jaz sighed. Taylor was perfect. He was the Mr Dreamy of Saint Christian College with his gorgeous tan, flawless skin, sexy smile and those summers' day blue eyes. He was a Michelangelo sculpture, chiselled and smooth. His jeans hugged his waist and the two top buttons were undone on his black dress shirt taking her focus for the moment.

He was also her best friend.

'Yeah, just sending Minka home.' Jaz leaned in and gave the Uber driver Minka's address as Minka sat staring out the window at Taylor. Jaz wasn't the only one who found him divine.

'See ya.' Jaz shut the door, and Minka shot her another one of her famous glares. Still no offer of thanks. Typical. Did Minka not realise what she'd just been saved from? Did she not care? Maybe she was too busy being angry because it was Jaz who saved her.

'What happened?' asked Taylor as he watched the Uber leave.

'Two guys were taking her down the alley for a good time. No matter how mean she is, no one deserves that,' she said with a shrug.

Taylor's eyes shot open in surprise and then he smiled. Jaz did her best not to melt.

'I would ask if you're okay, but I know better. I'm sure the other guys ended up worse?' Taylor reached for her hand, inspecting the redness appearing on her knuckles. 'Looks like you gave them a few?'

'Yeah, they didn't want to walk away. I had to convince them.'

Taylor sighed. 'I know you can take care of yourself, Jaz, but I still worry. You should've got help. Don't go off on your own, please?'

Jaz liked the way he kept hold on her hand and squeezed it gently.

'I know. I didn't think, I just acted. Next time I'll get help, okay?' Although Jaz doubted she would. She never stopped long enough to think about the danger factor.

'No, let's just hope there's no next time.' Taylor shook his head, as if he wasn't sure what to do with her. 'Do you want to go back inside?' He let go of her hand and placed it on her shoulder and smiled before sniffing the air and wriggling his nose.

'Um, no. Minka was sick and there seems to be a lingering smell. I wanna go home and shower for a long, long time.'

'Hmm, good plan. Come on, let's share an Uber,' said Taylor, shooting her a sympathetic smile.

It took three minutes for one to arrive and they both slid into the back, Taylor gave the driver directions. Heavy drum African music filled the car, rendering them both silent for the duration of the trip as they snaked their way through the streets of Perth. Jaz sunk back into the seat, enjoying being in Taylor's company, except for the vague smell that kept wafting through the car. Her shoes badly needed a clean.

Jaz stopped the Uber just down the road from Anna's house. 'I'll see you at school,' she said to Taylor as she climbed out.

'Take it easy, Jaz. Say hi to Anna for me.' He waved as she shut the door and watched the taxi leave.

With a sigh, Jaz turned and walked close to the tree line, keeping to the shadows. She didn't want neighbours dobbing her in.

When she came to Anna's huge house, she took her shoes off and hung them off her arm. Climbing up the nearby tree, she worked her way out across the large lilac branch to reach the roof of the house and towards

Anna's window. Having been best friends and almost-neighbours since childhood, this entry to Anna's room was a well-worn path.

When she climbed in, Anna was playing a game on her computer, as usual.

'Hey, you're home earlier than expected,' said Anna swivelling in her chair. Her room was huge with a queen-size bed and a wall-mounted flat-screen TV. But it was her computer set-up that looked like it belonged in a video gamer's den.

Anna's strawberry blonde, almot red hair was piled up on top of her head in a loose bun, two pencils stuck through it. She'd obviously been engaging in one of her favourite pastimes: studying.

'Yep, kinda fizzed out. I swear trouble just follows me,' said Jaz sitting down on the end of the bed. All she wanted was shower, put on her pjs and crawl into Anna's bed.

Anna turned off her screen and walked over to her. 'Oh no. What happened? What did you do?'

'Hey, what makes you think I did anything?'

Anna smiled. 'Years of experience being your best friend.' She jumped onto the bed beside her. 'Okay, dish!'

'First I need a shower, and then I'll tell you everything.'

'I'll be here waiting.'

Jaz got up and headed to the massive en suite, the large tiles cool on her feet and easing the pain from wearing heels.

She glanced in the wide mirror at her long, black hair, her olive skin that came from genetics and not the sun, and wondered if Taylor would ever see her as anything other than his friend. It was probably hard when they'd been besties since childhood and this crush had only surfaced in the last year. It was something she was finding hard to figure out. She couldn't lose him as a friend.

She would have pondered this further if the lingering smell of Minka hadn't crawled up her nose and made her gag. Minka had better be nicer at school now. But in the back of her mind Jaz knew she was expecting the impossible. Some things in her life would never change.

CHAPTER 2

'WHERE THE HELL is it?' Jasmine mumbled, lifting up black folders, shoving aside magazines and pens as she searched her desk. 'I'm sure I left it here!'

Her dark-painted nails scratched through her silky, black hair as if searching for a clue. She paced to her Queen size bed, kicking a pile of black sheets and a dark purple doona out of the way before bending down to search the black cavernous space underneath. Amid the odd socks and shoes that lay undisturbed, three old school books collected grey fluff beside a rag doll, minus its eye, long ago left abandoned – but still no sign of the necklace.

With a heavy sigh, she sat back on her heels and examined her surroundings. The dark grey carpets and deep purple curtains made it hard to see anything in the spacious but messy room. Not that she'd ever admit that to her mother; she'd had a pink fit when Jaz picked out her colour scheme, and had refused to help her paint the walls, still trying to convince her that maybe a light blue or yellow would be better than grey. But it was Jaz's room and she felt comfortable in the darkness... except when she couldn't find stuff, though that could be due to the fact her room needed a serious clean.

Slapping her hands over her eyes, she racked her brain trying to remember the last place she had seen it. She'd left it on her desk after her shower that morning.

Realisation struck Jaz like a hit to the head with a cricket bat. 'That little bugger!' she growled, wishing she'd thought of him sooner.

Jaz strode out of her bedroom, down the wide corridor to the other end, straight into her brother's room, and stumbled. Argh! It was so bright she had to wait until her eyes adjusted before she could start looking. The glint of her necklace hung from his bedpost, taunting her from the other side of his perfectly clean room. She was sure his shoes were colour-coded, along with his clothes. Jaz put her necklace on over her head, the medallion dropping between her breasts. She was about to leave but yanked at the crisp white sheets on his neatly made bed. A smile curled on her deep red lips. She knew he would hate that, Mr Oh-So-Tidy Simon, but he might think twice before going into her room. And what normal fourteen-year-old had a room that clean anyway.

'Jasmine, are you coming or not! We need to leave now or we'll all be late!' echoed her mother's voice up the staircase.

Jaz bellowed back as she grabbed her black school bag and headed down to the foyer. 'Yeah, yeah, keep your shirt on, Mum.'

She watched the expression on her mother's face change from her normal calm to irritation as she looked Jaz over with her sharp eyes. Tasha Thomas's blonde hair was pulled back into a hard bun and her cream skirt suit was immaculate. It went with the face she was making: like she was just about to 'tut tut' along with an exaggerated eye roll.

'Jasmine, *tuck in* your shirt please,' Tasha said as she gestured to Jaz's white school shirt. 'We pay good money for you to attend a top school and I just wish you would be a little appreciative of what you have. You'd look so pretty if you did your hair and didn't wear so much... black.' Tasha's eyes roamed down to Jaz's thick black stockings and Doc Martens. 'Oh God, I'm going to get another call from them, aren't I? And is your skirt getting shorter or do they make them like that now?' Tasha's eyes were drilling holes in her daughter's red tartan skirt.

Personally, Jaz couldn't see what was wrong; all the girls wore their skirts this short. She didn't even mind the stupid thin black tie they had to wear, the guys had to wear it too.

'You look like a high-school dropout,' sneered her brother, who was waiting patiently by his mother's side with his shirt crisp and folded into his pants as carefully as origami. He was short for a fourteen-year-old, like his hormones hadn't kicked in yet, still baby-faced with soft blond hair, fair skin and their mother's blue eyes.

'Better than dressing up like a fifty-year-old school teacher. You're just missing the tweed jacket.' Jaz snorted at her own joke.

Simon was about to open his mouth but he was cut off.

'That's enough, you two. Into the car.' Tasha checked her diamond-encrusted watch as she followed them both out to the sleek, silver Mercedes. At the door, she stopped Jaz and reached for the necklace around her neck. The medallion slipped into her mum's hand. 'Jaz, I told you not to wear that. Why can't you keep it in your room, where it will be safe?'

'It's safe on me, Mum,' said Jaz pleadingly.

Tasha gave her a pained look. 'But what if it's lost or someone spots it and steals it? It's eighteen-carat gold.'

Jaz had heard this all before. 'It's all I have of him. Please, Mum.' The only reason Jaz had it was because she'd found it while snooping through her mother's things a few years back.

'I wish you hadn't found it, Jaz. I wish I hadn't told you it was from your biological father.'

Jaz sighed. 'But he's not alive, and seeing as you won't tell me anything about him, I think of this as a compromise,' she said slipping the medallion back down inside her clothes.

The few times her mum had opened up and let some details slip – telling Jaz how much her smile was like her dad's, or that she was strong and determined like him – Tasha's eyes had not been able to hide the truth: she had really loved him at some stage. Jaz had no idea why it all went south. Tasha refused to tell her anything, except that he'd died in a car crash. So, this was her life. Clinging to a pendant of a man she knew nothing about.

Her mother sighed. 'Okay, okay, you win. Just please keep it hidden under your clothes. Come on, we have to go.'

Jaz smiled on her way to the car. Her mum was getting soft in her old age.

'I'm in the front, knucklehead,' Jaz said as Simon reached for the car door.

The sprinklers popped up and began watering the dark, green lawn as Tasha pulled out of the paved driveway and onto the road. Simon called out from the back seat, the leather squelching under him as he leaned forward. 'Mum, don't forget I have my computer lessons with Dad after school, I need to be on time, please.'

'I won't forget, darling. How about you, Jasmine, do you want a ride to Pax's today?' asked Tasha, keeping her eyes firmly on the road ahead.

'No thanks, Mum. I don't mind the walk, it warms me up before my workout.'

Tasha sighed again. 'I do worry about you walking down there. It's not the best part of town.'

'Come on, Mum. I'm old enough to take care of myself, you know that. Why don't you come down for a workout? It's been ages since we've sparred together... and Pax keeps saying he hasn't caught up with you for so long!' Pax ran The Ring, an old friend of her mums and a relative of Anna's. So he was practically family.

Tasha risked a long glance at her daughter. 'I know, darling. I'll try to make it one day so you can beat me up, yet again. But I'm so out of touch with all that now. Work keeps me so busy.'

Jaz slouched in the front seat as she swallowed her mother's excuse. She'd been coming to the gym less and less, spending more and more time at the law firm, and Jaz missed her. It was her mum who introduced her to the gym, before Jaz could even walk, and then as she grew spending every afternoon there teaching her martial arts as if her life depended on it. But these days her mum's job and social calendar kept her pretty busy. She had married her step dad, Paul, when Jaz was only a toddler. They then had Simon and she slowly morphed into a career woman a wealthy wife. Paul had been rich and his job still payed big bucks. Yet Jaz felt as if she didn't belong, instead The Ring felt more like home.

Jaz stared out the tinted window watching the two-storey houses flash by. Her pulse started to throb in her neck as they approached Taylor's house. His dad's red SUV appeared first, stationary in the wide, circular driveway, Taylor's blue Mustang beside it. Craning her neck she watched the jarrah double doors but they didn't open; she glanced back to his Mustang.

'Would you like us to go back so you can get a better look at Loverboy?' Simon teased.

Jaz swung around fast, her hand flying. Simon had been ready, hiding behind his school bag, but the force she'd used caused his bag to slam into his face.

'Mum!' he whined.

'Jasmine, I wish you would behave,' Tasha said, hardly flinching.

'He's baiting me.'

'And you're falling for it.'

Jaz crossed her arms and Simon slunk back into the leather seat, both travelling in silence until they pulled up outside the large metal gates of Saint Christian College.

'Bye, kids!' Tasha yelled through the car window as they climbed out. Simon said goodbye while Jaz raised her hand in a half-wave and took off along the pathway, her hair flying behind her.

'Hey Jazzy, over here.'

Anna Johnson, best buddy in the world, waited by a shady tree that grew in the corner of a large manicured lawn, in front of the towering brick school. Teenagers ambled past into the building, while others gathered outside waiting for friends. As soon as Jaz saw Anna twirling her hair she knew she must have something to tell her; it was such sign whenever Anna was trying to contain herself. Jaz threw her bag down on the lawn as she joined her best friend on the wooden seat. Anna sucked in a deep breath, her green eyes bulging.

'Go on, spit it, I can see you're dying to tell me something!'

Anna's soft green eyes brimmed with excitement and the small freckles on her delicate face highlighted her fair skin. 'You'll never guess what happened this morning,' she teased, finally releasing her hair from her fingers.

'Um… you hacked into the school's computer again to see what grade you got in English?'

'Don't be a knob! No, I got here early because Mum had to get to work, and you know who was here, sitting right here on this very spot?' Anna was practically bouncing on the seat.

'Calm down, anyone walking past would think you were trying out for the drama club. Honestly, that's the last impression we want to give.'

Anna rolled her eyes while Jaz smiled.

'Ricky?'

Anna nodded.

'Really? Did he say anything? Did you talk to him?' Jaz pressed.

'Well, no… but he might have if I had got close enough,' said Anna with her standard cheeriness.

Anna might have been the brightest person Jaz knew, but she could also be utterly clueless. 'Anna! Tell me you talked to him… did you chicken out?' Jaz rested her arms on Anna's shoulders and shook her, already guessing the answer.

'Well, yeah, I was kind of scared.'

'You git! He was probably waiting for you; maybe he was making a move.'

'He had his nose stuck in a book, I doubt he was waiting for me,' said Anna screwing up her cute freckled nose.

'But everyone knows we always sit here, it's our spot and nobody comes near, unless they're new or unbelievably stupid.'

'Who's unbelievably stupid? I hope you're not talking about *moi?*'

They both looked up. 'Taylor, don't sneak up on us like that,' said Jaz, trying to hide the discomforting feeling that surged through her, as it always did around him. As usual he managed to make a pair of black school pants look delectable, and with his blond hair flicked up at the top he could have easily come from a modelling shoot. Usually she preferred the strong soldier rustic type. The bouncer from the other night flashed before her eyes, but she pushed it away, he was way out of her league.

'So, do I get to find out what you were talking about?' he said raising a perfect eyebrow, his school bag hanging from his shoulder. He could make the simplest things look cool.

Anna shook her head and tried to hide behind her cascade of strawberry blonde hair, but Jaz jumped in. 'Ricky was on our seat this morning and Gutless Wonder here didn't go talk to him.'

Anna sucked in a breath and shot daggers her way.

Jaz put her hand on Taylor's arm, enjoying the warmth through his shirt. 'Anna, it's only Tay, he's like… been our friend since the first grade. He probably knows more dirty secrets about you than I do!'

Anna relaxed, and almost smiled as she squinted up at Taylor. 'You know, you might just be right. How lucky we are that you don't blab to your other friends about us.'

'I wouldn't dare. Jaz would likely kick my butt and have me begging for mercy,' he said giving Jaz a wink. 'Besides, I don't think they would be interested in you two rejects,' Taylor finished jokingly. The girls automatically lashed out. He caught Anna's hand but took a hit to the guts from Jaz. 'Oomph, no fair, Jaz,' he said rubbing his belly. 'You know it doesn't do much for a bloke's ego when he's always getting beaten up by a girl. Blokes like to be the stronger ones... or at least think we are.'

'Oh please, somebody give him a tissue,' Anna laughed.

Jaz smiled. 'Maybe next time you'll think twice about a smartarse comment. You know we don't like your other friends, they're very snobby and just plain mean.'

'Yeah, and why is it that you like them again?' asked Anna tilting her head to the side. But they weren't expecting an answer. They knew that Taylor moved in different circles with his family, and that deep down he liked being popular. But he'd never once dissed them and because of their friendship all the other kids left them alone. Besides the odd snide comment from Minka when he wasn't looking.

A short blast rang out over the PA and small groups slowly merged together as they headed inside the building.

'Come on, we better get moving. I've got Mr Noble up first and you know how he likes to make a spectacle of anyone who's late, so I'll catch up with you two later,' he said before taking off. 'Oh, Jaz, you gonna be at training?'

Her heart pounded an extra hard beat as she nodded.

'Cool,' he replied before striding off into the merging traffic of uniformed bodies.

Anna watched her friend for a while before speaking. 'And you think I'm chicken... When are you going to fess up your feelings for Tay?' she asked as they moved off.

Jaz reluctantly took her eyes away from Taylor's lean figure. 'Come on, Anna, it's different. We've been friends too long, I can't risk losing that. Besides,' she added sadly, 'I know he doesn't feel the same way.'

'How would you know when you haven't even asked him?' Anna said before putting her arm around Jaz's shoulders. 'Don't worry, we'll sort something out. Come on, let's get to another exciting lesson of biology, whoopee… not. You might be able to dissect a frog; I know how much you love gross stuff.'

Jaz smiled. 'And Minka likes to faint at anything gross-related. That would be a highlight.'

'Remember the last time she fainted and hit her nose?' Anna laughed.

Jaz smiled. 'You always know how to cheer me up.'

On her way to her form room she passed a circle of guys on the inside quadrangle who looked like they were shoving someone around. Jaz kept walking, more concerned about getting to class, but in the gap of the guys she saw a familiar face.

Simon.

Then she heard what the guys were saying, teasing her brother, trying to goad him into a fight. She skidded to a halt just as one guy punched Simon somewhere near his chest.

That was it. Nobody teased her half-brother but her. Throwing her bag down she pushed her way into the middle of the bullies' circle to stand in front of Simon.

'You okay, Si?'

He was rubbing his chest, but he nodded.

Now she turned to face the older boys. 'Think it's funny, do you? Like picking on people smarter than you? Well, now you can deal with *me*. Who's first?' She stood there challenging them, waving them on with her hands while daring them with her eyes.

One of them, the ring leader she guessed, was solid and wore a stud earring in his left ear. He puffed out his chest and laughed. 'I don't hit girls,' he said. Jaz hadn't seen him before, and so she assumed he was new and hadn't yet heard of her.

'Well, I don't discriminate,' she said, raising her hands. In the back of her mind she knew this was a bad idea. She was already on thin ice at the school over the years for fighting.

The other guys took a few steps back. They didn't look so tough now. Jaz was itching for one of them to make a move just so she could bust their butts. The one with the earring, who had hit Simon, stood tall, shaved head and a sneer on his lips as he tried to intimidate her.

'You come near my brother again and you'll have to deal with me. I don't like bullies.'

A boy with face fuzz and pimples leaned over and whispered something to the dude with the earring before he turned and left, taking the rest of the crowd with him. Earring-boy gave her an unimpressed glance before turning and following the others.

'I guess your reputation is still alive and well,' said Simon as he picked up his scattered books.

Jaz put her hand on Simon's shoulder. 'If they bother you again, you tell me.'

'You can't fight all my battles, Jaz,' he sighed while putting his bag on his shoulder.

'And why not? You got the brains, I've got the brawn, together we're unbeatable,' she said with a laugh. 'Come on, we better get to class before we're both in trouble.'

'Thanks, sis,' he said before turning and running towards the nearest door.

Jaz followed along at a slower pace. She was a little disappointed no one had thrown a punch. She did love a good fight, but usually it was with her mates at The Ring. Maybe another day, she thought.

CHAPTER 3

Jaz was mesmerised. Yes, the wooden bench seat in the gymnasium was hard on her butt and her white breeches were a bit tight, but Taylor occupied the rest of her thoughts. He was just so cool. Okay, so the get-up in fencing wasn't as revealing as a pair of footy shorts, but it was the way Taylor moved that was wonderful, his steps so graceful, his arm speed so quick and his riposte so decisive. Jaz wasn't great at remembering all the names of positions and techniques in fencing but that didn't matter, she could still make the moves.

Taylor was right into fencing, and anything else different, including his passion for guns. His dad was the Deputy Commissioner of Operations for the police and had a huge gun collection. Taylor had shown her a few times over the years, and he would ramble on every time his dad acquired a new gun. He probably thought she was interested but Jaz just liked the way the words rolled off his tongue and the way he spoke so passionately.

'Hey, you? Finished practice?' asked Anna as she walked into the school's large gym. It had grandstands on either side of the court, and two fencing mats were set up in the middle, where Taylor and Reece were bouting.

Jaz lifted her mask up off the bench so Anna could sit down. 'Just about.'

They watched for a few minutes as Taylor won another point.

Anna sighed. 'Wow, Taylor makes it look so sexy.' Jaz glanced at Anna, who held up her hands. 'Hey, I'm just saying... no wonder you joined.'

'Hmm.' When Jaz had joined the fencing team – mostly to be near

Taylor – she hadn't realised how much she would need fast reflexes and pinpoint precision. Over time, though, she'd found that fencing was a battle of the body, mind and spirit between athletes, and she got that, it was an extension of what she did at Pax's gym. Now she enjoyed it as much as Taylor did and she liked beating the other boys. She liked being the only girl on the team.

She watched as Taylor lunged to finish his attack, then she turned back to Anna. 'So, did you memorise a few more books in the library?'

Anna rolled her eyes. 'Don't mock me, because you know you need me. I'm the smartest friend you've got.'

'Anna you're the smartest kid in the whole of Perth. And of course I'm glad that you're my friend – and not just because of that marvellous mind of yours. So, you coming to The Ring too?'

Anna tossed her long hair over her slim shoulder. 'Yep, never know when Pax will be off. He's always been capricious.'

'He's been *what*? Stop showing off! How many times have I asked you not to use big fandangled words I don't understand? Speak plain English, please.'

Anna laughed, her green eyes sparkling and her freckles creasing in her smile.

'Thomas, over here, now!' shouted Coach Belmore, who was dressed in their team tracksuit of red, black and white.

Jaz swore under her breath as Coach Belmore pointed his finger at her. He probably fancied himself as a modern-day Zorro with his pointed triangle of facial hair on his chin. She collected up her mask and picked up her weapon before heading towards the coach and the rest of the team, as Anna pulled out a book from her bag and began to read.

Taylor was just putting his mask down near his feet as she stood next to him. 'Hey, what's Coach want now?' she whispered to him.

He ran his hand through his hair and adjusted it. 'Pep talk, I reckon.'

Jaz loved the way he leaned in close when he answered. He smelled divine, like an expensive men's aftershave.

'Okay, Team Amaris! This year it's our turn to win,' shouted Belmore, even though the six of them were huddled closely around him. Jaz was sure she felt spit spray and leaned back a fraction.

'We have these two, who are going to do us proud.' He motioned to Jaz and Taylor. 'But they can't do it alone, so don't forget training on Thursday; that's *you*, Sutton!' He pointed to the largest guy in the group, who almost snapped his head to attention. 'Macintosh, don't forget your plastron, and Benson please, for the love of God, remember your sabre. It's no good fighting with your hand, son. Right, off you go. Get some rest.' Coach Belmore clapped them off as the boys headed to their change rooms while Jaz went to the girls rooms.

She packed up her gear and dressed in her cargo pants and black hoodie, and put her Dr Martens back on. As she headed back to Anna, Jaz was busy putting in her earphones for her phone when an arm closed over her shoulder. She didn't need to look to know it was Taylor. Why couldn't he kiss her as easily as he put his arm around her? But no, he always kept things chummy between them, as if she were his best *male* friend. Seriously, was he ever going to notice she wasn't one of the boys?

'What're you listening to?' His breath caressed her cheek as he spoke.

'Hayley Williams.' And when she got a blank stare, she added, 'You know, from Paramore.'

'Oh, yep. What else? Still listening to Pink too?'

She smiled and nodded. For a guy who knew Jaz so well, he was completely blind to how she was feeling about him.

'You off to the gym?'

'Yep, with Anna. Pax is off on one of his adventures. What about you? To the firing range?'

He laughed, so sweetly it sent tingles down her back.

'Yep, they got a new Schmidt & Bender scope I wanna try out. You should come with me next time and I can show you.'

'Sure, sounds great. It's been a while.' She'd no sooner finished than Taylor nodded.

'Can I give you ladies a lift?' he asked as Anna joined them.

'Oh yes, please. Come on, let's go!'

Anna looped her arm through Taylor's and they left the school gym. Outside it was almost deserted except for the after-school-sports kids leaving. Jaz noticed a guy with a full-on beard leaning against a black car. He wasn't the usual type to hang around here. Clean-shaven and expensive suits were more the norm, not black jeans and a demin jacket. The other thing that struck Jaz was how his eyes were watching them; more to the point, Anna and Taylor.

Jaz caught up to her friends but kept her eye on the guy with the bushman's beard. He had that biker vibe about him, maybe he was a dealer for the rich kids? After Taylor helped Anna into the front of his Mustang, Jaz got his attention. 'Hey, Tay. Do you know that bloke?'

She didn't point but gestured with her eyes to across the road.

'Nup, why?'

'Don't know.' She shrugged. 'He was watching you like he knew you.'

'He probably just likes my car. It's not just a chick magnet,' he said with a laugh.

Jaz climbed into the back while Taylor and Anna sat in the front. As he drove off, she couldn't help but glance back. The guy was still there watching them leave. Maybe he did just love a good classic car?

On the ride to The Ring, Anna and Taylor chatted about guns. But Jaz couldn't wait to get to the gym. She loved it; it felt like home and she didn't care that it was in a rough neighbourhood. They lived in richville in between the Swan River and the Indian Ocean, but The Ring was in a whole different area, no designer gardens or multi-storey houses. Just the scraps left when development took over the area. The wealthy wanted to clean it up, to push all those people out and redevelop the area, but Jaz liked it. It felt real.

'Still rubbing Saint Michael's back?' Anna was looking over her shoulder, watching Jaz play with the pendant around her neck. An eighteen-carat gold disc depicting Saint Michael. Her finger ran over the engraving on the back. *Salvatore*

'Yeah, I can't help it.'

'Saint Michael the Archangel, field commander of the army of God, leading God's armies against Satan's forces,' said Anna. 'I bet he was hot. Your dad.'

'I guess I'll never know.' From time to time she would wonder about him, especially those days when she felt so different. Her silky, black hair and darker skin made her the odd one out in all their family portraits, but her blue eyes kept the link to her mum and her brother. When she saw them in the mirror, that's what she clung to. She didn't even have a photo of her biological father, nothing, zilch. Only the medallion.

'So, where do you think Pax is off to this time?' asked Taylor, changing the subject.

'My bet is overseas somewhere.' Anna smiled.

'Ha, talk about hedging your bets, would you like to be more specific and pick a country? I reckon he'll be off doing another bloody course in something,' said Jaz.

'Probably on how to prune bonsai trees,' added Anna before laughing.

It's true. Pax loved doing all sorts of weird courses. He had certificates in everything from Thai cooking to Woodwork 101.

Taylor pulled up next to the uneven footpath alongside a big, white, rectangle building with a flat roof and THE RING painted across the front in blue and red, now faded and flaking. Pax lived next door in a house that was built like Fort Knox with window bars and alarms. A must, apparently.

'Thanks, Tay,' Jaz said as she stepped out of the Mustang. 'See ya tomorrow.'

'Yeah, don't shoot anyone living.' Anna smiled and waved energetically as he drove off. 'Kinda wish we were going with him. I like spending time with Tay and I know *you* do,' she said with a wink.

Jaz sighed. Yes, she did.

When Jaz walked inside the gym, she was greeted by the smell of the mats, the leather from the gloves and sweat. She took a deep breath, feeling right at home. Maybe she was weird, but she didn't care.

Inside, a boxing ring stood in the back corner of the room with a large floor mat in front of it. A few boxing bags and speedballs were along the side wall where Jimbo, a large, black guy with huge muscles, pounded away. Jimbo was a regular, along with Niles, who was a very tall furniture removalist with no hair, and Tick, a twenty-five-year-old half-Asian street-smart guy who had reformed himself by coming to Pax's gym instead of getting drawn up into the street warfare. Tick could kick higher than any-one she'd seen and he was helping her learn his secret. There were a couple of other guys who came seasonally, and Bags, who taught the boxing classes and Jaz loved the most, but this lot were the main crew.

Then there was Pax.

'There's my girls,' his warm voice spread over them like hot gooey chocolate. He was sixty-odd, middle filling out – too much beer apparently, though Anna reckoned it was his love of pastries – but he still had most of his dark hair and wore steel-rimmed glasses when at his computer. He smelled like cinnamon and coffee.

'Hiya, Pax,' they both said, each wrapping their arms around him.

Pax was Anna's great-uncle and he'd brought the gym before they were born. He was a computer geek like Anna and the words computer and gym just didn't seem to go together. But if you knew Pax, then you knew of his love of Muhammad Ali.

Pax was also the grandfather Jaz never had and the reason she and Anna were friends. Tasha would bring Jaz for training and Anna would be on Pax's knee at the computer. Being the same age they hit it off straight away, even though they were opposites it didn't seem to stop them growing an amazing friendship over the years.

'So, where to now?' Jaz asked, nodding towards the stuffed black carry bag beside him.

Pax tapped his large nose. 'Ah, you'll just have to wait and see when I return.' The same old answer. 'Think bright colours, beautiful landscapes and water.' The same old clues too.

'Are you going to Hawaii? Bali?' Anna asked. But Pax just smiled and shook his head. They followed him into his office, positioned behind a huge glass window that was also a two-way mirror. Pax said he'd had it installed so no one could watch him playing games on his computer and he could see if a new customer came in.

'Think quick.' Pax threw his set of keys to Jaz, which she caught with one hand. 'You right to run the place for me again?' he asked.

Jaz laughed and rolled her eyes. This was nothing new. Over the last two years Pax had started giving Jaz his keys to the gym while he was away. She looked forward to these moments of responsibility and loved that Pax trusted her.

'I know,' sighed Pax. 'You run it more than I do. I should probably pay you more.'

'She'd like that,' added Anna. 'Can I use your stuff while you're gone, Pax?'

'Sure thing, sweets. Just stick to the simple stuff, hey?' In other words, don't go hacking into 'major' stuff. 'I don't wanna come home to the cops,' he laughed as he caressed Anna's check. 'All right, I'd better head off or I'll miss my flight.'

'Ohh, I told you it'd be overseas,' said Anna.

'Come on,' groaned Jaz. 'He could be going to Sydney, that's not overseas.'

'Oh, yeah.'

'And you're supposed to be the smart one,' Jaz joked as she wrapped her arm around Anna while following Pax through the back door to the small carpark.

He gave each of them a kiss on their forehead, his whiskers scratching as he said a final goodbye. 'See you in a few weeks or so.' Never anything solid; typical Pax. Footloose and fancy free.

He climbed into his little red hatchback, throwing his bag in the back. Pax reckoned he didn't need a fancy car, someone would only pinch it around this neighbourhood. He wasn't a materialistic person, didn't need status or flashy things, hence his gym.

'I'll be at the computer,' said Anna after his car had zoomed out of sight.

'Okay.' The breeze blew a few strands of hair across Jaz's face as she looked down at her hand and the big bunch of keys, an eight-ball hanging off them. 'Guess I'll go clean some mats,' she said as she followed Anna back inside.

CHAPTER 4

Jaz picked at her salad as the cafeteria chaos settled to its standard lunchtime hum. Anna sat on the other side of the wooden table, poking her fork at a stubborn bit of carrot that was refusing to play nice.

'No point starving yourself, it won't change how you look. Besides, I heard chubby cheeks are in,' came a nasally upper-class voice.

Jaz didn't have to look up to know Minka was standing there with her standard *You're the scum I scrape off my shoe* face.

Anna dropped her fork and tried to look unaffected, but Jaz knew better. She saw the twitch in the corner of her smooth lips and the hurt in Anna's eyes. Poor Anna believed what they told her. It pissed Jaz off to think that Minka thought herself above everyone else, enough to mess with other people who had never done anything to her. It was this schoolyard bullshit that really irked Jaz, made her so keen to finish school.

Jaz caught Anna's eye and winked. 'Really? Well, I definitely heard that looking like a broomstick was out. Maybe you could grab the one shoved up your arse and fly away. Off you go.' Jaz waved to where Minka usually sat with her clique.

'Bye-bye,' added Anna, who was looking much better. They both went back to their lunch, leaving Minka to scoff and mutter under her breath as she sashayed away.

'Thanks,' said Anna as she finally speared a carrot.

Jaz dropped her fork ready for a rant. 'You know I don't understand school and this so-called pecking order. It will all mean jack crap after we've left. And you would have thought that saving Minka would count for something, but if anything she's ten times worse!' Jaz watched as Minka sat next to Taylor, resting her hand on his arm while making sure Jaz was watching. 'How does he put up with her?'

'Easy, it's called being a two-faced bee-atch and Minka's got it down pat!'

Jaz laughed and held up her hand so Anna could give her a high-five.

Ten minutes later, as they were finishing, Taylor came by with Minka, who was so close to him you'd think they were stuck together with double-sided tape. While in Taylor's company, Minka was polite and civil (if even a little over-performed), but the moment his head was turned, her ugly side reared like the venomous snake she truly was.

'Hey, the joy of brushstrokes and paint smears with Miss Burnstein. You coming?' Taylor asked with a shake of his blond hair.

She almost said yes. *Yes, a thousand times I'd go with you, Taylor.* But when Minka spoke in that high-pitched whine – 'Yeah, come with us.' – and looped her arm through Taylor's and smiled so sweetly Jaz thought she'd soon be in a sugar coma, Jaz stood up. 'Nah, I've got a few things to do. I'll catch you later.'

As Jaz rose, Anna quickly scrambled to follow.

'What?' Jaz said, catching Anna's expression.

Anna laughed. 'Really, you have stuff to do?'

'Hmm, no. I'd just rather scrub the men's loo with a toothbrush than walk next to her.'

'Okaaay. So, I'll see you at the end of school?' Anna asked as she unlocked her locker and took out a few books. Jaz just grabbed her bag as the class bell sounded.

'Nup, I'm gonna cut.'

'Jasmine Thomas!'

'Well, I have to. That heinous bitch has made me cross, so I'm gonna go to The Ring and unleash some frustration. I'll catch you tomorrow, okay.'

Anna was still glaring at her until Jaz hugged her goodbye.

'Tomorrow, okay?' Jaz repeated as students filed past them and into their classrooms.

'Yeah, tomorrow. Don't get caught leaving!'

Jaz flicked her hair over her shoulder, the white of her shirt making the dark strands stand out. 'You know me.'

'Yes,' said Anna with her hands on her hips as she watched Jaz leave. 'Yes, I do.'

Jaz took the corridor to the left, past the last stragglers, and up a set of stairs that headed towards the teachers' staffroom. This was the key to her escape: heading right towards the lions' den and facing the danger head on. She crouched down past the long window, avoiding the chatting and coffee-drinking teachers who had a free period, and pushed through the outside door that led to a small balcony. It was a dead end, but next to it was the sports shed and she could make the roof by climbing over the edge of the balcony. Just as she was about to go she saw one of the teachers come out, a phone pressed to their ear and chatting away.

Jaz cursed. She was going to be caught for sure.

The teacher paused as if the conversation on the phone got serious. It was all the time Jaz needed. Without looking back, she went up and over the peak on the sports shed to the other side. The large brick wall of the school boundary was just beside it. There was a three-metre gap but a well-placed tree branch gave her a simple jump, swing and drop onto the top of the brick wall. A little jump to a pine tree on the other side and she was home free. While behind the cover of the tree, she dived into her bag and pulled out her thin hoodie to hide her uniform. Then she began the twenty-minute run to the gym; all the while her eyes kept a sharp lookout for teachers and the local tattletales. This area was home to a few oldies who had nothing better to do all day except look out their windows to report stray school kids. It hadn't taken her long to figure out which houses to avoid.

Jaz ran hard for the last ten minutes, increasing her speed until the gym came into view, then she slowed down. She didn't have to open the gym today, because Bags was here already doing his boxing classes. Tick and Niles had keys too; Pax trusted them all, and they banded together to keep the place running while he was away. Jaz had school and the others had day jobs but somehow they all managed it.

'Hey, Jaz,' said Bags as he threw a blue towel over his wide shoulder. Bags was in his forties, tall and an aspiring writer, but he'd always been a boxer. His dad had been a well-known one, a good mate of Danny Green and had taught Bags everything he knew, though Bags didn't fight professionally like his dad. He much preferred to teach boxing. Bags said getting his fingers busted made it too hard to type and he never knew when his creativity might strike.

Bags reached out his muscled arm and rested it on Jaz's shoulder. 'Jaz?' he said, leaning his head to one side, his eyebrows raised. 'Are you cutting school?'

'No, I've got a free period,' she said with a straight face. She could see Bags weighing up her words.

'Yeah, and I'm off to have a mud facial and get my toenails painted.' Bags laughed as he brushed his hand over his prickly short hair. Then he looked at her with those hazel eyes, which probed deeper. It was the concern she saw in them that made her fess up.

'I just need to let off some steam. My buttons have been pushed.'

'I have some free time, wanna throw some punches?'

Her lips tugged into a huge grin. 'Really? I'd love to… and I'm already warmed up.'

Bags pushed her off towards the locker room and swung his towel at her like he was herding sheep. 'All righty then, go and get ready.'

Jaz practically skipped to her locker, and changed into her crop top and yoga pants. She threw her school uniform into her school bag before heading out to join Bags in the ring.

'Up you come, sunshine,' he said, parting the ropes for her to climb in before handing her gloves. Bags, who was nicknamed because he really was a punching bag to his students, put on the hand pads.

'All right, start with a few jabs.' Bags widened his stance ready for her attack. His muscles flexed and rose like balloons filled with helium. Another reason Jaz loved the gym so much: all the guys were so fit. Not that she was interested in any of them like that. Christ, most were old enough to be her dad, but she could appreciate the work they put in to keep their muscled forms.

Jaz settled into a rhythm, pounding against the pads on Bags' hands.

'Bloody hell, Jaz,' said Bags shaking out his hands. 'Whose face are you imagining?' But he didn't wait for her answer as he got her to do some uppercuts.

After another thirty minutes, when he was sure that she was hurting, he called a stop. 'That will do you today, I think you've vented enough. I know you could keep doing this all day if I let you.'

'Thanks, Bags, that was great,' said Jaz in between deep breaths.

'No worries. Look, I better head off. Say hi to the guys when they get in and I'll catch you soon.' Bags threw her towel over the top of her head.

'Righto, bye.' Jaz towelled some of her sweat off as she watched him leave. She had the gym to herself. This was so much better than school, even if she had mats to wash today.

Ten minutes later Jaz had her earphones blaring music, bucket and sponge by her side. Dark silk cascaded over her shoulder and shook with each push of her arm as she scrubbed the large blue mat. She stood, throwing the sponge back into the bucket and then broke out in a little dance as she sang a few lines from her favourite Avicii song. As she bopped away and squeezed out the sponge, a sudden tap on the shoulder made her jump.

'Yeah,' she yelled as she turned and pulled out her earphones.

The tall, gorgeous guy in front of her smiled and she dropped her voice down a few decibels before asking, 'Can I help you?' She wouldn't mind helping the stranger with deep dark eyes that gave her chills. Or maybe it was the way his jeans hung off his hips. Why did he seem so familiar?

'Is Pax here?'

'Nup.'

'It's still his gym, yeah?'

Jaz flicked her hair from her eyes before answering and gave the stranger a head-to-toe inspection. Why was he so familiar? His grey T-shirt fitted his muscled chest to perfection. God she loved working at the gym.

'Yep.'

Who was he and how did he know Pax? He didn't look that old, maybe twenty-five at most, so what would he want with Pax? His body was long and lean; he definitely kept fit, so maybe he was an instructor. A scary instructor at that. As handsome as he was, her radar was screaming 'danger' and she couldn't read his expression. His eyes were dark, almost menacing, like he could kill if he was ordered to. And that's when she realised why he was familiar. He was the bouncer from the nightclub. The one who reminded her of a soldier. She never forgot a pair of muscled arms.

'I've come to work out for a while. Do you have short-term memberships?'

She threw her sponge into the bucket with precision and nodded her head towards the front desk. He followed obediently.

'Fill in this form, sign here. The amounts per month are there: take your pick,' she said pushing the paper towards him. 'We don't get many new members here.' They hadn't had anyone new in five months, not that it seemed to worry Pax. He'd have to be making a loss but yet he never seemed to care, as if he'd keep it running even just for the regular five that always came. Jaz figured Pax wasn't ever short of money, he just didn't flash it about like the rest of his wealthy family.

'So, you been working for Pax for long?' Mr Mysterious asked.

'Yep, you could say I've been working here for most of my life, but I've been getting paid for the last seven. I'm running it at the moment while Pax is away.'

Those dark eyes were studying her closely; so closely Jaz felt like she was being slowly stripped bare.

'You seem familiar,' he said eventually. 'Have we met?'

'I think so. You're a bouncer, right? You probably don't remember me from a few weeks ago—'

'Oh, the girl in the black dress,' he said. 'How could I forget?'

Jaz swallowed hard. He remembered her and her dress. Wowzers.

Ryan began to fill in the paperwork. 'You know, I've been here a few times before and I don't remember you.'

Jaz shrugged. 'Yeah, well, I don't remember you either.'

She saw his eyes flash with humour. 'So, when will Pax be back?'

Jaz put her hand on her hip, and leaned the other one against the desk. 'Whenever he wants.'

The guy sighed. 'Are you always so curt?'

'Do you always ask so many questions?'

The guy smiled. 'My name's Ryan,' he said holding out his hand.

'I know,' she said shaking it. He tilted his head at her curiously. 'It's on your form,' she said pointing to his paperwork and laughing.

Ryan dragged his hand down his face before glancing at her.

'My name's Jaz, it's nice to meet you, Ryan. So, how well do you know Pax?'

'Um, we see each other from time to time and I try to keep in touch but it's hard with work. I'm travelling a fair bit but I'm home for a while and I'm going nuts with nothing to do, and so I'm here.'

Jaz watched him carefully as he neatly evaded her question, then she reached over into the desk drawer, pulled out a key and threw it to him.

'This is for your locker, which is through that door,' she pointed to the back corner. 'Showers and change rooms are also in there.'

'Thanks, I'll come back later.' He turned towards the door.

'Ryan?'

'Yeah?' He turned to face her.

Jaz walked to him and handed him a piece of paper. 'These are the times for the gym, and one of our regulars takes boxing lessons if you're interested.'

'Cheers, but I'm happy just doing my own training.'

She nodded. 'No worries. See you around.'

She watched him leave. Watched him walk past the window with his long stride and his cute butt. Then she turned on her heel and headed back to cleaning the mat, all the while thinking of his dark eyes and the mystery they held.

CHAPTER 5

RYAN HAD DRIFTED quickly from her mind when Taylor appeared at fencing practice, and her day got better when they teamed up to practise together.

'I liked it better when I could kick your arse easily,' puffed Taylor as he took off his mask and clapped Jaz on the back. He made the white protective gear look cool, while the rest of them resembled Froot Loops in straitjackets. 'But then again, it's nice to actually have a worthy opponent who makes me work for it.'

Jaz couldn't stop her smile as she took off her mask and walked with him towards the coach, who was already bellowing.

'Don't forget, the other school will be arriving in a few days. I want you kids ready by nine o'clock on Thursday. We'll meet again then. Chop, chop, off you go.' The coach scratched his goatee as they headed for the change rooms.

'What's Anna doing?' asked Taylor as they paused outside the change-room door.

'She's researching at the library... something that's way over my head... and then she'll come to The Ring.'

'You off to The Ring now?'

'Yep, no rest for the wicked. You wanna come and keep me company?' *Say yes, please say yes*, she silently begged. Taylor was leaning his shoulder against the doorway casually but if he leaned towards her a fraction, it would be much more intimate. Sadly, she could see the answer in his eyes already. She knew every silvery speck in them.

'Can't, sorry. We've been invited to Minka's dad's new girlfriend's gallery opening… some sort of abstract art. Minka wants me to be there.'

'Your girlfriend?' she teased.

'You know damn well she'll never be my girlfriend.' He pulled a face like he'd bitten into a lemon.

Jaz knew he wasn't interested but she liked to check. Taylor just hung out with her because all his mates were in her circle. 'So this art, is it painting with fingers?' Jaz suggested.

Taylor laughed and nudged her shoulder. 'I'll text you a picture of it and you can see for yourself. You might be able to pick a finger painting better than I can.' He squeezed her affectionately before pulling away. 'Catch ya later, Jazzy.'

'Yeah, bye, Tay.'

When Jaz had changed into her black trackies and hoodie, she decided Linkin Park was called for to vent some frustration, so she inserted her earplugs and started her pavement-pounding run to the gym. She was still trying to de-Taylor-ise when she got to the gym, so it took her a few minutes to notice a new body at the speedball. She stopped mid stride and gaped at the rippled back gleaming with sweat.

Ryan in his shirt was impressive. Ryan without a shirt was bloody amazing. With a dry mouth, Jaz went to Pax's office, sat behind the two-way mirror and found her gaze returning to Ryan's body. Now *that* was a specimen of a man. Yeah, Taylor was good-looking and his body was lean but Ryan had those extra years of filling out, of developing real muscles and strength. Several long scars traced across his back, some in the shape of a circle. Intriguing.

After refocusing and hydrating, Jaz moved to start her usual yoga routine. Not far from Ryan she placed her feet at the end of the mat in the corner and started her Ujjayi breathing before moving through the positions, a calmness settling through her as she enjoyed the stretches.

It was a while later that she realised Ryan was on a mat not far from her. He looked like he'd been doing stomach crunches, lying on his back with his knees bent and his hands behind his head. But after a while she didn't detect any movement. She glanced his way and met his eyes, and he smiled. The bugger was just lying there watching her, and he had the nerve to smile! She tried to ignore him as she finished, thinking of her breathing and relaxing her muscles.

'You all right?' she asked getting up and sending him her best *don't mess with me* look.

But Ryan just laughed at her discomfort. 'What was that you were doing, all that bendy, twisty stuff?' His voice held amazement.

Now she couldn't help but smile, her irritation gone. 'You've never seen yoga before?' Jaz asked, sitting down opposite him as he sat up. His naked chest glistened golden with a thin film of sweat. She continued her assessment of his body until she met his gaze. He'd caught her out and she felt a blush creep up her neck.

'My mum did yoga when I was a kid but I don't remember it being anything like that,' he said with a smile.

'This is called Ashtanga yoga. We had a teacher here at the gym who's since moved but I've kept doing it. I find it very rewarding.' *And it helps to control my moods*, she thought.

'How so?'

Jaz flicked her hair over her shoulder. 'Well, in a way, yoga is the controlling of the mind, and we do a breathing and movement system called Vinyasa. So for each movement you take one breath. It helps heats the blood, cleaning and thinning it so that it can circulate more freely. And the sweat helps take the impurities out of the body.'

'Yeah, I've heard that sweating is good. At work, we have an infrared sauna, which helps us recover from muscle injuries quicker.'

'What, being a bouncer?' Jaz frowned disbelievingly.

'Um, well I do other jobs. I'm not just a bouncer.' He waved her question away. 'And do you do this yoga every day?'

'I try to. My mum reckons it's good for me, she thinks I'm a bit hot-tempered.'

Ryan laughed, the sound soft and tingly to her ears, and for the first time she saw a glimpse of gold in his dark brown eyes.

'Besides that, it gives me inner strength and great flexibility.'

'Hmm, yes, I could see that.' He smiled when Jaz rolled her eyes. 'But stuffed if I could get my legs in any of those positions.'

'Yeah, you could with practice.'

'Are you offering to teach me?'

Jaz choked on her laugh. 'You're a funny one!'

'Well, I must thank you, anyway.'

Jaz's laughter died down and she looked at him strangely. 'What for?'

'Let's just say I didn't think I'd be able to laugh again, but you've proved me wrong. So, I'm grateful.' He smiled. It was genuine and warm but edged in sadness.

The air was still between them as she studied him. His eyes, as guarded as they were, hinted at great pain and loss.

'You've had it tough, hey?' Jaz asked quietly. It was the way Ryan had said the words, so full of sincerity and weight. She saw a flash of anger stretch across his tight jaw, as if he was replaying whatever it was that had caused him so much pain. But a second later he shut down, sealing his eyes with a steely glaze.

'Yeah, you could say that,' he answered softly.

Jaz felt the urge to touch his arm or grasp his hand and give it a reassuring squeeze, but hell, she hardly knew the bloke. He could be a raving loony for all she knew.

'Hey, Jaz!'

Jasmine turned towards the front door and spotted Anna, who was out of her school uniform and wearing jeans and a blue jumper. 'Hey, it's Anna Montana.'

Anna poked her tongue out as she walked towards them. Jaz waved to the guy opposite her. 'Anna, this is Ryan. Ryan, this is my best friend, Anna.'

'Heeeey,' said Anna slowly as her steps faltered and her eyes grew to plate size.

'How ya goin'?' Ryan's voice was friendly.

Anna tried to smile but she looked like she was going to melt. Jaz sighed and grabbed Anna's arm, steering her towards the office. She flicked her head back to Ryan. 'Catch ya later.' He nodded and returned to his stomach crunches.

'Who is he and why did you take me away from him?' asked Anna when they were in the quiet of Pax's office.

Jaz closed the door and then sat on the spare computer chair. Anna claimed the one by the desk.

'I was saving you from making a fool of yourself.'

'I wasn't!'

'Oh, please! If you'd stayed there any longer I would have had to fetch the mop bucket for your drool. Haven't I taught you enough about how to not show your emotions on the outside?'

Anna went a shade of pink and then snorted. 'Was I really that bad?'

'Uh huh,' said Jaz as she watched Anna lean on the table so she could look out the window.

'But he's so hot. Have you seen his bod! And those eyes, so mysterious. How did he end up here?'

Jaz raised her eyebrows in mock seriousness. 'Are you done yet?'

Anna giggled. 'Come on, are you telling me you don't find him attractive?'

Jaz flicked her eyes towards Ryan, who was now doing push-ups. His body was as straight as a flagpole and his arms rippled with each motion. 'Of course I do, what warm-blooded woman wouldn't. But…'

'But he's not Taylor,' answered Anna.

Jaz shrugged, unsure if that was what she was going to say. There was something about Ryan; something a little edgy and dark. She wasn't sure if she was fascinated by it or just bloody afraid.

Her phone beeped, and her gut knew it was Taylor. She pressed open his message: a picture of a canvas of colours in no order or pattern, kind of resembling a night on the curry.

It's worse than we thought, the artist used her sponge collection!

'Oh, is that from Taylor? I can tell, you've got that dreamy smile you reserve for him.'

Jaz tried to frown.

'Well, while you deal with Taylor, I'm gonna go surf the net. Tell him I said hi.'

And within seconds Anna was opening screens and infiltrating stuff far beyond Jaz's knowledge.

'Okay, master at work. I'll see you after I've cleaned the toilets.'

After trying unsuccessfully to think of a witty reply for Taylor, she set about scrubbing the gym toilets, and then finally sent him a picture of the urinal with her scrubbing brush in view.

Wanna come help me?

Ha ha, you're so funny!

As she left the bathrooms, Jaz glanced over to Ryan. His arms rippled with muscles as he did chin-ups, the motion smooth as if he were weightless. Yes, she was procrastinating. With a sigh she tore her eyes away and went back to work.

CHAPTER 6

'SO, ARE YOU nervous?' whispered Taylor as he came up behind Jaz. She jumped a little, but Taylor's smooth voice instantly set her body at ease. His shoulder touched hers as they watched the crowd moving into the school gym to find seating on the stands.

'Hmm, so many people.'

'You'll be okay, Jaz. Stick with me and you'll be right.'

'Well, let's go see Anna before I get changed. She's got a front row seat cos, get this, she doesn't want to miss any of the action,' said Jaz.

'She's a funny one. I think she's played too many of those fighting computer games,' said Taylor, cracking up.

'Tell me about it.'

Together they walked further into the gym to the grandstand on their left. Anna was at the end, and when she saw them she waved frantically, scooting across the bench seat to make room for them.

'How much did you pay for these seats, Anna?' asked Taylor with a chuckle as they sat down.

'Nothing, I just got here early, that's all. Besides when your two best friends are going to win, it's well worth the effort.'

'Ah, Team Aramis can win!' said Taylor impersonating Coach Belmore, causing both girls to laugh.

'My bet is on Taylor to win. No offence, Jaz, but you're, like, nearly the only girl in the competition,' said Anna glancing across the room. 'Oh, besides that large girl with the short hair on the other team, who I only just realised was a girl.'

'Don't count Jaz out, Anna. She's nimble and quick and she serves my arse on a plate to me at training more often than not.'

Jaz felt her cheeks glow from Taylor's praise.

'All right, ladies, as team captain I better head off before Coach starts calling me over the PA. Catch ya in the rooms, Jaz,' Taylor said before pointing his finger and waving it like a sword, just like Coach Belmore did at training.

'What a tosser.' Jaz laughed as Taylor walked away, past the large crowds, his head high.

'Yeah right, and you'd shag him any day,' said Anna bumping her shoulder against Jaz's. Jaz didn't have to reply, Anna's words were true.

Anna's hand latched onto her arm and squeezed. 'OMG, Jaz. It's the hunk of spunk,' squealed Anna as quietly as she could before putting her arm up and waving frantically.

God, had she not taught this girl subtlety? Jaz snapped her head in the direction Anna was waving. 'Oh! What's he doing here?' It was him, Ryan, the one with the scarred body.

'Maybe he's a scout, you know, come to recruit people for national teams and stuff.'

'Anna, I think you watch too many movies,' said Jaz.

Ryan lifted his arm in a wave when he got closer, causing his shirt to ride above his pants. Hard muscle.

'Hey, Jaz. And, Anna?' he said.

Anna glanced at Jaz and smiled, clearly pleased Ryan had remembered her name.

Anna turned back to him. 'Hi Ryan, great to see you again.' Anna shook his hand.

Jaz stood also, but it wasn't a greeting that came out of her mouth. 'Are you, like, stalking me or something?' She squinted her eyes and probed his brown ones for answers.

'Pure coincidence, I swear.' He raised his hands in surrender. 'I saw a flyer and thought I'd check it out. It's not like I had anything else to do. What are you guys doing here?'

'Um, this is our school,' said Anna.

Ryan's eyebrows shot up. 'School?' He glanced at Jaz, his eyebrows bent as he revaluated her. 'How old are you two?'

Jaz almost laughed at the surprise on Ryan's face. 'We'll be eighteen soon, last year of school.' She knew he was twenty-three as he'd put it on his membership. Jaz may have studied his form more than most.

'How old are you?' Asked Anna.

'Old enough to know your mothers wouldn't like me hanging around, or the teachers,' he said as he glanced around the gym.

'What are you – like, twenty-eight?' probed Anna.

'Really, do I look that old?' Ryan shook his head and a smile tugged at the corner of his lips.

Anna laughed. 'Well, we don't mind how old you are. Here, have Jaz's seat next to me. She's gotta go anyway.'

Smooth one, Anna. Jaz was about to move when Talia went past, her brown locks flowing over her shoulders. Talia spotted them, pulled a face at the school's outcasts before seeing Ryan, and just about stumbled. Her head may as well have been plastered on backwards for all the ogling she was doing. Jaz watched her run back to where Minka was sitting. She could see their curious glances, wondering what a guy like Ryan was doing with them.

'Well, I better head off. Gotta go Zorro,' she joked.

'Okay, Jaz,' said Anna scooping her up in a hug. 'Good luck. I'll be cheering for ya.'

'Cheers,' said Jaz sarcastically.

She felt strong fingers curl around her arm, and turned to face Ryan, whose eyes searched hers. 'Are you fencing today?'

'Ah, yeah. Are we not at a fencing tournament? Is that all right with you? Didn't realise I had to check things with my stalker.' She glanced at his hand. Ryan released it immediately but she could feel the pressure of his fingers tingling her skin. Instantly she remembered the way he'd looked at her at the nightclub, causing her to shiver.

'Sorry, just a lot of surprises today. Good luck, though.'

Jaz stepped out and watched Ryan take her place beside Anna. His khaki cargo pants rode up his legs a fraction, revealing a pair of commando boots similar to hers — well, his were flashier. But his rating went up a few notches on her chart. He smelled different today, some type of cologne. It was strong, not in the overpowering way, but sharp and alluring.

'Thanks, see ya after.' Jaz meant the last bit for Anna but Ryan nodded his head. She walked away still confused. Was Ryan innocent or was he really a stalker? She wished her gut would tell her something but it was too wound up with nervous energy. She'd have to think that through later. Right now, she wanted to impress Taylor.

When she joined her team, Coach Belmore was just starting his speech, and because of her interruption he decided to start again from the beginning. Jaz had the feeling he'd been practising in front of a mirror for weeks. Teaching them how to fence, Coach was brilliant — but motivational speaker he wasn't. Jaz totally blanked out during his speech because she was too busy watching Taylor tighten his breeches before putting his gloves on.

'Don't forget how to deceive, extending late in the lunge, changing line and drawing a parry and changing line again. Let's get out there and show them Team Aramis means business. All right, let's take our seats. Greenwich, you're up first; look lively, son.' Coach Belmore rubbed his hands together as he followed the team out to the gym courts.

Jaz followed Taylor and sat next to him in the plastic chairs against the wall where both school teams were stationed in two sections. With a nervous yawn, she glanced across the gymnasium towards Anna, who gave her a wave. Ryan's eyes were also watching her. She wished she had her hoodie on so she could hide inside it. Once again Ryan's gaze stripped her bare. It was as if he truly saw her for who she was – the person only Anna and Taylor were privy to – and it rattled her.

Jaz felt a hand on her knee, warm as it gave a gentle squeeze. She glanced at Taylor in surprise, and in reply he flashed his perfect row of teeth.

'Are you nervous?' he asked.

'No,' Jaz spluttered.

'Then why are your legs jumping?'

Jaz looked down and realised he was right. How long had she been bouncing them on the spot like that? 'Hmm, maybe just a little. I don't do crowds that well.'

Taylor leaned over so she could hear him easily over the noise of the crowd. 'You'll be fine, Jaz. Just block it all out, and do what you do at training. You've got a good chance of winning.'

Oh, his words sounded so nice and his breath tickled her ear. 'So have you,' said Jaz finally finding her voice.

They watched the first few bouts. Greenwich lost his, so did Benson, and next was Taylor, who won his in record speed. He was definitely the one to watch. His attacks were flawless.

Jaz was up next. Taylor tapped her on the shoulder and wished her luck as she walked over to the fencing strip and put on her mask. She saluted her adversary and the referee of the bout, with a wave of her sabre. Her body began to zing with nervous energy and she breathed deeply, clearing her mind. She sized up her opponent, in a blink of an eye; she knew he would be slower. His weight was slightly off balance and his movements were jerky, not fluid. They stepped up to the *en garde* line. Jaz had fifteen hits to win in order to move through to the next round. She was determined to survive until the end. Bags called it her devil instincts. Like a Tasmanian devil, she would latch on and not let go until she had succeeded. Giving up was not an option.

The bout started, Jaz lunged forward, saw her opponent attack and took a quick double step backwards causing her opponent's attack to fail, giving her the right of way and scoring a hit, or *touché*. In no time at all she clocked up the required hits. At the end of the bout, and another salute, she went and joined her cheering team and took her seat beside Taylor.

'Well done, Jasmine, you made nice work of him,' praised Coach Belmore.

Taylor nudged her shoulder and winked. It made her pulse jump.

They watched on as the rest of the bouts continued. They had two fencing strips, or *piste*, so when her next bout was up, Taylor's was on at the same time and she missed watching him win. She also won her bout and progressed to the third round. Her third-round competitor was shorter and she found it easier to target his head, and won convincingly. The beep of the electronic scorer echoed amid the cheering crowd. Her parents weren't here today, due to their work commitments, but it didn't bother her, she didn't want them to come and make a big deal out of it anyway.

Her stepfather, Paul, wasn't into sports of any sorts; he would have been just like Simon as a kid.

Taylor's fourth bout was against a guy of similar build but with a long neck like an ostrich. His white jacket had their team name, Excalibur, embroidered on the front in blue.

It was close, with both going hit for hit. Jaz's legs had begun to jump again as she watched carefully. Taylor's opposition matched him in speed, their hits fast but she could almost pick ostrich-boy's next movement, his downfall being his inability to hide his intent. She wished Taylor would notice but she guessed it was easier for her because she had time to study the opposition whereas Taylor was busy. The ostrich boy lunged forward in a super speed attack and Taylor stepped back but was slightly off balance and lost his footing, causing the ostrich to place a hit. After another *touché* the bout was over and Team Aramis's chances of winning crumbled.

It was like the whole crowd in the gym breathed in at the same time, sucking in the walls. The state of the team rested on her shoulders against ostrich-boy in the final.

Crap!

She wanted desperately to speak to Taylor and console him, but there was no time. Coach Belmore wanted to talk to them in the break before the final showdown. She'd never felt the weight of a whole team depending on her before, and it was that thought that brought her back to the ground with a thud. It had always just been Jaz against the world, but now the expectant, hopeful faces of her teammates filled her with as much dread as determination. She felt duty-bound to save them all.

The team dispersed on Coach's orders as he left Taylor, the team captain, to give the last bit of advice.

Jaz felt like every set of eyes in the gym were on them. But she found Taylor's eager blue eyes drawing her in and filling her with strength. His voice was calm, pragmatic.

'You can get him, Jaz. You're great at deceiving, and I think that's the only way to beat him. His body also gives his moves away; I just noticed it too late,' he sighed.

'Yeah, I picked that up.'

'Okay, remember late extension and changing line and throw in some feint attacks.'

Jaz nodded obediently. She'd do whatever he asked… but he never asked for the things she wanted to give. *Hold me? Kiss me?* Maybe if she won this bout?

Taylor pushed her towards the strip, his words of 'good luck' lingering in her ears.

She put on her mask and saluted ostrich-boy and the referees. She let him get the first hit in, letting him think she was an easy target. 'That's the only one you'll get for free,' she whispered.

After a few attempts, Jaz started going with her gut instinct, or tempo, as Coach Belmore called it. She had a good read on ostrich-boy, started to choose the exact psychological and physical moment of his weakness, and made her attacks. The gym faded away into the background. No longer could she hear any cheers or chants. It was just the beat of her heart and the swish of her blade with each cut.

Triple advance-lunge/*en garde*, triple retreat-lunge/*en garde*, *balestra*-lunge recover/*en garde*. She didn't think about her footwork, she let it come naturally, as it did with Bags in the ring. Her body moved on its own accord, and when ostrich-boy started to move his left shoulder she knew he was about to attack and met his sabre with a block. She could sense his annoyance with a) the fact that he was losing, and b) that it was to a woman. But all those thoughts did was make him sloppy.

Jaz won another point and the crowd's noise reached her ears. Just one more point for the win, and she already knew the move she was going to take. With a lightening lunge her arm shot out and the end of her blade pressed against his chest. The beeper went off as the crowd jumped to their feet. Jaz had just won the final.

In a daze, she staggered back to her team, trying to take off her mask as they all congratulated her.

Taylor hugged her and said something, but everyone was cheering so loudly she missed it. The crowd milled around as Jaz and Team Aramis were declared the winners, and she felt suddenly overwhelmed by all the commotion, a little uneasy. Her eyes started seeking out the green exit signs.

After the medal presentations, Anna and Ryan make a beeline straight for Jaz.

'Yay, you big star!' said Anna, proudly hugging her and inspecting her medal.

'Brilliant work,' said Ryan, his lip twitched as if wanting to smile.

She should probably feel grateful he even said something, even surprised he stuck out the whole event.

'Jaz, that was amazing! And to think you weren't even interested in fencing.'

'Why not?' asked Ryan, his brow creased. 'You're a natural.'

'Well, she only joined last year to spend more time with...' As Anna spoke, Jaz felt like her guts had been spilled all over the floor. She punched Anna in the arm to shush her up. 'I mean she's really good considering she hasn't been doing it for long,' Anna corrected and turned a pretty shade of pink.

Jaz blushed and lowered her eyes, thankful that at least Taylor hadn't heard Anna's words.

Ryan reached out to touch the 'Team Aramis' red stitch positioned above a sabre on her jacket, but he stopped short when he realised where it was positioned. 'So... Team Aramis... as in *The Three Musketeers*?' he asked.

Jaz looked up, her eyes twinkling like sapphires. 'Yeah, you got it in one. I had to ask Anna what it meant,' she laughed.

'Nice work out there. Very impressive,' he added.

Jaz shrugged off his compliment and tried to hide behind her hair.

'So, what are you doing now?' asked Anna.

'She's coming to celebrate at my place,' said Taylor as he wrapped his arms around Jaz and kissed her cheek. 'I knew you could do it, Jazzy.'

Ryan took a step back and Taylor glanced across at him, seeing him for the first time. He let go of Jaz and held out his hand. 'Hi, I'm Taylor. Are you a friend of Anna's?'

Jaz watched Taylor sizing him up, trying to find the connection.

'Name's Ryan,' he said shaking Taylor's hand and added, 'I'm actually Jaz's stalker.'

Jaz and Anna spluttered out laughter while Taylor raised his eyebrows in confusion. Ryan smiled and Taylor nodded his head. 'Ha, funny dude.

Well, you're all welcome to come back to my place. I think we should go out tonight. It's Friday, so we should celebrate in style.'

'Cool, I'm in,' said Anna.

'Thanks but I better head off, things to do,' said Ryan.

'You feeling too old for us now?' Jaz asked.

'More like I'd hate to cramp your style. I'll see you later.' He paused, about to leave but glanced at Jaz, his eyes holding hers meaningfully. 'Congrats on your win, you deserved it. You have great footwork.' He stood staring at her as if he couldn't believe it himself. Then he turned and walked out of the gymnasium, taking all the female eyes with him.

Now that he knew her age, would he still flirt with her like he had at The Ring? Would he treat her differently? Taylor took her hand and dragged her towards the team, and that was the last she thought about Ryan as she was swept away in the celebrations.

CHAPTER 7

'Okay, here's our new fake IDs,' said Anna handing them out to Taylor and Jaz as they stood in his bedroom. They were staying the night at Taylor's because his dad – much to Taylor's amusement considering his dad was a cop – was always busy with work and didn't ask many questions.

'These look real,' said Jaz. 'I better not let Mum find it.'

Taylor shook his head. 'My God, you could go into business selling these. Dad would freak. Anna, you have a scary talent,' he said grinning at her. 'Where do you get this stuff?'

Anna shrugged. 'You'd be amazed, Tay. Pax has so much stuff, I kinda just borrowed the bits I needed. I don't think he will notice, at least I hope not.' Anna bit her lip. 'I'm sure I can persuade him it was for the greater good of our youth.'

'Well, I don't know about you lot, but I'm going to get changed and then we're off dancing.' Jaz grabbed her bag and headed into the spare room where they were sleeping. Anna followed excitedly.

Twenty minutes later, Taylor banged on their door. 'Come on, you two! Surely you're ready by *now*.'

Anna cracked open the door and whispered out. 'Do you know how hard it is being a girl? The pressure to look good isn't easy. Statistically speaking, a —'

'Anna,' said Taylor cutting her off before she began her tirade. He pushed the door open so he could see them. 'You look amazing,' he said, blushing slightly and hooking his finger nervously into his trendy jeans.

'That's what I've been telling her,' said Jaz as she pushed Anna out. 'Little black dresses always work, especially teamed with heels.'

Taylor glanced at Anna's elegant shoes, then to Jaz's feet, covered with flat knee-high boots. He raised his eyebrows.

'What? I might need to run or something,' said Jaz.

'You're always prepared for everything, Jaz. But they're still sexy boots,' he added, taking in her off-the shoulder top, free-flowing hair and the big hoop earrings Anna had insisted she add. She couldn't help but smile.

'I think we're ready to go. So, where to, Tay?' Anna looped her arm around his, while Jaz went to his other side, and the three headed down the passage.

'Well, I was thinking, seeing as Anna's done such a fab job on our IDs, that we should see if we can get into Ramblers.'

Anna squealed. 'Really?'

'That joint is all anyone talks about.' All Jaz could think was, *Wait until Minka hears we went to Ramblers with Taylor. Oh, she'll just be green with envy.* 'Let's do it.'

'Let's go, girls.'

As they climbed into the waiting taxi, Jaz couldn't help but feel excited. The three of them off for a night of fun. They laughed and joked all the way into Northbridge. They probably gave their taxi driver a headache but nothing was going to spoil their fun.

'Hey, I told Mum we were watching the latest *Vampire Diaries* season. Everyone cool with that?' said Anna as they got out of the taxi onto the lit street.

Taylor paid the taxi man before he added, 'Yep, righto. But I doubt your folks will call to check. They trust us.'

'Huh, I don't think my mum trusts me. I have to tell her everything and she always knows when I've been up to something. It's like she has a sixth sense.' Jaz pulled out her phone. 'See, she's already texted to see if I'm okay!' With a groan she handed her phone to Taylor to keep in his jeans pocket. She had no room for it in her sexy black skirt.

'No, your mum just has a great bullshit detector, Jaz. Always has,' said Anna. 'I've never been able to lie to her face. Oh my God, we're here,' she said nervously, flapping her hands.

'Okay, Anna. We're trying to pretend we are over eighteen,' Taylor said with a smirk.

Anna ran her hand past her face, turning cool and collected. 'Right, got it.'

They walked towards the dark building. If the big sparkly RAMBLERS sign wasn't blinking above the door, you wouldn't have even noticed the building in the street. It gave off a sleek, important vibe, something the owners had no doubt wanted. The queue of sexy women and good-looking guys out the front also gave it away.

The three friends barely spoke as the line crept forward. They were trying to keep cool and seem older; not too much older, though; they weren't far off being eighteen.

'ID please,' said the large bouncer in his black T-shirt with a white R on the front.

Obediently they showed him their cards as his sharp eyes sized them up. His neck was as thick as a tree trunk, and Jaz found herself wondering if she could ever beat him in a one-on-one fight. Would her skills be any good over someone so strong and big? With a bit of luck she'd never need to find out.

Without a word, he nodded them through the door. They headed inside and up some narrow stairs while sneaking victory glances at each other, surprised they'd made it in.

The music was pumping and shaking through their bodies as they merged onto the crowded dance floor. Huddling together, they headed for a space near a wall.

Anna kept her face calm but her voice was excited as she half-yelled, 'We're here, we're here. Now what?'

'This is so awesome,' said Jaz taking in the room. There was a bar in the far corner along with some tables and sitting booths and the rest of the floor was filled with people dancing, while the DJ played music from up on a mezzanine floor among the flashing lights.

Her hand was tugged along as Taylor dragged them into the centre of the room. 'Let's dance.'

And dance they did. Four songs later, a cute guy had turned around and begun dancing with Jaz. She didn't know him from a bar of soap, but he was older and could move, so she had fun dancing alongside him.

'I need a drink,' mouthed Anna after a while.

Jaz nodded, her own throat parched. She followed them to the booths and grabbed a seat while Taylor and Anna headed for the bar.

'One drink won't kill us,' he said ten minutes later as he put them on the table along with a water bottle. They didn't argue. Jaz loved sitting back, watching everyone, from the bartenders to the DJ and the dancers on the floor having a great time. She didn't know if it was the alcohol or the music or maybe a combination of both but she felt a warm buzz through her body and couldn't keep the smile from her face.

'It won't be long and we can do this whenever we want,' said Jaz leaning over to Anna.

'Ah, the life of an adult.' Anna smiled. 'Come on, time's a'wasting, more dancing needed,' she said, finishing her drink, getting up and dragging Taylor with her.

Jaz got up to follow them, noticing a few eyes watching her. So many cute guys, and to have them looking at her was kind of cool. She certainly never elicited this reaction at school. Most of the guys there were scared of her; well, that's what Taylor had told her once. So, maybe she knew how to take care of herself, and if that meant they were scared of her, then none of them was man enough for her. At least that's what she tried to tell herself.

Trying not to lose Anna in the crowd, she bumped her way through. ''Scuse me. Sorry,' she called as she pushed in.

Being this close to people, hemmed in tightly, put her on edge. She reminded herself it was just a crowded dance floor and she tried to relax, when suddenly her arm was grabbed tightly. The pressure didn't ease as she tried to plunge forward through the congested crowd, towards her friends. The grip on her arm felt like a threat, it sent her heart racing as she fought against it. She was being pulled backwards away from her friends. Had she been caught by the police or a bouncer? Or was it some creep?

Drawing a breath she tensed, planted her feet firmly and turned to face her possible attacker.

'Jaz, what the bloody hell are you doing here?' the strong voice growled. She would have breathed a sigh of relief if Ryan wasn't looking like was ready to kill her; and that if he wanted to, he could. His eyes were menacing and scary, but she wouldn't let that put her off.

'Ryan! Man, you scared me. Will you quit following me?' she said shaking his hand from her arm.

He was studying her carefully amid the strobing lights and incessant thump of the music. She could tell he was trying to calm himself as he took a deep breath before saying slowly and gently, 'I'm not. You must be following me.' The tone in his voice was more controlled, not like the initial abrupt harshness.

'What? What makes you think that?' she asked while watching his eyes as they flicked around the room. Did it wear him out to be so alert all the time?

'I'm working here tonight.' And as if to prove it, he pointed to his black T-shirt embossed with the white R.

'Oh.' She admired the fitted T-shirt over his lean body. Anna was so right about him being hot.

He bent down, speaking near her ear, his breath caressing her skin. 'And if I was doing my job, I would be kicking you out right now. How did you even get in?'

Ryan smelled good. A clean mixture of soap and deodorant as if he'd just stepped out of the shower and came straight on duty.

Jaz glanced up and smiled, and tried to bat her eyelids. Hey, it always worked in the movies. 'I have my secrets.' She could see Ryan was trying hard not to smile. His jaw was tense as he fought it off.

Raising a strong arm, he held out his hand, palm up, waiting. 'ID?'

With a sigh, she pulled out her ID from its hiding place in her bra – she found it cute that he averted his eyes – and placed the warm card into his hand.

Ryan studied it carefully. He glanced at her and then studied the card again. 'Where did you get this?' he queried.

'I can't give away my sources,' she said to him frankly. 'It's good, right?' With a quick movement, she swiped the card back and hid it back down her top.

'Hey!' Ryan ran his hand over his head when he realised he wasn't getting the card back. 'Jaz, please. Where did you get it? Who's selling them to you?'

Jaz saw the look of concern and suddenly hoped he wasn't a cop.

'Are you going to dob us in to the cops? Are you a cop? If you are, I can't tell you anything.'

'No, Jaz, I'm not.' He sighed while surveying the room, yet he was still focused on their conversation. 'I just want to know. You'll be fine, I promise.'

Jaz thought about it for a minute, then pulled Ryan closer and whispered in his ear. 'It was a home job, we did it ourselves.' Jaz figured if she implied they all had done it, then Anna couldn't get into trouble.

'Really?' Ryan looked dubious. He opened his mouth again, but no words came out.

'We just did it for us, we're not selling them or anything like that.' Had she done something wrong by telling him this? Her heart raced.

Ryan must have seen her panic, because he put his hand on her shoulder kindly. 'It's okay, Jaz. Your secret's safe with me.' His sudden attitude left her slightly confused, and she watched as his eyes flicked to the side as if something else was also holding his attention. 'Look,' he said, 'I've gotta go, but please be careful tonight. Don't leave your drink unattended.' His eyes came back to her for a second and she saw fiery warmth in them. 'A pretty girl like you could attract a lot of attention.' He took his hand away; it paused by her hair as if he was going to touch it but then dropped quickly. With a deep breath, his eyes flicked back to the far corner of the room where the noise level had gone up. 'Ah, shit.'

'What?' Jaz asked. 'What's up?'

Ryan's eyes darted back to her and then back across the room. She couldn't see over the heads of the people, but Ryan could. What was going down? A fight?

His eyes came back to her again. 'Can you do something for me?' His gaze was serious and dark, as if his life depended on this simple request.

'Sure.'

Ryan bent down towards her ear. 'I need to sort out that fight, but can you go sit over there and watch that man in the corner? He's wearing a fedora and a white suit. Can you see him?'

Jaz glanced across to where he'd motioned with his eyes and caught sight of the man. He was hard to miss. He looked important and reeked of money. Maybe he owned the club? 'Yeah.' She nodded.

'Keep your eyes on him and tell me if he meets up with anyone new. If he does, use this to take photos but pretend you're texting someone.' He put his mobile into her hand. 'Can you do that?'

'Yeah, but—'

'Look, I gotta go. Just do what you can. But I'll be back, just make sure to watch him, please. Thanks.'

Ryan disappeared. She was left surrounded by a dancing crowd and his phone in her hand. *His* phone. This was all too weird.

Jaz moved through the crowd to the bar and bought herself another drink, then positioned herself opposite the fedora guy.

Why would Ryan want her to watch this man? Maybe he was the club owner and Ryan didn't want to get caught doing something? Heck, was he out the back robbing him? Really, Jaz had no idea what she was doing. Could she be aiding a criminal?

She took a sip of her drink and fiddled with Ryan's phone. It was plain, Jaz opened the camera and aimed it at the fedora guy but made it look like she was just typing a text. As her heart rate increased, she checked the flash was off.

What the hell am I doing?

Before she could answer her own thoughts she saw movement at fedora guy's table. A man in a black suit had joined them, shaking his hand. Jaz took a few happy snaps of them both. The photos wouldn't be so great in the nightclub but you could just make out their faces from the single lights that hung down on a wire, low over each table.

She took another sip of her drink and then glanced around. There looked to be a big scuffle over by the far wall. God, she hoped Anna and Taylor weren't near that. Far too much was going on at once.

Jaz glanced back to the table opposite her and just about panicked when she saw fedora guy and his black-suited friend getting up to leave.

'Oh shit, now what?' she mumbled. Did she stay here or follow them? *Come on Jaz, think quick*, her brain screamed.

Leaving her drink, she got up and watched the men head towards the bathrooms. She practically ran into the corridor that led to the toilets, afraid to lose them. *Crunch.* She shouldn't have stressed. They were chatting just behind the wall and she'd slammed right into the guy in the black suit. Instinctively he reached out to steady her as she almost slid down him. Jaz gripped his arm and gathered herself, her heart racing.

He shrugged her off and withdrew his hand but not before she saw the small snake tattoo on his wrist. 'Sorry,' she said. It came out a bit wobbly from her nerves.

'Here, take these and bugger off,' he said as he pressed a small plastic bag into her hand and pushed her away.

That's when Jaz realised: they thought she was drunk or drugged. She'd never felt so relieved, as she dragged herself along the wall trying to keep up the appearance of being inebriated. She stayed close to the doorway, but hid behind a pole just in case they came back out. In her hands, the packet with pills scared her. Did that guy think he was doing her a favour by giving her these? Instantly Jaz wanted to throw them away, but to where?

'Hey, I found you.'

Jaz jumped.

'Jesus, Jaz. Is that what I think it is?' said Ryan snatching it from her hands and putting it in his pocket. 'What the hell do you think you're doing?' He stared at her like she'd grown two heads.

'Chill. It's not mine,' she said. 'Some man with the fedora guy gave it to me.'

'What? So, it's not yours?'

Jaz slapped her hands on her hips and tried to burn holes in him with her eyes.

'Good. Great. I'm glad. So, this guy… where did he go?' Ryan glanced around the room.

'They're just in the corridor by the toilets. They could be still there. But I got photos.'

As he checked the phone he gaped, then looked back at her open-mouthed. 'Amazing.' Ryan looked to the doorway before resting his eyes on Jaz. 'So, the other guy was the one who gave you the pills?' he said in her ear.

'Yep.' He was so close she had to resist the temptation to grip his shirt and shake him. 'Ryan, what's going on?'

He tucked his phone away into his jeans before bringing his focus back to her. 'Look, Jaz, you've helped me heaps just now. One day I hope to repay the favour. But I think it might be best if you head off, okay? It's not safe in here at the moment.'

'That doesn't tell me anything,' she said with a frown.

'Now's not the time to go into it, Jaz.'

She glanced at Ryan's pocket. 'What are you going to do with the drugs?' Just saying the words made her heart race, or was that due to the fact that they were ear to mouth so they could talk without being over-heard and that the sensation of his breath against her ear was something wild? His body didn't touch hers, but was close enough she felt his power. It was very intoxicating, even if she was a little afraid.

'Destroy them.' The rumble in his voice made it sound like he was going to kill people, not flush pills down the toilet.

'You really have a beef against drugs,' she said. Had he seen firsthand their disastrous side effects?

'Yes, I do. And for a bloody good reason, Jaz. Never go near them, it's not worth it.'

Would he ever share that reason, one day? He reached out for her arm, gently this time, and brought her in closer still. The effects of both her drinks, combined with Ryan's aftershave, were making her light-headed. She was also losing the feeling in her legs. Were they still attached?

'Jaz, please go home. I'll feel better knowing you're home safe. We'll talk later.'

And then, without even a goodbye, he was off through the crowd. Just the pressure from his touch and the scent of him left lingering, taunting.

Jaz was a little flummoxed. What did Ryan mean when he said he wanted her 'safe'? What did any of it mean? This whole night had been weird, and she found herself wondering if someone hadn't spiked her drink, causing her to hallucinate. Feeling vague, she started to wander back through the crowd looking for her friends.

'Hey, Jaz, we've been looking for you. God, don't scare us like that, we thought we'd lost you!'

'I'm okay, Anna. I just ran into Ryan and he had to break up a fight. I think we should leave.'

'Oh, we saw some of that, it was big,' said Taylor. 'Are you okay? You look a little hazy.'

'I had another drink and I'm not feeling that flash,' she lied. What else could she say? *I did some weird spying for my hot stalker and I was given drugs and I'm totally confused by all the events.*

'Let's go. That fight freaked me out and my feet are killing me,' said Anna. 'I'm so glad Tay was there.'

Jaz smiled and agreed, and together they headed for the exit.

At the last minute, Jaz glanced back and saw Ryan watching her leave. How was it that in a crowded room she could find him as if he were a lighthouse on a rocky cliff? He was standing by the wall, no doubt waiting for the men to return from the passageway. Ryan nodded towards the door and mouthed, 'Go'. She didn't need to be told twice.

Riding in the taxi back to Taylor's house, Anna started talking about the club and wondering if they should go again next week. And while Taylor and Anna made plans, Jaz just laid her head against Taylor's shoulder to rest. She was too caught up to talk with them. The whole night was just a mix of Ryan's face now, and she couldn't force his image from her mind. There was just something about him. Danger. Mystery. Smoking hot. What did she just get herself into?

CHAPTER 8

'COME ON, THINK you can take me?' said Tick as Jaz stood on the mat in front of him. 'Little miss, I'll toughen you up. Come on.' Tick launched a high foot at her head.

Jaz stood still, watching Tick's scare tactics, as his foot rushed past her nose by inches.

A panicked shout rang out behind her. 'Jaz!'

Ryan ran towards the mat, bag in hand and a worried expression on his face.

She laughed; he probably thought Tick was going to slaughter her. *I'll show him*, she thought as she threw the first punch at her opponent.

Tick blocked her punch and fired off one of his own. Jaz saw Ryan from the corner of her eyes. He was about to run in and rescue her. How sweet. But his step faltered yet again as Jaz threw up her hand and blocked Tick's oncoming fist. Not only did she block him, she followed it with a knee to his gut that connected. Tick's stomach was not soft, either; it was rippled with muscle and was like kneeing a brick wall.

Ryan's bag dropped to the floor along with his jaw, but she focused on Tick and unleashed a frenzy of kicks and punches.

'Oh, you think because you won a fencing tournament that you can hurt Tick now, hey?' Tick taunted.

'I don't know. How did that last kick feel?' Jaz asked, her pink lips curling up into a cheeky smile.

Ryan hadn't run in to stop them, in fact he had walked to the edge of the mat to watch, so she assumed by now he must have realised they were just sparring and having fun.

Jaz jumped and swung her leg out as she spun, and if Tick hadn't moved his head back in the nick of time, it wouldn't be sitting on his shoulders. Her foot brushed past his nose by millimetres. She laughed at using his own move against him.

'Remember,' said Tick, 'it's get in and get out.' And he showed her what he meant by slapping her face and sliding away and down so her return swing missed him. 'Be on your feet ready to instantly move down and away.'

After ten minutes, Jaz put up her hand and called a truce. The slap Tick gave her still stung her cheek but it also made her feel alive and invigorated. 'Enough, I've still got stuff to clean,' she laughed. 'I don't need blood on the mats too.'

Jaz hugged Tick as they laughed, and compared fresh bruises.

Ryan put his hands together and clapped. 'Well, that was brilliant.'

Jaz smiled as she wiped the sweat from her brow. 'Hey Ryan, this is Tick. Tick meet Ryan. He's just signed up for a few months.'

Tick held out his tattooed arm, Ryan shook it as he admired the artwork.

'So, you saw me take it easy on Jaz then, huh?' said Tick full of bravado.

Jaz scoffed and flicked her towel at him. 'Bullshit, Tick. You weren't holding back.' She felt pumped up, her skin tingled from the workout.

Ryan chuckled while they argued. No one had taken it easy on the other and it was just how Jaz liked it. Sometimes they went a little far and she went home with a split lip or a blood nose, which would cause her mum to complain. Then she'd have to remind the guys to not aim for her face.

'Well, I'm gonna hit the shower. Catch ya later,' said Tick as he walked off. The words JUSTICE were etched in black across his shoulders.

When Jaz turned and headed towards the office, Ryan followed. 'Well, you're full of surprises.'

Jaz took a drink from her water bottle; she felt a bead of sweat run down her neck, over her collarbone and down to her fitted black sports top.

'Anything else you can do that I don't know about?' Ryan asked as he hooked his thumb into his jeans pocket.

Jaz laughed. 'Well, I can handle a toilet brush and you've seen me scrub the mats.'

Ryan scratched his chin as he replied, and tried to hide his smile. 'Yes, your talent really has no end,' he teased. They gazed at each other for a moment. 'So… where did you learn to fight like that? Obviously not from a cereal box. Did Tick teach you?'

Jaz sat on a computer chair as Ryan leaned against the doorframe. Her black shorts rose further up her lean legs as she crossed them. A bruise was starting to show on her upper thigh.

'Sort of. It was originally my mum, but the guys at the gym kinda finished the job.' Jaz reached over to the desk and picked up a photo in a wooden frame to show Ryan. The picture was taken in the gym and showed her mum – with short, spiky blonde hair; so different to now – helping Jaz to stand on one of the blue mats.

'You look so much like your mum. How old were you?'

'I was one. Really? You can see a resemblance? I've got my dad's darker skin while the rest of my family is lily white.'

'You've got her high cheekbones and blue eyes,' said Ryan glancing at her. 'Your mum's pretty.'

Jaz nodded as she gazed into space trying to fight the heated flush she could feel building.

'She brought me to the gym before I could walk. Mum and Pax go way back, so she was always coming here and she taught me all she knew about karate from day dot. You spend every day in a gym and you soon start to pick up bits. The other guys help too. Bags taught me to box, and Tick's shown me the street-fighting stuff.'

'So, you have a mix of all sorts.'

'Yep, I love it all, it's a great way to clear the mind and forget about crap that pisses you off.'

'Hmm, remind me not to come across you in a dark alley.'

'Ha, try telling my mum that. She still worries about me walking home! When I was a kid she was so overprotective, I couldn't play in the park without her worrying I'd gone missing or been stolen when she'd lost sight of me for two seconds.'

Ryan took a last glance at the photo and put the frame back on Pax's desk. 'So, you really have known Pax longer than me.'

'Pax is family. I know everything about him... and yet sometimes I feel I know nothing.' Jaz glanced to the wall where certificates were displayed in simple black frames. Ryan coughed and cleared his throat.

'So... are you going to tell me about last night? What was all that about?' Jaz chewed her lip, watching Ryan. She found him fascinating, and after last night she was dying of curiosity.

'Well,' he said moving into the office and shutting the door. 'You know when I told you I wasn't just a bouncer, that I did "other stuff"? Yeah, well that was the "other stuff".'

'So, what are you, like a qualified stalker?' she asked.

Ryan ran his hand over his chin. It was shadowed with stubble, making him look rugged and a little sexy. Jaz found it hard to be cautious around Ryan. She should be, she didn't know him but something about him just didn't seem cruel or dangerous. Not towards her, at least.

'I guess you could call it that. I get paid to keep scumbags off the streets. But I'm a good guy and you can trust me, Jaz.'

'We'll see.'

He laughed. 'I'm sorry I put you in that position last night, but I really couldn't afford to miss who the guy in the white suit was meeting. You have no idea how important those photos you took were, and even better were the fingerprints we lifted off that plastic bag.'

'Wow, really?'

'Yeah, not that it helped much, as he's not on our database, but it's a start.'

'So, are you, like, an undercover cop?'

'Something like that.' He shrugged. 'That's as much as I can tell you, but just know that I work for the good guys.'

When he smiled like that, Jaz found it hard to think of him as anything but good.

'So... I suppose you're the *it* thing at school after winning the comp?' he asked.

Jaz laughed but it was edged with bitterness. 'Ha, like that would ever happen. You can't turn a scullery maid into a queen, and if by some miracle you could it would probably be just for a laugh.'

Ryan folded his arms. 'Like that, is it?'

'Yeah, school sucks. Some kids just have no idea about the real world. They can't live past their phones, flash clothes and status. I can't wait to leave and do something with meaning, earn my own money and be self-sufficient.' She leaned back in the chair, watching him. 'What was it like for you? I suppose you were popular.'

'What makes you think I was popular?' asked Ryan with a hint of a grin tugging on his lips.

'Well, you know…' she rolled her eyes. 'Cos you're all right looking and all.'

Now he laughed outright. 'All right looking?'

Jaz threw up her hands. 'Well, Anna thinks you're hot and you do turn heads wherever you go.' She wasn't ready to tell him she agreed with them.

He shook his head but a little blush crept up his neck. 'I wouldn't really know. I left school at fifteen.'

'Really, how come?'

Ryan stared at the cream-coloured wall behind her as if it held a secret. 'I joined up with the group I'm with now. They trained me and taught me things. But for the couple of years I was at high school, I don't recall being popular. I was far more interested in sports than anything else. Training took up a lot of my time.'

Jaz sighed. 'Yeah, tell me about it. But I mean, that's a good thing. I wouldn't give up my afternoons at The Ring for anything, it's my place. And I like the fact that it's here and not some fancy gym for the wealthy. It makes me feel like I'm living in the real world and not some fairy land.'

Ryan nodded and their eyes met and held for a moment as they fell into a comfortable silence.

'Well,' he said eventually, 'I suppose I better go and work out. Maybe one day, you and I can have a showdown like you did with Tick?' he asked.

A wide grin spread along Jaz's face. 'That'd be great. You better go practise!'

'Oh, you sound so confident.'

'Maybe. Your muscles don't scare me,' she said rising out of the chair and putting her hand on his biceps. 'One thing I've learnt from the boys in the gym is to never underestimate the little guy.'

Ryan's eyes danced with playfulness. Jaz put her hands on him and began to push him back towards the door but his wrist held her attention. Something about it tugged at her memory. 'Oh, I just remembered something. Does it help to know that the guy in the black suit has a tattoo?'

Ryan's eyes bulged. 'Really? Where? What did it look like?'

Jaz held his arm and made a circle on his wrist with her finger. 'It was right here, about this big.'

Reaching for a pen and a sheet of paper, Jaz set out trying to sketch the snake tattoo from memory. 'That's sort of it. But it was a bit smaller, like the size of a twenty-cent-piece.' She held the sheet up to Ryan.

Ryan studied the page, then folded it in half. 'You are awesome, Jaz. Did I mention that?' He leaned down and kissed her forehead before heading for the door. He paused with his hand on the doorframe. 'Jaz, just to be clear: you can't tell anyone about what happened at the club or about my work. Okay?'

'Yeah, sure.' But Jaz was still shocked at the kiss he'd planted on her. How had they become so comfortable with each other in such a short time? Was it being in a dangerous position at the club, knowing some of his secrets, or was it just that they connected?

'Thanks. I gotta deal with this. I'll see you soon.' And then he was gone. Meanwhile Jaz had a million more questions for Ryan rolling around in her head. Life certainly was much more exciting with him.

CHAPTER 9

JAZ FELT HER eyelids begin to drop, her chin resting on her palms with her elbows on the desk as Mrs Eckleston droned on and on about some Greek god and the essay she wanted them to write. Yes, maybe she needed to pay attention but Anna would have all the details. Besides, Mrs Eckleston's plain, even tone was sending her to sleep like the whine of the jets on an aeroplane. Momentarily she let the force of gravity win and let her eyelids close. She felt her body relax into the darkness, as if she were alone in her comfy bed with the doona pulled up around her. Maybe she should snap out of it; she'd hate to succumb to sleep and begin to drool or even worse, fall off her chair. But yesterday's spar with Tick had worn her out. She had pushed hard, wanting to impress Ryan. Instantly his mysterious brown eyes flashed behind her lids, the gold flecks glowing as if he was laughing. She felt her own lips curl into a smile.

'Wakey, wakey.'

The words echoed as her hands were smacked away from under her head. Jaz flung her eyes open.

'I don't know why Taylor even bothers to be friends with you. I guess he feels compelled to help out the less fortunate, always taking in feral animals. I'm surprised he hasn't caught some mangy disease yet.'

Jaz didn't bother to move, even though the bell had gone and kids were filing out of the room. 'Why, Minka, back on bitch duty already?'

Minka stood over Jaz, obviously enjoying the dominant position. Her cronies stood either side of her, but back half a foot so everyone knew who was top dog.

Not to be intimidated, Jaz rose slowly, almost on her tippy toes so she could tower over them all. 'Does it worry you that Anna and I are still Taylor's friends after all these years?' Jaz asked. She swung her bag up on her back and made sure it hit Minka, forcing her to step back so Jaz could pass. Jaz could see the safety of the corridor. The next class was already coming into the room.

'That's all you'll ever be to him. He has better taste, he doesn't do butch,' snarled Minka as she stuck out her foot.

Jaz tripped and felt the classroom move as she saw the floor coming closer. Swiftly she kicked out her other leg, planted it heavily, and managed to right her body before she sprawled all over the carpet like a pancake that had missed the pan. Minka had stepped up her game, being bitchier than normal. Then Jaz realised... the school ball was coming up. Was Minka feeling threatened?

Jaz could see Anna outside the door and quickly joined her.

'Hey you!' said Anna. 'You look flushed, are you okay?'

Jaz had a smartarse comment about Minka ready to leave her lips but it was swallowed as bony shoulders bumped into her back, pushing her through the door like a bulldozer. Anna rolled her eyes in their familiar way that said she'd already guessed. 'Minka.'

Minka's cronies didn't move off, instead they started an onslaught of criticism.

'Those freckles are hideous, Anna. Ever heard of make-up?'

'Commando boots! This is Saint Christian's, not the army.'

'She's obviously the guy in the relationship.'

Minka lurked in the classroom, listening to each slanderous word she'd probably coached them on.

'So, when are you two going to come out of the closet?' asked Crony One with the long, red pitchfork nails.

'I heard they're coming out at the ball and wearing matching outfits of black plastic and whips,' laughed Crony Two, aka Angelica, whose push-up bra was either really, really good or Daddy had recently paid for a boob job.

'Yeah, didn't you know, we got them from your mum's collection she uses for her special clients,' retorted Jaz, then briefly wondered if that might have been a low blow. But it was common knowledge that Angelica's mother had once been an escort girl before finding her rich husband. But hey, they had started this slinging match, and Jaz hated to give them the last word. Sometimes they needed to be dealt their own crap to see how they liked it.

Angelica's face began to glow a deep pink and Jaz almost expected steam to emanate from her ears. She'd hit her target, full on bullseye.

'Well, you're just a piece of shit that... that... no one likes you or even wants you here... you're... you're scum!' Her big breasts shook with her fury.

Jaz saw Minka take a black high-heeled step forward, as if sensing her girls losing control, but just as quickly she paused, before retreating behind the door.

'Hey Angelica, aren't you late for class?' came Taylor's voice from over Jaz's shoulder.

Instantly the cronies shrank back and pasted on sickly sweet smiles.

'Oh, hi Taylor. Yeah, we were just going.'

'See you later, Taylor,' they sang with the innocence of a dove. *Yeah, right,* thought Jaz. *More like crows that pick out your eyes, camouflaged in white paint!*

'Thanks, Tay,' said Anna with a big sigh of relief.

'Don't let them worry you. They're just threatened by your brains.' Taylor threw his arm around Anna and gave her a squeeze.

'Are my freckles that bad?' she asked, covering her nose with her hand.

'No, she was just being a cow. Take no notice,' Jaz reassured her.

'You only have a few freckles, Anna and they're so cute.' Taylor pulled her hand away as Anna blushed. 'So, would you girls be interested in coming to the range with me this arvo?' Taylor smiled at Jaz, and she felt like melting to the floor. 'Come on, guys, it's been ages since you both came with me.'

'Yeah, sounds great. I'll get Bags to run the gym this arvo. I'd like to shoot something,' Jaz said, thinking of Minka.

'Cool, Tay. Sounds like a plan,' agreed Anna.

'Great. I'll swing by your place and pick you up.'

Minka took the opportunity to step out of the classroom. 'Oh, hi, Taylor,' she said sweetly. Jaz reckoned she was waiting for her invitation to the range but it didn't come. Jaz felt like snorting with laughter at the impatient look on Minka's made-up face.

'Hi, Minka. Come on, Anna, we better get our seats.' Taylor directed Anna through as they weaved their way into the classroom Jaz and Minka had last been in. 'Catch you later.'

'See you after school,' Jaz said, mostly for Minka's benefit.

Minka grunted and walked off with a click-clack of heels. Taylor had never taken her to the range. He had gone with a couple of his male mates once or twice, but girl-wise, it was only ever her and Anna. Jaz couldn't even imagine Minka holding a gun; she'd likely shoot herself in the foot.

Jaz walked quickly down the corridor to her next class, knowing that she was going to be late. At this moment, she couldn't care less – she was spending the afternoon with Taylor, and even better, it had put Minka's nose out of joint.

During her next class with Mr Peel, who was always facing his blackboard, she typed out a text to Bags asking if he could run the gym this afternoon.

No probs Jaz

Mr Peel began scratching at the board with his chalk. He was in his late fifties with a big bushy beard and skittish eyes that seemed afraid to face his teenage class. Taking advantage of Mr Peel's weird behaviour, she fished her phone from her bag, put on her latest playlist and shook her hair over her ears… just in case. She picked up her pencil and began to doodle in the top corner of her page as she did some serious dreaming about the best-looking guy in school asking her to the ball. But as if Taylor would ask her.

CHAPTER 10

AFTER SCHOOL, JAZ was having a dilemma. No, correction: she was having a major meltdown! What the hell was she going to wear? She walked around her room in her black bra and undies, churning through piles of clothes on her bed and floor. She wanted to look nice for Taylor; maybe this would be the day he'd notice her. Well, you know, notice her as more than just the friend he saw every day.

She held up a cream leather jacket her mum had given her for Christmas and looked in the full-length mirror. It was a cool jacket. 'Nup, trying too hard!' she sighed and threw it over the end of her bed.

Honk, honk. Shit! He's here already. Jaz dived into the pile on the bed and pulled on a black singlet and black hoodie. She scanned her room and ran to the far side to drag on the pair of grey cargo pants she'd left draped over her computer chair. Crap! Shoes! Oh, and socks. Quickly she yanked open the top drawer on the bedside table, lucky-dipped a pair of black socks before picking up her Dr Martens by her door and ran towards the stairs.

Downstairs the house was quiet. Her mum and Paul were still at work and Simon was in the computer room, no doubt. With a swipe, she grabbed her house keys off the marble benchtop before heading back to the computer room. She'd got the guilts. Mum would freak if anything happened to Simon. While she was at work he was Jaz's responsibility. Even when she was at the gym, she was the closest to Simon and had to always have her phone on her.

'Hey, Geek Boy,' she said as she opened the door. The large room had one wall covered with books, and on the other side were two jarrah desks each topped with a huge computer. Half a computer lay open on a side table, its technical guts on display. Computers! Jaz wasn't totally computer illiterate; she knew how to check her emails, Facebook and use programs. But Simon, well, he could build a new one. That's why she never liked Anna coming over... she and Simon would start their geek speak and Jaz would be lost after mainframe.

'Hey, GI Jane,' Simon replied without taking his eyes away from the computer.

'Tay's taking us to the range, so if you need anything just call, okay?'

'Yeah, yeah, I know the drill. Don't shoot yourself!'

Jaz shut the door and ran outside, dying to see her friends again.

'Hey, Jazzy!' smiled Taylor from inside his shiny Mustang. His arm hung out the window, clad in a long-sleeved red T-shirt. He wore his reflective sunnies, even though it was overcast.

Jaz opened the back door and slid across the seat.

'Glad you could join us, Jasmine,' said Anna turning around in the front seat, her tone teasing. 'We've been waiting for ages!'

'Hi guys. Sorry, let's go.'

On the main road, Taylor planted his foot, leaving some tread behind and a whole heap of smoke. 'Jaz's folks are gonna love you,' squealed Anna who was gripping the door handle.

Jaz was flung back in her seat with her half-socked foot flying around in the air.

Taylor snickered with glee. 'How ya going back there, Jaz?'

'Fine and fricken dandy, no thanks to you. Bloody hoon,' she laughed as he swung the car sideways again, causing her leg to fling to the right window. 'I'd love to see the cops pull you up and then have your dad hear about it,' Jaz teased.

'You both know he'd kill me.' After Taylor mentioned that, his lead foot eased to the speed limit.

It was a twenty five-minute drive to the range, through the suburbs towards the hills.

'Can I drive on the way back?' Jaz begged after finally getting her boots on. She had her licence but no car.

'Jasmine Thomas! You know no one drives my baby but me. She's temperamental, fussy and has to be treated with care.'

'Just like her owner,' added Anna with a smirk.

'Burn.' Jaz laughed as she and Anna high-fived.

Taylor ignored them as he turned off the main road and into a bush reserve on the outskirts of Perth. It was dense and green; almost feel like being out in the country.

'See here? That's where the new training facility is going up. Dad said that all the groups will be able to use it — Australian Federal Police, Detectives, SWAT, SAS and other special forces.'

'So, will it be like a big paintball skirmish where they all run through the bush?' asked Anna.

'Some of it. It will have set-ups for bush scenarios, buildings and vehicles. Also areas where helicopters can land or hover above. I can't wait to watch them in action at the big viewing tower. Dad said it should be finished in a few months.'

Taylor's enthusiasm radiated from his eyes as he lifted his sunnies onto his head. He parked his Mustang and they headed inside a building that looked like an old clubhouse, aged red brick overgrown with shrubs and tall gum trees. It was once an old pistol club but the police had taken it over after it closed and turned it into their own training range.

Inside they signed in to the officer-on-duty. Taylor was well known to the officers because of his dad, but also because he practically lived at the range.

'Hey, Stewie!'

'Back so soon, Taylor. And with the ladies this time?' Stewie was a retired cop who, along with a few others, now worked full-time at the range, cleaning the weapons, keeping up stock and offering pointers on how to shoot. He was still in shape and had the tough buzz-cut to go with it.

He signed them in and gave them a wink. 'Off you go and have some fun. Derik is out the back and will fit you out.'

'Cheers, Stewie.'

The girls followed Taylor into a room set up with stalls for close-range shooting with handguns. Derik was sitting in the corner on a chair reading a paper, his blue trousers and boots the only part of him visible.

'Business must be slow, Derik,' asked Taylor.

The newspaper flopped down and Jaz could now see Derik's round face and short hair. The orange colour of it glowed like a halo. 'You could say that. It comes and goes.' Derik threw his paper on the floor beside him and stood up. 'Hi Jaz, Anna, long time no see. So, what can I get you all?'

Derik pulled a set of keys from his pocket, walked into a small office room and inserted a key into the big solid vault behind him. Then he pressed a few numbers on the keypad before it beeped and he turned the handle and opened the door. Jaz could see him through the small square hole in the wall, which acted as a serving window.

'The Browning 9-millimetre will do us for now, cheers Derik.'

'Just the one between you all?' Derik smiled when Taylor nodded. He seemed to like the idea of one gun between three teenagers better than one each. He handed the gun to Taylor while he locked the vault and opened another one for the ammunition.

Taylor held the gun out on his flat palm. 'So, who's first?'

Jaz and Anna both shrugged but Anna reached for it first. Jaz much preferred to use her hands as a weapon.

'Come on, you were scared the first time and I got that but now you know what you're doing,' said Taylor.

Take two thirteen-year-olds who had never seen a gun before and not long out of playing with dolls... well, yeah, they'd been scared. But Taylor's dad had been with them at the start and the adrenaline rush from holding a terrifying weapon and firing it had eased their nerves. 'Remember, Anna, it's just like the plastic one you have at home for your computer game.'

Anna snorted. 'There is the difference that my plastic one doesn't kill people, Tay!'

Taylor loaded the gun with ease. Jaz loved how calm he was around the weapons, how clever. He knew them in minute detail, which wasn't surprising for the son of a cop who tended to spend a lot of time cleaning and pulling apart his gun collection. If Jaz went to their house on a weekend, she would sometimes find them with guns dismantled on the table, as if it was as common as a father and son doing a jigsaw puzzle.

Anyway, Taylor looked so sexy when he was shooting. He'd stand tall and it was like he aged five years, looking like a man. Today was no different.

Anna took the gun and walked to a booth. She put the gun on the table while she put on her earmuffs. Taylor, Derik and Jaz put theirs on too.

Jaz tensed with Anna's first shot – it had been nearly six months since they'd been here – but by the eighth and last shot Jaz was comfortable with the sound.

Derik pressed a button and a sheet with a body outline came towards them.

'Not bad, Anna, only missed three shots,' said Derik as they all adjusted their earmuffs so one ear was free to listen.

'Um, Derik, did you not see where the other ones hit? Look, I have one shot that actually hit his shoulder, the rest would have sailed past.'

'Someone's rusty. See, if you came more often you'd be as good as me,' Taylor said with a smirk.

He took the gun from Anna, reloaded a new clip and fired out eight shots in a new booth in rapid succession.

'Damn!' Jaz couldn't stop the words from leaving her lips. He brought the target closer and she cursed again. All his shots had hit the target's head. Anna looked at Jaz, her mouth open in awe.

'Just how much time do you spend here?' Jaz asked.

Taylor shrugged, but he was definitely on a high from showing off. 'At least once a week,' he said with a cheeky grin. 'Sometimes three.'

'Crap, you've got so good.'

Jaz actually saw him blush at her praise. He was so cute with his cheeks glowing pink.

'Your turn.' Taylor handed her the gun and she reloaded it. The feel of the cold metal was nice against her calloused hands.

Already the adrenaline was pulsing through her veins as she took aim. Jaz was competitive, so of course she was trying to remember everything Taylor and Derik had ever told her about how to aim and fire. She also wanted to impress. With her stance ready, she pulled the trigger and felt the power of the gun explode with each bullet she fired. All too soon, the clip was empty. Her heart thumped as she remembered to breathe.

'Look at you; I can see that determination in your eyes. It's the same look you give me before you whip my arse at fencing,' said Taylor after he watched her put the gun down and take off her earmuffs.

Derik whistled as the target came near. 'Not bad, Jaz. Not bad at all.'

She had four shots make the target's head, three that were borderline and one that missed. Yes, she would have preferred that all of them hit the centre of the target's head, but beggars can't be choosers.

'Another round, I think, and then I want to show you guys the scope. More clips please, Derik.'

As Derik retrieved more ammo, Jaz engaged in one of her favourite pastimes: studying Taylor. Neither she, Taylor nor Anna knew what they were going to do past school, but Jaz believed that Taylor definitely needed to do something with guns or follow in his dad's footsteps. He seemed so happy and at home here. 'Maybe you should work in here like Derik after school, Tay. Then you can practise all you want. You're already here most of the time.'

'What about you, Jaz? You gonna run The Ring full-time after school, seeing as you nearly live there?' he teased.

'I don't know. Maybe? Better than going to college or uni. Don't think I'm cut out for that. Have you thought about it anymore, Anna?'

Anna shook her head. 'Nup. I guess I'll always have a job at Dad's business, but it just seems so boring to do that. I want to do something better than just computers.'

'I hear ya,' said Taylor. 'Dad wants me to follow in his footsteps but that's just it: they're his footsteps, not mine. I might try the SAS instead or something like it.'

'I agree. There's so much out there, and I can't think of one thing I want to do except make a difference. I don't want to be like Minka and worry about what I'll wear at each new function, I want to do something with meaning, like work at foreign camps helping the starving in other countries or even join the forces... I don't really know. That's the whole problem.'

'I'd like to be able to still see you both, every day if possible,' said Anna, her green eyes etched with sadness.

Jaz and Taylor threw their arms around Anna. 'Us too. What a crap thought. I can't imagine not seeing you guys every day,' said Jaz.

'It won't come to that.'

The girls eyeballed Taylor. 'Can you promise that?'

He shrugged and smiled weakly. 'There's all this technology we can use to stay in touch.'

'That's not the same,' sighed Anna.

'Well, this is morbidly depressing! You still have half a year left yet.' Derik shook his head. 'Here, go shoot something, you'll feel better.'

'Cheers, Derik. You're so thoughtful,' said Anna.

'Besides, we shut at five today and I think Taylor would die if he couldn't show you the scope. He'd have to wait another six months for your next visit,' Derik chuckled.

'No, we'll be back before then, won't we, Anna?'

'Too right, Jaz!'

CHAPTER 11

JAZ WAS BACK in the gym the next day after school, although her mind kept wandering back to the firing range. It had felt like the old days with Taylor, when they were inseparable. Now with high school and pecking orders it didn't happen so much. She missed those days. But the three of them had vowed to go together again soon. At least within a six-month period!

Jaz had just finished cleaning some sweaty gym equipment and was changing into her black crop top and yoga pants. With her skin tone, she could wear white easily, but she just couldn't bring herself to wear it. It was too bright, plus she was never one to stay clean; dirt just seemed to find her like metal filings to a magnet.

She tied her hair up into a quick braid as she walked out of the change room and towards her yoga mat. But who should be standing in her way? None other than the hunky, mysterious guy with those rich eyes that could go from haunting to come-hither in a millisecond.

'Jaz, you're back!'

'Um, yeah, I do work here,' she said with a sarcastic look. 'Gee, you make it sound like I was gone for a week.'

'Felt like it.'

Jaz paused two steps from him and studied his body, clad in a blue singlet and black track pants. 'Aww, you missed me. How sweet!'

Ryan laughed and followed her to her yoga mat. 'Can I take you up on the yoga lesson today?'

Now it was Jaz's turn to laugh. 'What, you mean the lesson I never offered?'

He cracked a smile. 'Yep, that one.'

'I suppose. Come on then, pull that mat over. I'll try to break it down to an easier level for you.'

Ryan threw her a look that said he didn't like being accommodated for. *Well, Mr I-Can-Do-Anything*, she thought, *I'm not going to make it too easy.* 'So, we start with some breathing. Just stand at the edge of your mat.'

Ryan did as she asked and followed her movements.

'Now, this is the Upward Dog,' she said as she stretched her back. Ryan was halfway there; not bad for a beefy bloke. 'Then bum up into the Downward Dog.'

'Is there any barking in this too?'

Jaz looked sideways at him as they both rested in the Downward Dog pose. 'You're kidding… that's the best you could come up with?'

'Yeah, lame, sorry. I've been away from civilisation for a while, I'm a bit rusty.'

'I'll say,' laughed Jaz.

She took Ryan up into a lunge position, left leg bent out in front with the right stretched out the back, and then got him to twist his upper body to the left side with his elbow on his left knee and hands in a prayer position. Jaz did it with ease, her balance great; Ryan, however, got the wobbles and fell… right into her.

His face went the slightest shade of pink. 'Oops, sorry. I lost my balance.'

'Yeah, no shit, Sherlock.' Jaz gave him a smile. 'Don't worry about it, that one's really hard, especially for a beginner.'

'Only you could be so condescending and nice at the same time,' he laughed before trying the position again.

'Your breathing needs to be more controlled, but I won't worry you with that much because you're still learning the positions.' Jaz didn't want him to feel too bad about his lack of flexibility, so she didn't let him know how far she'd brought the positions back to basic. Ryan struck her as someone who liked to be well prepared, and if he didn't know something he would practise until he could do it a hundred percent right. He was taking the yoga very seriously and she liked the way he'd followed her every move and direction. She'd half-expected him to take the piss out of her the whole way through, but when she gazed at his own sculpted body, she realised he'd never do that. His body was his temple. A damn nice temple too…

Jaz suddenly realised that she had held the same position for much longer than necessary… hey, she was a little distracted! She moved him through the final routine.

'Now just lie here for a bit, relax and breathe in and out and draw energy back into your muscles.'

'Hmm, I like this part the best,' Ryan, mumbled in a relaxed, half-asleep voice.

After a few minutes, Jaz sat up and crossed her legs. 'Well, how was that?'

Ryan rolled onto his side and rested his head in his hand. 'Much harder than I thought it would be. I could feel all my muscles working.'

Jaz nodded her head. 'Yeah, it doesn't just stretch your muscles. You did well for a first-timer. More flexibility than I would give your body credit for.'

Ryan shot an eyebrow up. 'And what's that supposed to mean?'

'Um… well, you know. Someone with your muscled physique can sometimes find it hard to stretch.' *Sheesh, Jaz, blush much*, she thought as she felt the heat burn in her cheeks.

'Well, thank you for the lesson, you were great.' There was a moment of silence. 'Um, this is where you say "any time"?' Ryan laughed.

'Really, you want me to put you through that again? I didn't take you as a sucker for punishment,' she chuckled back.

'I liked it. It was something new, and I'd like to get better at it.'

That didn't surprise Jaz. Ryan was just as competitive as she was. Funny that in such a short time she seemed to know a lot about Ryan, or maybe he was just easy to read.

'Well, if you're here this time each day, I'll take you through it,' she offered.

'Cheers, Jaz. You're a gem.' Ryan cleared his throat as he stretched his large fingers out on the blue mat. 'So, where were you yesterday? Get detention?'

Jaz laughed. 'As if. I don't get caught.'

His eyebrow shot up again; it was a cute look on him. 'Oh really! What do you get up to?'

Jaz smiled and shook her head. 'I'm not spilling my secrets unless you're going to spill yours.'

The stare of steel on Ryan's face said she wasn't going to get his secrets any time soon. Jaz sighed. 'If you must know I was at the firing range with my friends.'

Now Ryan's ears perked up. 'True? What kind of friends do you have? Are they the offspring of the mafia?'

Jaz laughed so hard she almost snorted. 'You come out with some funny shit.' Jaz's braid hung over her shoulder and she played with the end of it. 'I was with Anna and Taylor, who you've already met.'

'Ah, yes. I can't imagine sweet-looking Anna at a firing range. What were you kids doing there?'

Jaz's skin prickled at the word 'kids'; she would be eighteen soon!

'Well, ain't you just a Mr Know-It-All! Do interrogations much?' she asked.

'Yeah, a few,' he replied, and she had the feeling he was telling the truth.

'We've been going for years, since we were twelve. Taylor's dad is a cop and Taylor loves anything deadly. He'd join the Army just so he could use a grenade launcher, I reckon.'

'Really? So, what were you shooting with?'

'A Browning 9-millimetre.'

'Good choice, the Browning has strong recoil, so it's great for training, and being just that bit heavier makes a lighter gun like the Starfire 9-millimetre a breeze to use.'

'Yeah, I noticed that,' said Jaz dryly.

'Did you?' asked Ryan, his interest levels going through the roof.

'No, you dumb arse, why would I know shit like that? I just go there and fire the weapon Tay gives me.' Jaz flashed him a look she hoped said, *Who the hell do you think I am, Vin Diesel?* 'But you, on the other hand, seem to know a lot about guns. Do tell…' she asked curiously.

Ryan's face was guarded. She'd give fifty bucks to know what he was thinking. A minute later, after she'd just about died with anticipation, he finally replied.

'In my line of work we have contact with weapons.'

'"*In my line of work we have contact with weapons!*" Where did you get that from, your job description? Dude, that is weird.'

Ryan's intense gaze crumbled as he laughed. 'Sorry. Yes, I have played with a few guns. But I'm interested… Does Anna shoot too?'

'Oh yeah, all three of us try. Taylor is like the weapon expert, his dad has a collection of guns and Tay knows everything about them. He also can shoot the pants off us. Yesterday he landed all eight shots in the target's head. He's brilliant.'

'Is that so? Hmm.'

'Anna and I were a bit rusty, but it had been six months since we'd been.'

Ryan sat up; he was wearing an expression of awe.

'What?' Jaz asked. 'What's that look for?'

Ryan ran his hand over his short cropped hair. 'I just can't believe it. You're like the perfect package, the ideal woman.'

Jaz's eyebrows met as she screwed up her face. What did Ryan mean by that? She might have thought he was hitting on her but his expression was completely different. It was as if he'd found a missing notebook or something; nothing like attraction. Which was funny, because she was sure she'd seen him gaze at her with desire, once or twice. Maybe her romantic sonar was just off kilter.

'Thanks… I think. Hey, I've been dying to know if that tattoo drawing helped?'

That pulled Ryan away from his thoughts.

'Yeah, it was a huge help, Jaz.'

'Sooooo, can I ask what it was about?'

Ryan chewed his lip for a second as if he were raging an internal war. He sighed, glanced around the room to check they were alone and then sat up cross-legged. 'I guess it can't hurt to tell you we were trying to track a drug cartel. We had information about the guy in the white suit but no evidence he was in league with this other group. Until you spotted that tattoo. It's their mark. So, now we know he's involved, we just have to get some solid proof.'

'How will you find proof?' she asked.

'That's something you don't need to know. And this conversation goes no further, right?'

Jaz crossed her heart. 'Yep, figured that. Are you an undercover cop?' She just wanted to fit Ryan into a job description, to understand what the hell it was he actually did.

'In a way I am, but I don't work for the police force.' Ryan stood up. 'Well, I'm gonna go hit the speedball for a bit.' And then he walked off.

'Conversation over, got it,' Jaz mumbled.

While Ryan pounded the ball, Jaz set about cleaning. Fifteen minutes later she stopped to watch the fluid motion of his muscles at the speedball, the way the sweat rolled over his skin, making it shine. Jaz cleared her throat. 'Um, Ryan, I'm going to have a shower and then close up. Sorry to kick you out.'

He paused. 'No, that's fine. I'm nearly done here anyway.' Sweat dripped from his chin and soaked into his singlet. Jaz was going to need a cold shower.

She walked off, leaving him to finish.

Jaz went to the change rooms, and a few minutes later she heard another set of taps turn on a few cubicles down. Pax had an all-in-one change room, so he'd put curtains on all the showers, except on her shower, which had a lockable door.

But that didn't stop Jaz's mind from realising there was a naked bloke a few metres away, a nice yummy bloke at that. With a shiver, she reached for the soap and buried her head under the water to drown out her thoughts.

CHAPTER 12

IT WAS DARK outside the gym as Jaz stood near the light switch waiting for Ryan to come out of the change room. Drops of water seeped through her hoodie from her damp hair. Why was it, no matter how much she squeezed the water from her hair, and rubbed it with a towel, it still seemed to seep moisture. Jaz flicked it back over her shoulder just as Ryan entered the room.

'Waiting for me?' he asked.

'No, I just like standing here all night.'

Ryan cracked a smile as he walked towards her, his short hair glistening. As for the rest of him, his tantalising scent reached her first. He wasn't drowning in aftershave like most of the boys at school, who layered it on so thick you'd think they were trying to attract girls from schools three hours away. Ryan was refreshing without being overpowering.

'Will you be back tomorrow?' he asked.

Jaz cocked an eyebrow. 'Why, you gonna miss me again?' she laughed.

Ryan ignored her taunts. 'I was hoping you and I could spar together, like you did with Tick that day?'

'Now that sounds like a plan. Tomorrow it is! Prepare for an arse-whooping,' she said nudging him. The contact sent a zap through her, causing her skin to bristle.

'What makes you so sure you'll win?'

'Nothing... just trying to psyche out my opponent,' Jaz said with a wink.

Ryan shook his head and smiled. It reached up into his eyes as the deep chocolate swirled irresistibly with gold.

'Can I give you a ride home?'

'Nah. Thanks, but I like the walk back. Gives me time to unwind with my tunes. I keep telling Mum if she wants me safe she should get me a car. But I think the idea of me behind the wheel scares her more.'

'Okay, if you're sure. Just be careful out there. Not a nice hood to be in at night.' Ryan gave her a wave and headed to the back door towards the small car park behind the gym.

'Yep, I'm sure.' Jaz flicked off the lights and leaned against the door. She didn't need light, she knew her way around this gym blindfolded. There was something calming about being in the gym after hours; the darkness, the linger of sweat, even though no bodies were inside, no sounds except for her breathing. She flipped the closed sign on the door and locked it before pocketing the keys. Outside was dark, considering it was only seven o'clock and the streetlights were in full bloom. Jaz took a quick look up both sides of the street as she put her music on and lifted her hood over her wet hair. It was cold and her breath left an impression in the night air.

She waited until the Evanescence song came on before moving her commando boots down the uneven pavement. It was on her second step that she felt the first raindrop. *Damn.* All she could do was hope it didn't get any heavier. And wonder if she should have taken up Ryan's offer. Jaz wasn't going to run home tonight, mainly because she was too slack to get dressed properly and had only put on her white singlet under her hoodie, without her bra. Too much bounce was bad, so she would just have to endure the rain. It wasn't heavy at the moment anyway.

A block down the street she saw a group of guys turn onto the path from a dark alleyway. There were five of them and they smelled like trouble, and her belly flipped, warning her to be careful. It was the way they walked, the tattoos, the clothes; the way they pushed each other as they talked. She kept her head down and her eyes in front. She walked close to an old factory shed, making herself insignificant and giving them plenty of room to pass. Through the music playing in her ears she could just hear them whistling and trying to talk to her but she ignored them and moved on with her hands stuffed deep into her pockets. A few steps and she was past them, breathing a sigh of relief as she went on her way uninterrupted. The wayward spots became more regular as the rain got a bit more serious.

And that's when she felt a hand on her shoulder, right when she thought she was safe.

She was spun around to face the men, who circled back around her. One of them tugged at her clothes and pulled down her hoodie, ripping out one of her earphones. Another one whistled when he saw her face.

'Look at what we got here, fellas. Hey, beautiful,' said the largest one. He was solid like a rugby player and Jaz didn't fancy picking a fight with him. Not when his eyes flicked about skittishly. Was he on something? Possibly. If he was, that made a dangerous combination.

Was she scared? Hell, yes. Did she think she could take them? Maybe.

It depended on whether they were just regular guys looking for trouble, or guys like Tick who knew how to fight. What were her chances, and against five? A tall skinny guy with a ring through his lip and one in his eyebrow pulled out her other earphone.

'Hey, we're talking to you. Wanna help us celebrate?'

She could hear their breathing as they waited for her reply. She felt like a deer sitting in front of a lion as it waited for her to make a run for it. Let the chase begin. This was just a game for them.

'No thanks, my parents are waiting for me to get home.' Maybe they would let her go. Maybe they wouldn't. Jaz needed to keep her cool. She couldn't panic, she needed a clear head.

'I'm sure we have plenty of time,' asked another, who was wearing a black beanie and puffer jacket. She instantly disliked his slanted smile.

Jaz took this moment to run, trying to leave suddenly without warning. But there were too many of them and one managed to hook her hoodie and yank her back. The material pulled tight against her neck cutting off her air momentarily. When the material was released she gasped for air and felt hands all over her.

One had the nerve to go for her chest. Jaz didn't have time to think about her situation, instead she just launched into a kicking and fist-flying frenzy. She wouldn't go down without a fight. She connected with the guy in front. Her fist found his nose. He stumbled back as blood begun to pour down his face. The guy with the beanie was next as she aimed a kick to his groin, sending him down swearing, hands cupping his family jewels.

Hands reached around her neck; it was the muscly guy. She could tell by the strength of his grip as air was squeezed from her throat. Another guy punched her face, leaving her dizzy for a moment while he followed up with a few more to her ribs. Each blow was more intense as she struggled for breath. The one holding her started to drag her along the ground, back to the side of the factory shed. She reached out a hand, catching the edge of it. Rusty tin slid past her fingers. Her other hand grasped at the arm holding her neck. Was this how she was going to go out? Were they going to rape her? Leave her for dead?

Not if she could help it.

Jaz planted her feet and pushed backwards as hard as she could, knocking the guy off balance. His arm loosened its grip, allowing her to spin around and punch him in the kidneys. She would have followed up with a kick to his privates but the other three were still coming at her.

And then there was the rain, going about its own business.

Jaz wiped the drops from her eyes as she aimed a kick high and got one of the advancing guys in the head, sending him sprawling sideways against the tin wall of the old factory. The crack of his collision echoed out into the night like lightning. The guys swore at her, calling her names and looking very pissed off. No longer were they interested in taking her home; they wanted to exact revenge on her connecting hits and punches. Clearly they weren't expecting a fight.

Blood filled her mouth as a fist connected with her lip. The taste on her tongue ignited a primal need to return the favour. She swung a punch back and gave the yellow-eyed guy a solid crunch. Blood smeared her hand as his teeth left an imprint.

'Get the fucking bitch,' wailed another who was off to one side.

From her quick count, three were still trying to get up off the ground; one was holding his nose, and the other she could take.

But then he flicked out a knife. An overhead streetlight glinted off its smooth shiny blade.

Oh, shit.

She saw two more blades being unsheathed beside her. Okay, the odds were really stacked against her now. An uninvited image entered her mind: her body drawn into the shadows, sliced and diced into bits. Who would find her body? Would they recognise her?

She had no other option but to keep her cool; this was the fight of her life. Jaz took on the immediate threat in front of her. They circled each other. He with the knife. She with her hands. The blade seemed small but the damage it could inflict was great.

He struck out with the knife. Jaz dodged it. She watched his movements, saw the rain dribble into his eyes and waited for her time. He lunged again. She counter-attacked with a swift kick, using her boot to knock the knife from his hand and sending it flying to the road.

Jaz then spun around and shot out both arms to get the other two guys with knives. One blade cut across her hand, causing a red line to appear, and she wasn't sure what happened with the other knife. The guy was still armed, she had to keep moving. The blood was slippery through her fingers, the rain making it run faster. She was hurting all over but told herself this was just like the training sessions with Tick and the others. *Move past the pain and keep going. Breathe. Mind control.*

Jaz was trying her best but the extra knives were making it hard for her to get to them. Every time she hit one down they just got back up. Did she have a chance of running away from them? It was looking like her last option. Run for help. She knew she should scream but wasn't sure if she was capable. She'd never been a screamer. Wouldn't know how to start. She'd always dealt with things quietly. Refusing to call for help. Would that now be her downfall?

Beanie-guy lunged forward with his knife, and she ducked out of the way before throwing a punch to his kidneys then followed it up with another, sending him sprawling backwards. She snatched his hand with the knife and bent it back until he dropped it in pain, then she kicked the knife into the gutter. She then pulled Beanie-guy into a tight headlock. She intended to use him to get away. Somehow. At the moment she was playing it by ear.

She said a silent prayer, hoping she would survive this. The guy still wedged underneath her arm started to fight, so she tightened her grip, squeezing the air from him just like they'd done to her. She had one at her mercy, but what about the others? They'd all bounced back and were getting up and coming towards her. Blood down their faces. She had hurt them, but not enough to stop them.

As her mind raced about what to do next, the guy closest to the road fell suddenly with a thud. It was like he had narcolepsy; he lay there, still. But she hadn't even punched him.

Someone else had.

The remaining three were in a half-circle around another person. Jaz's jaw dropped as the rain eased off.

'Ryan,' she mumbled, relieved.

Jaz watched in horror as the blond-haired guy without a knife collected the bit of cut chain lying by the factory door and started swinging it. Ryan took off his jacket and wrapped it around his left arm, his eyes never leaving his opponent. Then he faked a move and the guy launched his chain. Jaz winced as she expected the worst, but Ryan had the chain wrapped around his arm and dragged the guy in so quickly he didn't know what had hit him. He maimed the guy with a poke to the eye and a knee to his nuts before throwing him back. Two left. A guy with a knife lunged at Ryan, and Jaz yelled out his name in horror. Her voice distracted the guy, making it easy for Ryan, who'd held up his covered arm and attacked with the other. With a sickening crunch, Ryan bent his attacker's hand, the knife falling to the ground.

The last guy jumped on his back and dragged Ryan to the ground.

In a blink, Ryan had picked up the knife from the gutter and slashed it against his assailant before kicking out the legs of the last guy standing.

Ryan stood, with bodies around him, and wiped the knife handle on his singlet before dropping it.

He looked perfect, as if he'd just dusted off his hands after baking. Instead, he'd just laid out four armed guys faster than Jaz could kick one.

'Are you okay?'

She just stood there, open-mouthed, with the guy under her arm starting to wriggle again. 'Let me go, I'm sorry,' he begged.

Ryan stepped towards her, grabbed the guy she was clutching onto like a Gucci bag and laid him out with his buddies.

'You should have maimed them, and then they wouldn't keep coming at you. Go for the eyes or the testicles.'

Jaz stood there dumbly. Ryan was picking now to give her a lesson in self-defence!

'If you want to survive, you have to get dirty and think outside the square.' Ryan was unravelling his jacket from his arm as one of the guys began to move. He stepped towards the guy and swung his leg, kicking him hard. Jaz flinched.

'Come on,' said Ryan as he grabbed her arm and pulled her towards the road.

'What are you doing here?' she finally managed as they ran to his car.

'You're just lucky I drive this way home. I saw you beating up on the homies and came to lend a hand. Sorry, I would have been here earlier but I got a phone call. I hate to think... if I was any later.' He opened the door. 'Quick, get in.'

He practically lifted her in before slamming the door. Next thing, he was beside her, putting his SUV into gear and driving off. Jaz looked out the window at the guys under the streetlight. Five motionless bodies. Had Ryan killed them?

'They'll be fine... eventually,' he said as if reading her mind.

When they were well away from the area, Ryan pulled over. He switched on the interior light, put his hand up to Jaz's face, and caressed her chin.

'Are you okay?' he asked, tilting her face to check for wounds.

'You've already asked me that,' she replied plainly, trying to flick his hands away.

'Yeah, but you never answered me.' Ryan moved her arm out of the way and touched her lip.

'Is it bad?' she asked.

'No, just a small split, a swollen cheek, and... oh.' Ryan pulled his hand away when he saw that it was covered with blood.

'Oh my God, Ryan, are you okay?' Jaz's heart lurched as she saw just how much blood was on his hand. 'You're bleeding? Did you get cut?'

'No, it's not mine.'

'One of them?'

'I don't think so.' Then his eyes grew large and filled with fear.

'What... what is it?' she managed.

Ryan leaned over to her side of the car and started feeling her. 'Do you want us to get a room?' she joked.

'Only you, Jaz, could joke at a time like this. I think it's *your* blood,' he stressed.

'What! I was cut on my hand but it wasn't deep.' She showed him her hand covered with blood, but the cut wasn't bleeding much.

'Does it hurt anywhere?'

Jaz thought about it: her ribs hurt, her feet and hands, her lip, head and a few other spots, just the normal pain. Except for the stinging on her arm, which was slightly different.

She held her left arm up for Ryan to inspect. 'Here.'

He pulled her arm gently across so he could see it better in the light. Blood was trailing along her hand, dripping off her fingertips.

'Oh, that's not good,' she said weakly, amazed at how freely her blood spilled.

Ryan sucked air in between his teeth.

It was hard to see anything against the black of her hoodie but when he pulled the material, a hole appeared in the jumper. Red blood stood out against her skin, staining her clothing around it.

'Oh shit,' mumbled Jaz. 'Is it bad?'

Ryan ripped her sleeve further and she felt his fingers probing her skin. 'Yeah, I'm afraid so. You'll need stitches. It's bleeding badly.'

'All in your car too. Sorry.' Jaz tried to mop it up with her other sleeve.

Ryan pulled off his singlet, causing her to momentarily forget everything. 'What are you doing?'

He didn't answer, instead he wrapped his singlet around her arm. 'Now hold that tight to stop the bleeding.'

'Oh, yeah, thanks.' *What's going to stop my shaking?* she wondered. Maybe having no shirt on was part of his plan to distract her. Well, it was kind of working. The dull interior light cast shadows along Ryan's muscled abs. She concentrated on counting them.

'I'll take you to the hospital.'

Jaz withdrew her arm and clutched it to her chest. 'I'm not going to a hospital,' she said shaking her head. 'I don't care how much it's bleeding.'

Ryan was taken aback. 'Jaz, it won't hurt that much, I promise.'

Jaz laughed. 'No, it's not that. I can't tell Mum about this or she will freak. And I definitely don't need a hospital lady calling her up. Mum would never let me go back to the gym again, let alone walk by myself.'

'Come on, Jaz.'

'No, I'm dead serious. You don't know my mother. She's paranoid as it is. I used to play soccer until one day I went off with someone's dad for ice-cream without telling her, she freaked out and never let me go back. I can't go to a hospital. Can't you just give me a few bandaids and we'll call it even?'

'I'm afraid it might need more than that.' He bit his lip as he thought. 'How about I take you to my place and we get you cleaned up and take a better look at it?'

Jaz let out a long breath. 'Yes, I'd like that heaps better. Thanks.' But after she spoke she wondered if she wasn't putting herself at more risk. *Ah, what does it matter, Ryan just saved my life! He can't be that bad.*

'Okay.' He turned off the interior light and drove back onto the quiet road.

As each streetlight flashed past she got a glimpse of his upper body.

'You know, you were awesome back there. Thanks for saving me.' What else could she say? No other words could express just how fast and methodical he'd been. Now she knew why he looked like he did: he was a bad-arse fighting machine. He was her new superhero.

'No worries,' he said. 'You weren't bad yourself.'

Despite bleeding, aching and realising just how close she'd come to something truly scary, Jaz smiled. The adrenaline coursing through her was topped off with Ryan beside her, giving her the best feeling ever. What a night.

CHAPTER 13

'WHAT *ARE* YOU trying to do?' asked Ryan as they pulled up outside a big roller door.

'Text one-handed.' Jaz attempted a smile but it was weak, she suddenly felt tired. 'I'm just letting Mum know I'm staying at Anna's for dinner and then letting Anna know that I'm at her place in case Mum calls.'

'I see.' A smile tugged on the corner of his lips.

Jaz put her phone back in her pocket. 'So, this is your place?' There was not much to see except for a big fence out the front.

Ryan pressed a button on his key ring and the roller door begun to move up. He drove his car along a short paved driveway into an open shed.

Without a word, they got out and he led her out of the shed to his home.

A security light flicked on and Ryan rattled his keys and pushed open the door on his house. Jaz followed his half-naked body closely down a hallway, past a kitchen and through the lounge room, down another tiled hallway and into a bathroom. One thing she noticed on her travels through his house was how tidy it was. Almost to the point that it looked like a house out of a magazine, so bloody spotless no one could actually live there. No books or coffee cups lying around, no pictures on the walls, just some artwork and ornaments that looked like they came from Africa. Her room looked like a bombsite in comparison.

His bathroom was nice; white with a charcoal grey theme. It had a large bench with a sink in the middle, and very few personal items.

'Do you even live here?' she asked. Without warning, Ryan picked her up and plonked her on top of the bench. She was almost eye-to-eye with him. It would help to keep her eyes above his neck and not on his very naked and glorious chest.

'Like, where is your toothbrush and stuff?'

'In these things called drawers.' As if to prove he had some, he pulled one open. Jaz saw a toothbrush, deodorant and shaving gear. It was neat and clean, not jumbled up like everything in her drawers.

'Hmm, you're very tidy. Don't come to my house unannounced, will you?'

Ryan grabbed the bottom of her hoodie and began to lift it up. At this point Jaz was too shaken up to care and lifted her arms like an obedient toddler. He managed to get it off without moving his makeshift bandage, he was gentle, but she did suck in a breath as pain crept in as her adrenaline subsided. It was when her hoodie was a bloody heap on the floor that she realised what she had on underneath. Her hair was still dripping from the rain and it was seeping further into her white singlet, making her suddenly wish it wasn't so tight.

Ryan flicked on the heater light switch – she didn't want to know how he could tell she was cold – and she noticed a small tattoo under his right arm. It was just one word: *Forever.*

'Stay there while I get some stuff to clean you up with.' He'd cleared his throat before he spoke and when he did, the pitch was all over the place.

Ryan came back with a small towel and a first-aid kit. She flinched when he began to remove his bloody singlet from her wound, and again when fresh blood appeared as he threw away the temporary bandage. With a knowing speed he cleaned up the area. Then Jaz nearly fainted when he produced a needle and a thread.

'What the hell!'

'You need a few stitches, Jaz. Now, I'm sure that if you can take on five guys, then you can handle a little pinprick.'

Jaz gritted her teeth as she waited for the needle to pierce her skin. 'Damn you, Ryan. Where did you learn to sew people up, anyway?' she asked, partly because she was curious but mostly as a distraction as she felt the first pull of thread. She sucked in a shaky breath.

'With my job they teach you how to be self-sufficient. It comes in handy.'

'Really? You gotta sew people up? What are you, a Rambo medic?'

He laughed but he kept stitching her wound together with precision while she tried not to pass out.

'Mainly it's for sewing myself up.'

'Say *what*? You stitch yourself? Sounds scary and awful.' Slow breath in and out. She was not going to faint on him now. Instead she willed her body to relax and not think about it.

'You see that mark on my left arm near the top?'

Jaz let her eyes gaze past his chest over to his arm where she saw a thin long scar. With her free hand, she traced it, causing Ryan to flinch under her touch. 'You stitched this up?'

He nodded and she heard him snip at the thread.

'You did a good job.' Hell, an amazing job if he did that one-handed. 'How long ago did you do that?'

Ryan packed away the needle and straightened up. 'Two years ago, give or take. So, what do you think?' He held her arm up so she could see his workmanship.

Jaz rolled her arm around for closer inspection. Eight small, neat stitches closed up the cut. 'Wow, I'm impressed. Mum will never notice.' She glanced at Ryan, whose eyes were trying to politely avoid her chest. 'Thanks, Ryan. Not only did you save my arse but you patched me up like a pro. Thanks. I owe you one. No actually, that's two now.'

'It was my pleasure, but let's just call it even. The info you got at the club makes us square,' he replied as he wrapped a bandage over the stitches. Then he leaned past her to wet a flannel so he could gently dab at her split lip.

Jaz got another good look at his tattoo as his hand held her head gently. '*Forever.* Does that have some sort of special meaning?'

Ryan tensed a little before nodding.

'Well, are you going to share?' He paused and looked Jaz in the eyes. She felt her heart pick up the pace as his dark eyes clouded over in mystery. 'Come on, did I not endure you sticking me with a needle without complaint? Share a little, it won't kill you.' But the pain she saw in his eyes made her think otherwise. 'I'm sorry, you don't have to.'

'There *is* more to this tattoo, you just can't see it,' he said, so quietly.

'Huh? What do you mean?' Jaz instinctively looked to his lower torso and then wished she hadn't.

Ryan turned and left the bathroom, his damp track pants hanging divinely low on his hips.

She was just about to go find him, to ask if she had upset him, when he returned with a hand-held light. He flicked off the bathroom light, covering them in darkness. She felt Ryan move closer, his waist nudging her legs. Hairs on the back of her neck twitched in suspense.

Then a purple glow filled the bathroom.

'What is that?'

'It's called a black light.' Without further explanation, he waved it over his *Forever* tattoo and suddenly, as if by magic, more appeared.

'Wow, that is cool.' Jaz couldn't stop her hand from reaching out to his arm. Ryan's breath faltered as with a finger she traced two beautiful layered angel wings that glowed around the words etched in ink on his arm. Under the word *Forever* was the recently invisible initials *CC* and the year *2013*.

'CC? Who's that?' Jaz immediately thought of an old girlfriend, or a family member.

'My mate Chris. He died this year.' Ryan's voice was scratchy and deep. '*Forever* means I will never forget him or the way he died.'

Jaz let the rest of her fingers circle Ryan's arm and held him. 'I'm so sorry.' This explained a lot about his troubled expressions. 'I can tell it's been hard on you.'

He breathed heavily. 'Having you around has been helping,' he said with a smile.

Wow, really?

'Hey, what's this one?' Jaz had caught the edge of another tattoo and moved the black light closer to Ryan's chest.

'You don't recognise the Southern Cross?'

'Oh, yeah.' Jaz touched each star. She knew she shouldn't constantly touch him, but she couldn't help it, she was fascinated. It made her want a tattoo, because they were so damn sexy on Ryan. She could feel faint hairs under her skin, and her fingers itched to follow their path down to the top of his track pants.

'It's to remind me of home, of where I'm from.'

Ryan turned off the black light and switched back on the bathroom light. Jaz blinked rapidly, trying to adjust to the brightness. She preferred the dark. There was no way she could touch Ryan like she had in this light.

She studied him, looking back over his even skin to where she knew the tattoo was. 'So, why have it invisible?'

'It's just easier this way. It's not traceable like the guy with the snake tattoo.'

'Ah, got it. Because you're a secret agent guy.' She smiled. 'Ouch.' Her sore lip didn't like smiling.

'Let me finish.' Ryan went back to cleaning her lip. When he was done, he washed the blood off his hands, and Jaz watched the redness swirl down the drain. Her blood.

'Come on,' he said with a flick of his head. 'I'll find you another jumper to wear.' His eyes grazed past her chest and she felt her nipples push against her singlet. She had a feeling the jumper was more for his benefit. He led her into his bedroom and opened a drawer next to his immaculately made bed. It was a plain black doona cover with a few matching pillows. It looked so inviting, Jaz felt like she could sleep for a week. Ryan's matching pine bedside tables were bare except for an alarm clock and a photo of a couple she guessed were his parents.

'These your folks?'

Ryan didn't need to look to know what she was talking about. 'Yep.'

'Do they live nearby?'

'They are north of the city. My little sister lives close by too.'

'Cool.' Jaz turned to face Ryan. 'Man, you should see my room. It's nothing like this.'

He threw her a dark grey jumper. 'Here, I know how much you like hoodies.'

'Thanks.' Jaz pulled it on and smiled at its warmth. She loved the bigger size, it was loose and warm and smelled like him.

Ryan put on a blue long-sleeved shirt, and Jaz couldn't help but be a little disappointed.

'Hmm, I hope you're not expecting this back,' she said wrapping her arms around the soft jumper.

He raised one eyebrow in that funny little way. 'I guess not. So, you want a cuppa?'

Jaz sighed heavily as she followed him to the kitchen. 'How about a stiff scotch? I'm feeling a tad bit frayed and a little weak, which I don't like admitting.'

'I'm not surprised. Blood loss does that.' He went to the kitchen and made two strong coffees. The smell alone perked her up.

'Cheers.'

They went and sat in his lounge room, on a big deep brown suede couch, and he flicked on the heater.

Jaz used Ryan's long sleeves as a holder around her hot drink and took a sip.

They sat in silence. Every now and then, their eyes would meet.

Eventually Ryan spoke. 'You did great out there tonight. How are you feeling? You seem like you're handling it okay.' His eyes drilled her for signs of weakness. Did he expect her to flop on the floor and cry? Jaz didn't cry for anyone.

'I'm fine, Ryan. Honestly. I'll admit I'm a little shaky, I've never had to fight for my life before. And I wouldn't call fights with guys at The Ring real ones either; they don't fight dirty. So, all things considered I think I'm coping okay.'

'You're doing better than okay. You let me stitch your arm up without a flinch.' His pupils were huge, making his eyes more black than brown as he studied her openly. It wasn't like he was checking her out in an admiring way, more like he was seeing into her soul.

'Well, I guess when you have the guys at the gym beating you up, you tend to get a thick skin.'

Ryan chuckled. 'Somehow I think that's just how you like it. But that makes you who you are, Jaz.' He brushed his hand over his head. 'So, what are you going to do after you finish school? Have you thought about it?'

'Nup. Don't have a clue. Wouldn't know where to start. Maybe I'll just stay working at The Ring and throw in some travel.' Jaz pointed to a painted egg that sat on a little stand next to his TV. 'I see you have. Africa?'

'Yep, I get to travel around a fair bit.'

Jaz waited for him to continue… but he didn't. 'So, are you going to tell me some of your travel stories?'

'Nup. We don't have all night. I'd best be getting you back home before you're in trouble.'

Jaz checked her watch. 'Crap, you're right. I better get home before Mum starts ringing Anna asking to talk to me!' Jaz downed the last of her drink and found the caffeine tingled nicely in her belly. Her nerves had settled satisfactorily.

They put their cups on the jarrah coffee table and set off for the car. Fifteen minutes later Ryan parked a few houses down from Jaz's home. Jaz sat in the car, not ready to leave its warmth, or the company of Ryan. They had shared a lot tonight. He wasn't a stranger who visited The Ring anymore. He'd saved her life and had taken her home. She knew a little more about him; and yet there were still big blanks, things about him that didn't add up, things that maybe she should be afraid of. But there was something honest in his eyes, even when they took on the steel-like appearance that could send fear into her soul. Just like when he was fighting those guys. But beyond all that uncertainty, Jaz couldn't help feeling at ease with him, protected and safe. Of course it was strange, but Jaz was a strange one herself. Maybe that's why she liked him so much.

'Thanks for everything, Ryan. I'd hate to think… if you weren't… you know.' She felt Ryan's hand on her shoulder giving her a gentle squeeze. She lifted her eyes from her lap and met his. Understanding passed between them before he drew his hand back.

'Go on, you better get.'

'See you tomorrow at The Ring?'

'Sure will.'

His answer perked up her mood and she reached for the door handle. As she made her way home the night still smelled of the rain that had passed and for a minute, she remembered the attack. She shivered in fear. But as Ryan's SUV drove by, the terror of it left her. Ryan Fletcher filled her with warmth. As his name circled around her head as she looked up into the lit windows of her house. Home safe and sound.

CHAPTER 14

THE COLD MORNING chill seeped through the car window as Jaz's forehead pressed against it.

'If we are late because of you...' Simon's threat hung open. Jaz didn't even bother to reply. She was far too tired.

Last night she should have slept like the dead, but instead she'd lain awake, her mind a frenzy of thoughts. Jaz tried to blame the caffeine but she was deluding herself. Never in her wildest dreams did she think she would be attacked and fighting for her life. Most of her waking hours last night had been spent reliving every moment, trying to think of better ways to fight them. Ryan's words had come back to her. 'You should have maimed them.' She knew he was right; no matter how hard she had hit or kicked, the guys just bounced back like yoyos. Then Ryan showed up... another reason she hadn't slept so well. Who was he? Mr Secret GI Joe?

'Okay, kids, have a great day at school.' Tasha glanced across at Jaz as she stopped at the school gates. 'Oh, Jaz, couldn't you have tried to fix that up with some make-up? You look like you've been in a fight.'

'Well, I was, Mum. I can't help it if Tick got a bit excited. I should have fought him better too, I guess.' That had been her excuse for all the bruises and her swollen lip: a scratch match with Tick. Her mum had believed her, luckily, because it wasn't unusual. 'It's okay anyway, Mum, the school understands. It's not like years ago when they thought you and Dad were abusing me,' said Jaz with a quick laugh.

Her mum sighed but smiled. 'Yes, those were fun times,' she said sarcastically. 'Please can you tell the guys to take it easy on you? They should know better. Maybe I should come down to the gym and have a talk to them.'

'*No*, Mum,' groaned Jaz. 'Totally embarrassing. I'll do it, I promise. Okay? I'll sort it out. No need to do the overprotective mother routine. I'm nearly eighteen.'

'I just worry.' Tasha reached over and tenderly tucked Jaz's hair behind her ear. 'You remind me so much of your father.' Tasha smiled the same sad way she did whenever she mentioned Jaz's father.

'Really? Which parts?'

'Your colouring, your smile – and your defiance,' she added with a smile. 'Go on, you'll be late. I'll see you after school.'

'Bye,' she said heading straight towards the lawn area where her friends were waiting.

'You're late this morn… what happened to you?' Anna's eyes bulged.

Taylor drew in a shocked breath. 'Jasmine!'

Jaz laughed. 'Didn't you know, Anna, you accidently hit me with the Wii controller when we were playing tennis!'

'Me?' Anna said confused.

'Just kidding. I told Mum it was from having a scratch match with Tick at The Ring.' Jaz sat down on the seat and leaned her back against the trunk of the tree behind her.

'Your lip looks sore; it's a bit swollen.'

'You should see my ribs,' Jaz said and held out her fingers. 'My hands are tender too.'

'What the? You don't end up like this with Tick.' Taylor took one of her hands and gently held her swollen red knuckles, then saw the bandage on her hand.

Jaz nodded, the concern of her friends warming her heart. 'I was walking home from The Ring and got attacked by a few guys.'

'What!' Anna and Taylor yelled together causing some nearby students to turn their heads.

'What happened, did you snot them all?' asked Taylor.

'Well, I'd like to say I could hold my own against five guys, but…'

'*Five* guys! You were attacked by five!' Anna looked about ready to faint.

Taylor still held Jaz's hand, stroking it softly with his thumb. 'Holy shit, how did you get away?'

'Um, well it wasn't looking good but then Ryan showed up and opened a can of whoop-arse on them all. He saved me from... well, I don't know what they were going to do with me, but I can guarantee you they weren't taking me to a party.'

'Ryan? Really, he saved you?' Only Anna could see something romantic in this.

'That older guy from the fencing comp?'

'Yes, Tay, and he's not old, he's yummy. He goes to The Ring all the time with Jaz,' explained Anna.

Taylor glanced at Jaz for confirmation.

'Yep, and thank God too. He drove past on his way home and spotted me. He was amazing, Anna. And he stitched me up.'

'Huh?'

Jaz unbuttoned her white sleeve and rolled up her shirt to show her stitches. Taylor and Anna both leaned in for a closer look, narrowly avoiding knocking heads.

'What did that?' Anna's green eyes sparked with awe.

'A knife; a few of them had knives. I got a small cut on my hand too.'

'Jesus Christ, Jaz! Did you call the police?' asked Taylor.

'No, didn't have time, and after... well, let's just say they were in bad shape too. I think Ryan was more worried about trying to fix me up.'

The siren went and Taylor stood up. 'This is weird. I'm glad you're okay, Jaz, but I don't like this Ryan guy. He sounds a bit suss. Stitching you up instead of going to the hospital.'

'That's because I didn't want to go. You know my mum would have freaked, Tay. Ryan did a great job. It's all okay.' She reassured her friends.

'Just watch out, okay. Look, I better catch up with Dan. See ya in class.' He gave her stitches another glance before jogging off to join his mates heading inside.

Jaz did up her sleeve while Anna swooned back against the tree. 'You are sooo lucky. He took you back to his house?'

'After he took off his singlet to stop the bleeding.' Jaz couldn't help but share that juicy tidbit.

Anna's jaw dropped, just as Jaz expected it would.

'*No* way.' Anna sighed. 'Damn it. I say again, you are so lucky.'

Jaz was tempted to tell Anna about his tattoos but decided against it. It seemed too intimate to share. Funny, considering she shared everything with Anna. But this was personal to Ryan and he'd trusted her with it, and she didn't want to let him down.

As they picked up their bags and walked towards their class Jaz couldn't help but wonder what Ryan was up to today.

*

'The freak show has come to town. What happened to you? Someone finally tried to make you look better?' laughed Minka as she paused by Jaz's desk. Her blonde hair was shining like spun gold. She probably had a hairdresser dust gold leaf through it every morning before school.

For once, Jaz ignored Minka, and swallowed all her smartarse comebacks. Instead she picked up her bag, and left the classroom. School was finally over for the day and she wouldn't have the constant stares. The rumour mill must be working overtime. Everyone had given her a wide berth today; well, most of them. Minka wouldn't let anything stop her from taunting people unless they had something contagious.

'What? Is it that bad you can't share with the rest of us?'

Bloody Minka, Jaz thought, she'd followed her out of class. Jaz increased her stride, but as she walked towards the front of the school grounds she could feel Minka and Angelica behind her, no doubt gesturing rudely behind her back. No one could miss their overpowering perfume.

Jaz heard a girl beside her draw a breath. 'Oh, look at him, he's *gorgeous*.' She looked up, and no more than twenty metres in front of her stood Ryan. Tall, brooding, imposing and dressed in loose jeans and a black long-sleeved shirt. He smiled when he caught her eyes as she kept her steady path towards him. But inside she was flying.

'So, my creepy stalker is back,' she said coolly.

'Hey, Jaz.' Ryan watched as Minka and Angelica sashayed past, putting on their hottest smiles.

When he glanced back to Jaz she had her hand on her hip, shaking her head.

'What? I'm trying to spot their devil horns.' He gave her a wink.

'Were you now?' Ryan just accumulated a few extra points for immediately sniffing out bullshit in the form of Minka. 'So, what are you doing here?'

Ryan folded his arms in front of him. 'Just wanted to see how you're going, and I thought you might like a ride to The Ring.' He nodded to his car parked down the road.

'Hey, Ryan!' said Anna as she ran up to them.

'Hi, Anna. What are you up to? Do you want a ride to The Ring too?'

'Oh, yes please, that'd be great.'

Ryan turned around and headed to his car. Jaz threw Anna a look and said, 'I didn't know you were coming to The Ring today.'

Anna waved her hands around trying to shush Jaz. 'I have nothing else on.' She leaned in to Jaz's ear. 'Come on, he invited me. As if I'd say no!'

Grabbing Jaz's hand, Anna took off after Ryan.

Just before jumping into Ryan's car, Jaz caught Taylor's stare as he stood by his Mustang up ahead. The breeze ruffled his long fringe as his eyes threw caution at her. *Now, he worries about me!* she thought, a part of her hoping he was jealous.

She gave Taylor a reassuring smile and a wave before sliding into Ryan's back seat. Anna had silently called dibs on the front seat but Jaz didn't mind. She didn't want to think about the last time she was in that seat, bleeding.

'So, you saved Jaz last night, I hear.'

OMG! Should I just die now, thought Jaz as her face burned hot. The quiet computer type Anna was not! She was also on the debate team. It figured she'd jump Ryan with questions the moment she could.

'And were there really five guys?'

Jaz leaned forward, threaded her hand around the side of the seat till she found Anna's arm, and pinched it.

'Oww... I see you're not really the talkative type,' said Anna.

'Well, there's probably not much to tell, I'm sure Jaz has mentioned it all,' said Ryan. He glanced in the rear-vision mirror, his eyes watching Jaz for a second and she felt herself blush even more.

'Jaz isn't good with spilling the beans. If it weren't for the obvious split lip she probably wouldn't have said anything.'

Ryan raised an eyebrow. 'Really?'

'One time it took her a whole day to tell me that one of the guys had asked her out, and even then I found out about it on the grapevine first!

Could we just get to The Ring now, Jaz silently begged.

'Hello, I'm still in the car, Anna!' said Jaz. 'And I didn't tell you about Brad asking me out because it was just a prank. I knew it was crap when I saw Minka watching with that sadistic grin she gets on her face.' Jaz flicked her hair over her shoulder crossly.

'Soooo, Ryan,' said Anna, changing the subject. 'Where do you hail from?'

'North of the city. I grew up in Carine, went to school at Guilford Grammar and now live not far from here.'

Jaz's ears perked up. Anna had just got some major details that she'd never thought to ask.

'How come we've only just seen you around The Ring now?'

Jaz saw his hands tighten slightly around the steering wheel, and she could feel his body tense. Neither movement was really noticeable, but she knew that this was one of those questions he liked to avoid.

'I've been busy with work and I'm now on holidays and I'm not handling the whole "doing nothing" scenario, so I joined up at The Ring. Don't worry, in a few weeks I'll be gone again.'

That last part came with no warning, and left Jaz feeling unsettled; she even sensed Anna's disappointment. The car fell silent for the last few minutes of the trip.

When they got to The Ring, Anna went straight to Pax's computer to fire it up while Jaz walked in with Ryan.

'What?' he asked when he caught her watching him.

'So, when you go back to whatever it is you do, you won't ever come back here? To The Ring?' Jaz hoped she didn't sound too needy.

'Why, you gonna miss me?' He smiled but it didn't make her feel any better. 'I don't know, Jaz. I might just have to drop by whenever I get the time. Besides, you can't call me your stalker if I don't come around anymore, hey?'

'I guess not.' Jaz shrugged, but she smiled with relief. 'You wanna spar with me?'

'For real? You were just beaten up last night.'

'Nah, I'm good to go,' said Jaz.

Ryan scooped her up in his arms and squeezed her gently. 'So, me doing this isn't hurting your ribs at all?' he asked glancing down at her.

'Ouch! Okay, okay, you proved your point.' He put her down and Jaz held her ribs. 'Yeah, they're still a bit sore. Tomorrow, then?'

'You never give up,' he laughed. 'How about in three days. I gotta go somewhere over the weekend, so shall we book it in for then?'

Jaz studied him, immediately curious about where he could be going. 'Sure, Monday it is.'

Ryan smiled and stepped back. 'Well, I'm gonna go get changed and work out. Like you said, I might need it.'

Somehow, after last night, Jaz knew he wouldn't need anything. Her eyes trailed after him as he headed to the change rooms, and she was unaware that Anna had stepped up behind her.

'Such a cute butt,' she said as they watched him go.

Jaz turned around and slapped Anna's shoulder.

'He can't hear me!'

'He might have.'

'So, what was it like?' asked Anna.

'What was what like?'

'Hello, I just saw Mr Hunk practically hug you? You can't tell me you didn't notice his arms around you?'

Jaz shrugged and Anna scoffed, rolled her eyes and went back to her computer while muttering something about wasted moments.

The thing was, Jaz had noticed. She had noticed not just his arms but also his chest beating against hers and the warmth that came with it. Her ribs had only been a tiny twinge of pain amid the rest of her body, which was in tingles.

'I'm off to clean something.' And with that she headed for the storeroom, determined to scrub her thoughts from her mind.

CHAPTER 15

'HELLO, EARTH TO Jasmine, are you even listening to me?' Anna waved her hand in front of Jaz's face and then turned around in the direction Jaz was staring.

'What's so interesting about the cafeteria rubbish bin?'

Jaz blinked her eyes and focused on Anna. 'Sorry, what were you saying?'

Anna sighed. 'Never mind. What's up with you today? You've been in la-la land since first period.'

Jaz shrugged. Her mind was in a lot of places. Wondering how Pax was going, wondering if Ryan would be back today like he'd said, wondering if Taylor would ask her to the school ball. There was no rest for her teenage mind.

'Are you coming to The Ring today?' Jaz asked, trying to stay in the present with Anna.

'No, I've got a history essay due on Friday and I want to make a start on it. When are you going to start yours?'

'Probably late Thursday night,' said Jaz with a smirk.

'I don't know why you leave everything till the last minute, that's why your grades are crap. If you spent more time with your books instead of The Ring your marks would be as good as mine.'

'But Anna, it just seems so pointless. What is learning about some piece of art or algebra going to do for me after school? Diddlysquat, that's what. It wouldn't have saved me from those goons that attacked me. I'd rather be doing something with my hands.'

'Like wrapping them around Taylor?' laughed Anna.

Jaz rolled her eyes and pushed her lunch tray away.

'Hello ladies, I heard my name?' Taylor sat next to Anna.

Both girls flushed a little. 'Tay, what are you up to?' Jaz asked.

'Wondering if you girls have found dates for the ball yet?'

Jaz shook her head but Anna turned another shade of red.

'Anna, has someone asked you?' said Jaz. 'You didn't tell me?'

Anna played with her hair as the light through the cafeteria window caught the red highlights. 'Well, he only asked me this morning.'

'Who?' asked Jaz and Taylor.

'Ricky.'

'Oh, he's the tall one with glasses? Cute?' Jaz asked.

'Yeah, we were lab partners last term. He's really nice, so I said yes.'

'Hmph,' said Taylor. 'Well, I guess that leaves you then, Jaz.' He swung around to face her. 'Will you go to the ball with me?'

Jaz laughed, trying to hide the excitement that flushed through her body. 'Come on, Taylor, don't tell me you can't find a date. I'm sure half the school wants you.'

She reached across to straighten Taylor's tie as he spoke. 'That's actually the problem. So, will you save me from them all and go with me?'

She rolled her eyes for dramatic effect, pretending it was a hard choice. Inside she was doing a happy dance of epic proportions. 'If I have to. Okay.'

Taylor leaned over and kissed her forehead. 'Thanks, Jazzy, you're a life-saver. Catch ya later.' Then he was off again, back to his mates in the cool section over by the far wall.

'Well, well, well. Your day just got better,' said Anna. Her eyebrows were dancing across her forehead.

'Yeah, but really, I'm just a safe option.'

The siren went and they got up holding their rubbish. 'You're still his choice. It might mean something, and you'll get to dance lots with him,' said Anna.

'I have a feeling he would have taken you first. Tay just doesn't think of me any other way.'

'Jaz, there is a little thing called hope.'

After putting their rubbish in the bin, they walked towards their next class. Jaz threw her arm around Anna and couldn't help feel a little bit of hope.

*

At the end of the day, following their class together with Mr Noble, Jaz and Taylor sat on the steps outside school waiting for Anna. Jaz's commando boots lined up next to Taylor's expensive black trainers.

'Hey, it's that dude again,' said Jaz. She recognised the bearded guy from last time. He was leaning back on the car with a cigarette in his hand but she could have sworn he'd been watching them.

Taylor glanced over to where she'd gestured. The man looked down at his feet as if to avoid them. 'Maybe you have another stalker?'

'Ha ha, funny. I actually think this guy likes you,' she teased.

'Creepy.' Taylor rubbed his knees. 'So, Jaz... what's the colour for the ball? Black dress, black tie?'

'Tay, I might just surprise you and go a lime green,' Jaz laughed.

'Oh please don't. You need a nice blue dress to go with your beautiful eyes.'

Jaz choked. 'God, Mr Smooth, no wonder you're on every girl's radar.'

'Blame my dad. He was always sweet-talking my mum. How else would she let him play with guns inside?' he laughed.

'Hey, Jaz!'

She glanced up at the sound of her name. The voice was familiar and one she realised she had missed over the weekend.

'Ryan, you're back.' She tried to hide the enthusiasm from her voice. He was wearing his usual, shirt and jeans. Today's shirt was a khaki colour with buttons, military style. He was turning heads, as always.

Ryan held out his hand to Taylor. 'How ya going, Taylor?'

'Good, thanks.' Taylor shook Ryan's hand guardedly.

Ryan switched his attention back to Jaz. 'Can I give you a ride to The Ring today?'

'Sure, that'd be great.' Jaz stood up and turned to Taylor as Ryan headed to his car. 'Can you say bye to Anna for me, ta. I'll catch ya later.'

Jaz began to walk off but Taylor grabbed her hand, pulling her back.

'Jaz, just how well do you know this bloke? There's something about him I can't put my finger on. Just be careful, okay?' he said softly.

Jaz hugged Taylor. 'You're sweet, but he's all right, don't worry. Bye.'

As she was putting on her seatbelt in Ryan's car she could still see Taylor watching them.

'Your boyfriend jealous?' Ryan asked as he started his car.

'No, he's not my boyfriend. Tay and I have been friends forever. He just has a vibe about you and he's worried. But he doesn't know you like I do, you saved my life. You're not dangerous to me.'

'You know, he's got reason to be concerned. He has a good instinct. And just because I wouldn't hurt you doesn't mean I'm not dangerous,' said Ryan, keeping his eyes on the road.

'Oh I'm well aware that you can be deadly. I figured that out the first moment I met you. I just had a vibe that you were someone not to be messed with.'

Ryan chewed on his bottom lip as he pulled into a side street and parked his car. Her pulse throbbed as her senses went into overdrive.

'What's up?' she asked nervously. Yes, she felt safe with Ryan but there was still a big unknown about him, that mysterious part.

Ryan turned in his seat so he was facing her straight on. 'Jaz, would you like to be a part of something big?'

Taken aback she asked, 'Like what?' She shifted to face him.

Ryan spread his fingers over his knee, long, lean and strong. 'Let's go for a walk.'

After they were out of the car and walking down the path he started again. 'What if I could offer you the job of a lifetime? One where you can do great things for your country?'

Jaz raised her eyebrows. 'Sounds interesting. But?' She could tell there was more.

'But this conversation goes no further than the two of us. Can you promise me that?'

Jaz nodded and wondered what the hell she was getting into. Cars drove past as they continued along the path. 'I haven't told anyone about your line of work,' she said. 'I'm not about to start.'

'Great. Okay. So, you know a bit about what I do, right. Well, to put a name to it, I work for MTG Agencies. It's a black-ops organisation that works internationally. The government covertly funds us and we work together on important issues, like anti-terrorism and drugs. Basically, we do what we have to, to fight the bad guys.'

'Oh.' It was something she could easily see Ryan doing. He fitted that mould perfectly. It was a little strange to hear that something like this existed but then again there was so much that went on that not many knew about. A thought came to her. 'And you are telling me this because...'

'Because I want – I mean, *we* want – you to join us as an operative. Like me.'

Say what? An operative. Like him? Was he for real? Jaz was suddenly struggling to make sense of his words. In the end she just said, 'Okay. But why me?'

Ryan laughed, his deep chuckle making her smile. 'Most people are shocked to find out about this, and the first thing you want to know is "why you". Jaz, you are one-of-a-kind. We try to recruit kids with some talent – say, the fencing competition for example – and then we train them further on other skills. But you can already fight, you've already held a weapon. At first, I didn't want to see it. I don't like to recruit women but you just kept amazing me and in the end I couldn't deny that you're a possibility to join. Don't you see how far out in front you are already? Hell, they recruited me with much less. I went away on the weekend to get approval to speak to you. With the information I brought them, there was no hesitation. Jaz, MTG wants to recruit you.'

'So, what, be a secret spy like you?' Jaz asked.

'I guess so, that's one way of looking at it.'

'What would I do?' Her mind was racing with images of a Lara Croft cross with James Bond. Fancy gadgets and explosions, great outfits and cars.

'Well, first off we train you. But seeing as you are competent in most areas you will pass your assessment sooner, and you'll be allowed on duty. You will be trained in surveillance, tracking, codes, weapons and many other things to help you finish certain operations. Some undercover work, as we try to gain information. Things like that.'

Jaz drank in his words. If she didn't know Ryan she'd think he was making all this up and would laugh. But seeing the way he was at the nightclub and how he saved her from the attackers, his hidden tattoos and the scary stuff she saw in his eyes – well, it all fitted perfectly.

'Were you recruited this way?' she asked.

Ryan nodded. 'I went when I was sixteen. My uncle recruited me.'

'Your uncle? Did you know?' She stopped walking to face him.

'No, I didn't know about Uncle Tim. And now my family doesn't know about either of us.'

'Really? What is it they think you do?'

'They know I work as a bouncer, but MTG has a business face of a few fronts. Bodyguards, consultants, you name it, whatever fits. It's amazing how as long as you're happy they don't question your lifestyle. And when I go overseas for missions I just pretend I've been backpacking around.'

'I don't know if I could keep that a secret from everyone.' Jaz played with the hem of her tartan skirt. 'That's a lot of lying to people you love.'

Jaz regretted her words when Ryan winced. She saw the scars of those lies within him.

'Well, you have to, to protect them. Believe me, it's easier than you think. A lot of the blokes are married with kids and their families don't know.'

'Really? Wow, it's just a lot to take in, you know.'

Ryan reached over and put his hand on her shoulder. 'Yep. I do know.'

'So, I would be working with you guys to help bring down drug cartels and stuff?'

'More or less. You could just be following people, retrieving information that other operatives have collected and small things like that. Because you're young you have a great cover; no one would pick up on it, and especially being a pretty girl.'

Jaz felt a blush burn her cheeks.

'But you really think I could do this?'

Ryan sat watching her, as if he was crawling into her skin and reading her mind. She felt stripped bare under his gaze to the point her breathing became shallow and quick.

'I think you're a person who doesn't belong in a material world. I think you want to make a difference, and it's not every day you see a girl take on five blokes and sit through stitches.'

He smiled and Jaz was struck with how handsome he was. With his short clipped hair and stubble he was a Stephen Amell lookalike. *Arrow* was one of her favourite TV shows and she could see Ryan standing in for the role of Oliver Queen any day.

'It still seems a little weird; or I suppose unreal is the better word. It's hard to believe all this goes on.'

'I thought the same thing, Jaz. But I made up my mind to be aware of the world and to try to help make it a better place. Those were my reasons. Now you just have to figure out if it's what you want to do. I won't push you into it; it's got to be your decision.'

Jaz nodded as she chewed on her fingernail on their walk back to the car.

Ryan waited until he'd pulled back onto the road before he spoke. 'I'll leave you to think on it for a while, but ask me anything, okay.'

She studied Ryan as he drove, his straight square shoulders and perfect muscled arms and she remembered his scars. The job came with consequences. Ryan didn't have to tell her, she could figure that much out for herself. He stitched up his own cuts, for Pete's sake. God, she had some thinking to do. Well, she'd always said she wanted to do something important with her life after school. Maybe this was her chance.

CHAPTER 16

THE RING WAS already open when they arrived. Bags was giving a lesson to a weedy kid who looked about fourteen.

Jaz and Ryan gave him a wave and headed for the change rooms. Like her shower, Jaz had her own private corner, with a curtain. Her locker was nearby and she quickly got out of her school uniform and into her blue tank top and yoga pants. She was tying her hair up into a ponytail as she walked out, Ryan just in front of her. Without a word since leaving his car, they both began to warm up in their usual ways: Ryan with a skipping rope and Jaz with her salute-to-the-sun routine. After about five minutes, they faced each other on the big mat. Ryan was just starting to sweat across the top of his chest and his dark eyes were hard to read.

'You're ready for this?' he asked.

'Ready when you are.'

Ryan took a crouched stance and Jaz followed suit as they circled each other. 'I'll try not to get your arm, okay.' He glanced at her stitches, which were healing up nicely.

Jaz, not wanting to pussyfoot around, threw out the first punch but Ryan blocked it with ease. She didn't expect anything less from him. They kept circling each other, taking a shot when they had a chance. Jaz could tell Ryan was holding back, and she wasn't sure if she was glad about that or not.

She surprised him by throwing in a kick, which connected.

Instead of doubling over in pain, Ryan lashed out one of his own but it met her body at only half-force.

'Good, surprise is handy, make sure you use it.' He jabbed at her as if he had a knife. 'If someone came at you again with a knife, what would you do?'

'Kick it out of his hand; it worked for me once.' Ryan smiled at her bravado. 'But you put your jacket over your arm, didn't you?' she asked.

'Yep, one of the first things they teach you is that with a knife threat you should quickly wrap something tightly around your arm so that you can lead with it. It lets you take the knife thrust on it while allowing your fighting arm to strike without being cut.'

'I see. And you also said something about maiming?' Jaz asked after tapping him on the head with a soft punch. He smiled at her mocking attempt at a hit.

'Yes, to maim and not anger. If you make them angry it can give them extra strength, whereas maiming will take them out of the picture. It's a hard lesson to learn.' Ryan blocked Jaz's high kick. 'But the best thing you can do if caught is go limp.' He was starting to puff as he spoke and fought at the same time. 'A limp body is heavy and hard to handle and it gets you down low. They relax thinking they have you, and that's when you strike them.'

'What, with my fists?' Jaz said quickly as she ducked a punch.

'With anything you have. Shoes, keys, rocks, sticks — anything you can find; it's all surprise. A high heel to the eye is very effective.'

Jaz screwed up her face at the mental picture.

'I know what you're thinking. You can't imagine doing that, and it's hard to hurt another human, especially like that, but when it's you or them...' Ryan dropped to the ground and rolled, taking Jaz's legs out from under her.

They both lay flat on the mat catching their breath.

'Would you be teaching me all this stuff or do you have proper instructors?' she asked.

Ryan sat up and crossed his legs. 'Maybe, if I wasn't out on an op. Otherwise it would be other agents like me. They're great, you'd learn a lot from each one of them.'

Jaz rolled over on to her side and rested her head on her hand, their fight on pause for the moment. She studied Ryan, sitting in just his black shorts, his lean muscles shimmering with sweat. 'What was your last op, can I ask?'

She saw the clouds roll in over his eyes and for a moment regretted her naivety. She was just about to change the subject when Ryan spoke.

'I was sent in to rescue one of our undercover agents,' he said softly as he glanced around the gym.

Bags was still in the far corner with the kid, other than that they were alone.

Jaz waited patiently for him to continue, watching him struggle with it.

'There's this bloke who is head of a company that deals in illegal operations, drugs and so forth. We're always trying to infiltrate his mob for details, information and ways we can catch them out. But they're good, and one of our agents sent an SOS, and I was sent in to help retrieve him.'

'It sounds scary. Were you scared?'

'Yes, but that's what makes you cautious and careful.'

'Would I be doing stuff like that?' Jaz asked, her heart starting to pound in her chest at the thought.

He shrugged. 'Maybe one day, after you're cleared for duty.'

'So, you're not just a recruiter, then?' Jaz sat up opposite Ryan.

'No, after a big op we get time off, but as you can tell I'm still working a few other cases, like building information on that guy with the tattoo. While we're having our break, we're expected to keep our eyes open for new recruits. You know, check out events where skills are shown, ones that we can harness.'

'So that's why you were at our fencing tournament and how you found me!'

He took a few breaths as he nodded. His chest raising slowly.

'So, what do you think so far?'

Jaz buried her head in her hands. 'I don't know what to think,' she mumbled. 'It's all so surreal. Do you want an answer now?' She peeked through her fingers. ''Cause I just don't think I can give you one. I have the school ball coming up and I seriously need more time to digest this.' She felt Ryan's hand on her knee, spreading warmth like a hot pack. 'Mind you, a school ball must seem petty compared to all this other stuff.'

Ryan shook his head. 'No, Jaz, it's not. A school ball is important. I never got to go to one, so enjoy your youth while you have it.' He gently squeezed her leg. 'And take your time with your decision, because it's a life changer. Just remember not to repeat any of it.'

'You realise if I did, everyone would think I'd just gone loony! But don't worry,' she quickly added as Ryan threw her a look of caution. 'I promise I won't say a thing.'

Damn it, she was dying to talk to Anna and Taylor about this. What was she to do if she couldn't confide in her two friends? How could she make such a decision without their advice?

'I'm going to do some yoga and clear my head... well, attempt to clear my head.'

Ryan removed his hand from her knee and watched her get up.

'I'll talk to you later, Ryan.'

He looked so sad sitting there. As if he was worried he'd scared her away. But he never said a word. Maybe he understood she needed time to process this wealth of information.

As she got to her yoga mat, she heard Ryan start up on the speedball. He was hitting it hard, letting off steam. Did he feel bad about dragging her into his world? She shook the thought from her mind as she began her deep breathing and tried to clear her mind. It worked... for all of two seconds.

CHAPTER 17

'ARE YOU OKAY, Jaz?' asked Anna on Wednesday morning as they sat on their seat, under the tree, waiting for the siren.

'Huh?'

'You've been away with the fairies since yesterday. What's up with you?'

Jaz sighed. If only she could tell Anna what was really on her mind.

'It wouldn't be Ryan, by any chance?' asked Anna.

Jaz snapped her head up. 'What makes you say that?'

Anna threw her hair over her shoulder and nodded towards the school car park. 'Because you've been spending lots of time with him and he's hot. Also, he's over there trying to get your attention.'

'What?'

He stood there; all lean and sexy, jeans hanging low off his hips, grey shirt pulling tight across his chest and arms as he waved to her.

'I'm gonna go see what he wants.'

'Well, *you* can, but I'm off to first period because I don't want to be stuck sitting near Angelica. Can you believe she tries to copy my answers?'

Jaz laughed as she stood up. 'Yeah, well, I would too.'

Anna rolled her eyes as she threw her bag over her shoulder. 'I'll talk to you later! Watch him, I reckon he's got the hots for you.'

'Who?'

'OMG, Ryan of course.' Anna pulled her close.

Jaz shrugged. 'It's just a friendship, like the one Tay and I have.'

Anna pretended to cough and swore instead. 'Bullshit.'

'Okay, so maybe he's all right.' Jaz pulled a face. 'But he wouldn't be interested in me.'

'Why not? You're a catch. If I was a guy I'd dig you.'

Jaz laughed and pushed Anna away. 'Go on, go and get your seat.' Anna wiggled her eyebrows as she headed into class.

Jaz jogged towards Ryan, her hair sailing out behind her. 'Hey, what's up?'

'Well, I wouldn't normally condone wagging, but do you feel like cutting school? I have a feeling you're not averse to this kind of thing.'

Jaz felt the smile creep across her face and hoped she didn't look like a circus clown. 'What do you have in mind?'

Ryan nodded toward his car. 'Let's get out of here first before you get busted and they think I'm a schoolyard perve.'

Jaz burst out laughing as she followed Ryan. 'Don't worry, I'd just tell them that you're my stalker and I'm sure they'd be all right with that.'

Inside his car, Jaz pulled off her school tie while Ryan threw her a clean shirt. 'I thought you might need this. Sorry it's not...'

'What... girly? If you hadn't noticed I don't really do "girly".' It was black with white and red writing on the front. 'This is fine, thanks.'

Jaz unbuttoned her white school shirt, took it off and shoved it in her bag. She was used to getting around in crop tops at the gym, a bra wasn't much different. But maybe not for Ryan.

His hands gripped the wheel as he spluttered, 'It's... um... one of my favourite shirts from when I was young. It doesn't fit anymore but I haven't been able to throw it out yet.'

'Well, it will do just nicely.' She pulled it on over the top of her lacy white bra. With the black shirt, her tartan school skirt and black boots, no one would think she was wagging school.

'Hey, how come you weren't at The Ring yesterday?' she asked.

'Gee, Jaz. Can't your stalker take a day off without having you worry about him?' he chuckled.

'I wasn't worried,' Jaz mumbled.

He nodded as if he knew better. 'I just thought you might like some time to yourself to think, without me being around. Did it help?'

'Hmm... nup,' she laughed. 'So, what's today in aid of? Did you know I needed to go shopping for a ball dress?'

Ryan glanced across to Jaz, a frank look on his face. 'We are *not* shopping for a dress! You can get that thought right out of your head.'

'Gee, you're easy to stir up,' she laughed.

Twenty minutes later, they were walking down Hay Street in the city, their arms brushing with each swing.

'So, now what?'

'How about we go and have a coffee?' he asked steering her towards a shop.

'Are you buying?' she asked. Ryan nodded. 'Cool, how about muffin too, please? I'm famished.'

As they sat outside at a small round table waiting for their order, Ryan reached across and pulled her arm closer. 'This is healing well.'

Jaz tried to ignore the feather touch of his fingers against her skin. 'Yep, thanks to you. So, will I get to learn how to stitch up things too?'

'Well, if you must know, that was self-taught. There have been a few times I've been injured and I couldn't go to a hospital, mainly because I didn't want to have to answer questions.'

Jaz's mouth fell open. 'So, what – you're saying you learnt *by stitching yourself up?*' He nodded. 'Oh man, that's gross. I'd probably faint first time.'

Ryan shrugged as he stretched his long legs out under the small table. 'You'd be surprised at what the mind can handle.'

A waiter appeared with their cappuccinos and Jaz's choc-chip muffin, which she instantly attacked.

'Cheers,' she said after swallowing. 'So...'

'So?'

'Come on, I know you didn't let me wag school just for a coffee,' she said.

Ryan took a sip from his cup and licked his top lip. He then slid his sunglasses down from the top of his head.

'You are wise, my young grasshopper. No, I brought you here to observe.'

Jaz's forehead crinkled. 'Observe? Observe what?' she asked glancing around them.

'Nothing in particular.' He gestured around them. 'Look around, observe. Don't just look but *see*. Watch people. You can learn so much about their behaviours and facial movements. See if you can read their lips and follow their conversations.'

Jaz coughed on her muffin as she turned to Ryan. 'Can you read lips?' He smiled and nodded. Jaz's eyes grew wide. 'Have you done this around me?'

Ryan said, 'No.' But when he turned, she caught a hint of a smile on his lips.

Her mind whirled as she tried to think of all the conversations she'd had with Anna about Ryan. Had he lip-read some of those? *God, I hope not.* Jaz focused her attention onto her muffin while waiting for her embarrassment to fade.

'How do you learn lip-reading anyway?' Jaz asked eventually.

'With practice. See those two over the road, the ones that look like husband and wife? Well, she's getting up him for parking the car in a loading zone. He's holding a bit of paper, which is probably a ticket.'

'Oh yeah, I see. Huh, she looks pissed. Did she just call him an idiot?'

'Yep, see you're already picking bits up.'

'Hey, I've watched football on TV, it's easy to lip-read the swear words.' She watched the couple, trying to follow along the conversation. 'Hmm, this is way more fun than trigonometry,' said Jaz as she began sucking the froth from her coffee.

They sat there for another thirty minutes and Jaz watched the street, trying to read lips and take note. Ryan would point out little things she'd not even noticed. A bloke passing drugs off to a mate, and a guy in the shop near them lifting stuff from the shelves. She couldn't believe it was happening right before her eyes.

'Come on, unless we're going to have another coffee I suggest we move on. You always need to think of things like that. You'll be noticed otherwise.'

Noticed by whom, Jaz wondered. She was sure there was so much to learn, so much that she'd just taken for granted, so much lying beneath the surface. It was scary and exciting at the same time. Being here with Ryan was amazing. He was like the Yoda of agents. Not that she'd really know, she'd only met the one. She just had a feeling he was great at his job.

'Are you, like, a top agent or something?'

He laughed. 'I wouldn't say that. We each have our own expertise in different areas, but I'm still the youngest ever to be recruited and approved. I was eighteen when I went on my first op.'

'Seriously?' Jaz saw pride burning in his deep brown eyes. Here was a man dedicated to the cause.

'See this person in front of us, the big guy with the brown coat?' Ryan asked.

Jaz nodded, unable to speak while busy picturing an eighteen year old Ryan out on an operation.

'We're going to see how far we can follow him without him suspecting us. Now, this will be pretty easy because this guy wouldn't expect to be followed, but with the shady sorts, they're always on alert.'

Ryan showed her how to follow discreetly, from both behind and in front of the target.

'Why do you keep looking at your watch?' she asked.

'Good, you noticed that. Have a look for yourself.'

Jaz took Ryan's arm and looked at his leather band watch, but then she saw the difference. 'It's a mirror stuck on top.'

'It allows me to see behind me and up in front without detection.'

'That is so cool and yet so simple. But then again, I've never had the need to follow someone.' Jaz laughed. 'You really are a stalker,' she teased.

He smiled before continued. 'So, say like now, he's stopped to look in this window. It would look suss if we stopped here too, so we continue. However, the next shop is a coffee shop, so we keep going until we find a shopfront that's suitable for us to pause and look at. So, if I was on my own I wouldn't want to be looking in a lingerie shop or something.'

'But you could if you were buying your girlfriend something nice, or maybe if you're a perve,' said Jaz with a grin.

'You like calling me a perve and a stalker. You're lucky I don't have a complex.' Ryan pushed Jaz back in jest. 'So, now we're away from our target and I can use my watch just to keep him in sight.'

They kept following the guy in the brown coat for another half-hour before he got in his car and left the city.

'Shall we follow him by car? I can drive, you know.'

'As much as I'd really love to see you driving my car,' he said drily, 'I think we'll let this guy go home in peace.'

'I didn't like the note of sarcasm in your voice, Ryan. I'll have you know I'm a good driver.'

Ryan raised his eyebrows as if he didn't believe her. 'Come on, I've got another test for you,' he said with an evil grin.

'Damn, I take it back, maybe trigonometry would be better. So, what's next?'

'Follow me.'

They walked the busy city centre streets, people rushing past, others sitting reading newspapers. It made Jaz wonder what some of them were really up to. Was that guy really reading a paper or was he staking out a shop, or a person?

Ryan pulled her away from a few dress shop windows until they came to a huge Target store. 'Okay, you sit here opposite. I'm going to go in there, and you have to spot me when I come out.'

'Sounds easy enough.'

'Well, I might be disguised and I might be out in ten minutes or three hours.'

'Oh damn, really! I'll never have time to look for a dress if you take that long,' she whined but nodded her head nonetheless. 'All right off you go, I'll be watching.'

And watch she did. The doorway was large and people were in and out but she thought she could see them all okay. None were Ryan so far. But after twenty minutes she had to try hard to stop her eyes wandering off. This would be so much easier with her music. After another twenty minutes, and a few close look-a-likes, she was still sure he hadn't come out. Or was she? If she blinked at the wrong time, he could have slipped out unnoticed. What if he'd been wearing a hat? Oh crap, this was hard.

Ten minutes later, she felt like she was being watched. Abandoning her post, she looked behind her to see Ryan standing there. He was wearing a sexy leather jacket, a trendy surf hat and a stupid smile because he'd won. How could she have missed him! Anyone would have noticed someone that good looking, surely.

'Okay, obviously I suck at this! But on the plus side, I like that jacket on you.'

Jaz crossed her arms as Ryan sat beside her, ditching the hat on the other side of the chair. 'Hats aren't my thing, but you like the jacket?' Jaz nodded and was rewarded with another smile. 'It's a keeper, then. Don't worry, surveillance is a hard job; and in this case I knew you would be looking for me and I know how to blend in, hide behind a group and stay out of your line of sight.'

Jaz's phone went off as she pulled it from the waistband of her skirt. 'Oh no, busted. It's from Anna, wondering where I am. She said she was sitting all alone in the school caf but luckily Taylor kept her company. I'm now demoted to second-best friend.' Jaz laughed and texted her back. 'I just told her we went to The Ring for a workout.'

'You hungry?'

'Could eat a horse,' she replied.

They grabbed a bite at the Carillon food court before heading back, and as they passed a dress shop Jaz turned her eyes to Ryan. 'Look, normally a dress shop is the last place I'd be, but I can't go to the ball naked, now, can I?'

His eyebrows shot up and then he shrugged. 'Oh, I don't know, I think you'd be the best dressed there,' Ryan laughed.

'Pleeeeease, can we go in?' He sighed and she took that as a yes. Jaz grabbed his arm and dragged him into the shop. 'You can stand here and tell me what you think. I need a guy's opinion.' Jaz parked Ryan in front of the change rooms before heading off to find some dresses. She went for the blue ones; Taylor did suggest it, after all. On the way back she saw a silvery blue halter neck dress and grabbed that too before strutting past Ryan, who looked less than enthusiastic.

'Shouldn't you be doing this with your mum?' asked Ryan, whose foot she could hear tapping away impatiently.

'My mum works and just gave me money to find something. She probably thinks I'm not even going to go. But I have a date now, so I have to.'

'Uh-huh. Who's the lucky fella?'

Jaz burst into laughter as she walked out. 'I look like I'm being strangled. Check out all these straps. Any good?'

'No.'

She tried on the next one.

'You didn't say who you were going with?'

Jaz found his interest in her date amusing. 'Taylor is taking me. Just as a friend,' she said coming out with another dress on.

'No.'

And then another.

'No.'

'Damn you, Ryan, are you going to like any of them?' Jaz reached for the silvery one and slipped it on, then smiled at the image in the mirror. The dress started at the top in a silver halter and blended through to a vibrant blue. Fitted like a glove too. She sashayed out of the change room for Ryan's opinion. But she didn't need to hear it, because she could see it in his eyes.

'You like?'

'Definitely, that one is perfect. I even like it with your boots,' he commented.

Jaz hiked up the hem and showed them off. She felt giddy at the look in his eyes. There was heat simmering in the deep depths before he blinked it away and said quickly, 'Come on, grab that one and let's get going. I've had more than my quota of dresses.'

Jaz almost squealed with delight as she went to change. After paying for the dress, she looped her hand through Ryan's arm. 'Not a bad day's recon, and a dress and a jacket for our troubles.'

Ryan looked across at her and raised that funny eyebrow. 'Yeah, it wasn't *too* painful.'

'Thanks, Ryan, today was great,' she said meaningfully. 'Can we do this again tomorrow?' she asked.

He laughed. 'Not on your life!'

CHAPTER 18

AT ELEVEN O'CLOCK that night, Jaz jumped out of bed and stuffed it with pillows. She threw a jumper on over her singlet and stepped into her warm Ugg boots, tucking in her black pyjama pants. Quietly she opened her window and crawled out onto the small roof below it. She left the window open just a fraction before walking carefully to the garage roof that met the house. After scaling across the garage, she climbed down the lattice on the other side, dodging the rose bush at the bottom. Many times, she'd had to get Anna to pick out thorns buried into her hands, legs or backside after a failed escape.

She crept through the front of her neighbour's yard to Anna's house. Being only a house away was another reason they'd been friends since they were toddlers. The Johnsons had a bigger property and in their front yard were two big lilac trees among the landscaped gardens. Anna's dad had always wanted a tree house as a little boy so he had one built for his daughter. The girls had loved it, it had become *their* place and at least once a week they would sneak out at night and catch up in the tree house.

Jaz slid through the small front hedge, to the base of the biggest tree and climbed up the small wooden pegs stuck in its trunk.

'Howdy, neighbour. Was just lighting the burner,' said Anna. She was in the corner of the square wooden tree house, next to the window that overlooked the street. Jaz crawled in and over to the other corner and sat on a pillow. Yes, they'd put a few creature comforts in here over the years along with some goods. Once it was matches and cigarettes they'd stolen, when they went through a trying-to-smoke stage, but now their possessions included a gas burner, a couple of sticks and a large packet of marshmallows, a large mattress and a heap of pillows, two pairs of binoculars and a portable DVD player with a small collection of their favourite movies. Jaz threw a sleeping bag over her legs to keep out the chill. Anna was already rugged up in her pink fluffy dressing gown.

This place had always been their haven, a place they were alone to talk or just watch a movie together during the week. Most times, it would be two o'clock before they'd creep back to their rooms, their bellies full of gooey marshmallows.

'Here, check this out,' said Anna as she passed over a pair of binoculars. 'Looks like Mr Cooper is on the couch again. Do you think Mrs Cooper finally found out he'd been stopping three doors up for a little after-work fun?'

'Ha, quite possible.' Jaz put the binoculars down, picked up her roasting stick, and poked on two marshmallows before putting them above the flame on the burner.

'Mum's taking me shopping tomorrow for a ball dress, do you wanna come with us and get yours?' said Anna, pulling her marshmallow off and popping it into her mouth.

'Oh, I've already got mine,' Jaz said and then realised she'd have to lie to her best friend.

Anna scoffed. 'When!'

'Today. I left the gym cos Bags was there and went for a look-see and found the coolest silver-and-blue dress.' Jaz was rather scared at how easily the lie came out. If she took on the life of an agent, lying would be a huge part of the job.

'No fair. You should have taken me! Now I'm going to have my mum trying to convince me to go for some virginal white dress that covers me from neck to toe.'

Jaz laughed and nearly choked on her marshmallow.

'Sorry, do you want me to come with you anyway? I can pick out the really short revealing ones so your mum might come back to a half-normal dress.'

'Nah, don't worry about it. Mum's got dentist appointments for both of us. I'd hate you to have to sit through them and then have us spit all over you when we try to talk with numb lips.' Anna put a pink marshmallow on her stick and then eyeballed Jaz. 'Hey, what is it with that jumper? You must like it, you're wearing it a lot.'

'I don't wear this all the time!' Jaz said defensively.

'Jaz, I've seen you in it four times in the last week. Normally you wear your black one.'

'Well, this one's nice and big and warm, is that okay?' said Jaz, lifting the grey hood over her head as if to show its warmth. The jumper was always at the end of her bed and it was just the first one she picked up. That's all, she told herself. It had nothing to do with Ryan. It didn't even smell like him anymore.

'Oooh, touchy,' said Anna as she turned off the burner. Five marshmallows was their usual limit. 'Shall we watch a movie? Or you wanna talk and do the neighbourhood watch?'

Anna liked to call it that, instead of spying. When they were fourteen they saw an unknown van pull into Mr Cooper's place while he was on holiday. It looked suss, so Anna called the police on her mobile and they watched as the police arrived and caught the burglars carrying out the big plasma TV. Ever since then Anna felt vindicated for the spying they did. Really, it was quite entertaining. Ryan's words – 'Don't just look but *see*.' came to her. This was sort of like that. They noticed when things were different or unusual in their street. Like the time they caught Jessica, a fifteen-year-old who lived across the street, sneaking out of her house and getting into her boyfriend's ute. They'd also seen Mrs Bovell skolling liquid from a bottle when her husband wasn't looking. They soon found out that she was at sent to a rehab clinic for alcohol addiction.

Anna reckoned it was their own fault. If people wanted to keep stuff private, they should shut their blinds at night.

Either way it had given them plenty of entertainment over the years.

'How about we watch a movie. What shall we have tonight?' Jaz asked.

Anna flipped through the collection in the DVD folder. '*Sweet Home Alabama*? *The Ugly Truth*? *Avatar*?'

'How about *SALT*?'

'Okey dokey, *SALT* it is.' While Anna put the disc in the player, Jaz stretched her legs out under the sleeping bag and propped herself up against the wall of the tree house. Anna brought over her pillow for their backs and snuggled under the sleeping bag before putting the player on their legs.

'Lights, please?'

Anna reached up and drew a curtain across their window so the street-lights wouldn't shine in and their light wouldn't shine out.

'Cool, I love the action in this movie.'

Jaz nodded and wondered if she could pick up spy tips from the movie. She figured they had to base it on something, who's to say it wouldn't work in real life. As the movie played out, Jaz found her mind wandering to Ryan and their day in the city, and by the end of the movie she'd accumulated another stream of questions for him. What other weapons had he used? Had he killed anyone? Or seen someone die? How many agents were there in Australia and overseas? God, so many questions. But she figured she wouldn't get answers to a lot of them until she was sworn in as an agent. She was thinking about this stuff an awful lot lately. Did that mean that she wanted to do it? Jaz searched her mind, hoping for an answer, but nothing came to her. She just wasn't sure.

CHAPTER 19

'Are you ready for me, Thomas?'

'Bring it on, Fletcher!'

Jaz moved, shifting her weight from left to right, trying to pre-empt his attack.

'No holding back today,' she said. 'I'm not injured anymore.'

'All right, just remember you asked for it.' Ryan smiled like the devil.

'Just not my face, okay. I have a ball coming up. I don't want to look like the bride of Frankenstein.'

'Got it, no head shots... *or* groin shots, for that matter,' Ryan added.

Jaz laughed and threw a punch, trying to catch him off guard.

'Oooh, she's quick today. Someone came to win!'

'I always come to win.' Jaz laughed as she narrowly missed taking a hit to her stomach. *Damn, that was close. Pay attention, Thomas,* she scolded herself. It didn't help that Ryan had taken his shirt off to fight. It was hard enough to concentrate without his perfect chest and arms on display. Ryan's fist got her in the stomach, wind exploding from her mouth with the force. Jaz could handle the pain, just not the humiliation. *Concentrate.*

They'd been ducking and diving, punching and attacking with such force that after ten minutes Jaz was sweating so much she stripped off her shirt down to her small crop top. Hell, if he could fight shirtless, so could she... well, nearly shirtless. Her dad's necklace hung just above her breasts.

She saw his eyes flick to her chest and used this distraction to kick his feet out from under him. He landed with a thud on the mat and she quickly jumped on top to hold him down. 'That's a trick you taught me: distract and hit. Did you like it?'

'You learn fast.' Ryan smiled before turning his hips under Jaz and throwing her to the mat before quickly rolling onto her, holding her body belly down. 'But here's another one: don't ever let your guard down. Never think you have won and relax.'

Ryan had her pinned tightly to the mat. 'Okay, you win, let me up,' she begged.

'No.'

'*No?*'

'This isn't over. Anything is still possible, because everything has more than one option. Think hard, Thomas! Don't just give up because you think you're in an unbeatable position.'

Jaz did as he said and began to assess her situation. Quickly she pushed up and felt Ryan till backwards, hopefully just enough, then she sunk back down as her legs went up behind her as she arched. Thank God for the bendy yoga moves. She tried to grab him around the neck with her feet with the aim to drag him off to the side. It didn't go to plan but it was enough for him to reach his hands up to protect his face and that gave her the room she needed to buck and roll on her side and, rather scrappily, she pounced back on him. She would not win any awards for that graceless move, but like he said, when it's life or death, you or them, you do what you have to. Jaz trapped his legs down under hers and held his arms down.

'Like that,' she puffed just inches from his face.

His eyebrow arched up cutely and his breathing was equally heavy. 'Yes, just like that.'

Jaz tried not to focus on just how close he was, and just how much of his body lay pressed against hers. She diverted her eyes to the side and saw Ryan's tattoo on his inside arm. *Forever*, but it was the initials *CC* under it that she couldn't see that held her thoughts. 'Your mate Chris, was he an agent?'

Ryan nodded slightly. 'Remember how I told you my last operation was to go in and rescue an agent who'd been compromised?'

'Yeah.' Jaz was still trying to bring her breathing back under control. She felt Ryan's muscles straining against her, whether he was waiting for her to relax or maybe it was the current topic of conversation that had him wound so tight she couldn't be sure.

'Well it was Chris, and I… I couldn't get there in time. I saw the whole thing through my scope.'

Ryan's jaw clenched and his eyes went cold with anger.

'You saw your mate die?' she whispered. Jaz relaxed her grasp on Ryan as the reality of what he'd just said gripped her. 'Oh, Ryan…' She went to say sorry but he cut her off.

'They had obviously found out he was an agent, and he'd been summoned out to see the boss man. I was casing his house, which is on a huge block in the bush on the outskirts of the city.'

His eyes stared past her at the wall, his heart racing against her skin. He was underneath her still and yet he felt far away as he recapped the moment.

'His pool area is edged in a glass fence that overlooks a steep cliff off the side of a hill. I was on a nearby hill, seeing where I could get in to find Chris. I couldn't act but I could see them clearly.' He swallowed with difficulty. 'Chris and the boss were leaning against the glass fence, looking out over the bush, talking, when the boss's right-hand man – they call him Franko – pulled out a gun from the other side of the pool and shot Chris in the head. So quickly, I didn't have time to get a shot off. The boss then walked away while Franko pushed Chris over the fence and watched him fall down the cliff face.'

Jaz released his arms and sat up covering her mouth with her hand. She couldn't speak, couldn't find the words to express her horror. She slid off Ryan to the mat as he sat up. 'What…?' Her eyes probed his.

'What happened next?' he asked for her. 'Well, Franko and the boss no doubt dusted off their hands, had a drink and probably ordered someone to clean up the mess they'd left. I didn't stick around to find out. I took off down the hill to get to Chris.'

Jaz watched him, not daring to speak. She couldn't imagine what state Ryan would have found Chris in. She couldn't imagine seeing a wound in his head, let alone broken bones and scrapes from the fall. She shivered with repulsion. 'Was he alive when you found him?'

Ryan turned his head, as if he were looking out the front windows of the gym, but his expression was blank and unseeing. 'No, he would have been dead the moment he went over the railing.' He paused, only their steady breathing could be heard in the empty gym. 'It took me over six hours to carry his body back out to where I'd hidden my vehicle. We'd been best mates since I was recruited. I won't rest until I can avenge his death.' His tone was venomous.

Jaz saw Ryan swallow, his eyes set hard while her own filled with tears. She reached out for him, rubbing his arms, and rested her chin on his shoulder. His pain was still so raw, and she now realised just how well he'd hidden it.

She wanted to ask him how they'd covered up Chris's death for his family, but she knew that it didn't really matter. They would have found a way to hide the truth, and after all, it wouldn't change the fact that Chris was gone. Jaz swallowed her question and just sat there silently with Ryan as she blinked away her own tears.

It felt like hours, but maybe it was minutes, before Ryan turned to Jaz and smiled. He took a deep breath to steady himself before reaching out to touch her necklace as she dropped her arms from the embrace.

'Is this special? I've never seen you without it,' he asked as he tried to read the medallion.

'It's Saint Michael, he's an archangel. Apparently, he's, like, this commander of God's army against Satan's forces.'

'Sounds like a cool dude.'

Jaz grinned as Ryan's thumb ran over the medallion. 'I'm not religious; I wear it because it's from my dad. He gave it to my mum before I was born and it's all I have of him. He died.' Jaz turned the medallion over to show Ryan the engraving on the back. 'Mum hates that I found this and kept it. But I refuse to give it back. It's all I have of him.'

She watched Ryan read the engraving on the back. *Salvatore*. His body suddenly went rigid as his eyes flicked up to hers. 'Have you ever tried to find out what this means?'

'Well, it could be my dad's name or maybe his dad's name, or a favourite uncle. I don't know because Mum won't tell me anything about him or this. Anna and I Googled it, but do you know how many Salvatores there are out there? Mum threatens to take it off me if I ask too many questions.

She just reminds me that Paul is my dad, has been since I was two and that's all that matters. He loves me.' Jaz sighed. 'But still I see I'm different than them and I want to at least know something about my real father. Even if he is dead.'

'But what if it's not good, he's not good? Maybe your mum is saving you from something horrible. Have you ever thought of that?'

'Sometimes I do. Yet when Mum does talk about him, like when she slips up, I can tell she cared about him. I believe she loved him.' Jaz pulled her necklace from Ryan's hand and let it fall back against her chest. 'I got his skin tone and my mum's blue eyes. A rather weird mix,' said Jaz with a shrug.

'But it's what makes you so captivating.'

Ryan's voice was soft and quiet but the words he spoke reverberated through her body like he'd shouted them. Jaz was sure he was aware of the electricity sparking between them too.

'The name Salvatore certainly goes with my skin tone,' she added.

Cold detached eyes looked across at the far wall, in a way that brought chills to Jaz's skin. 'What? What's wrong?'

Ryan stood up. 'Nothing. It's not you. If we don't get moving again we'll probably seize up.'

Jaz took his hand as he pulled her up, but his eyes avoided her. Was he upset that she'd seen him at his weakest? She knew that blokes liked to pretend they were tough, and he was a secret super-agent, so it was probably twice as bad. Ryan went to walk away but she grabbed his hand. 'You okay?'

He tensed but then squeezed her hand, his shoulders dropping slightly. 'Sorry. It's not you.' He sighed. 'You know how you hate certain names attached to an awful memory or person?'

'Yeah,' said Jaz, instantly thinking of Minka. Just the sound of it grated up her spine.

'Well, I meet a lot of shady characters, so I dislike a lot of names. Salvatore just happens to be one of them.'

'Oh.'

'Don't worry about it, Jaz. It's just a name that rubs me up the wrong way. I can't help how I feel when I hear it.' Ryan squeezed her hand again before walking away.

Jaz didn't know what else to say, so she reverted back to what was normal and safe. Picking up her shirt she yelled to him. 'You know I won that round, don't you?'

Ryan glanced back, and for a moment his old playful smile returned. 'You hang on to that; it won't happen again.' But his face darkened before he turned back towards the change rooms.

CHAPTER 20

THE SIREN RANG out and you could feel the relief of five hundred students as they headed for the exit doors like stampeding cattle. Jaz was walking with Taylor. They'd had the same last class together, which was her favourite because he was in it. They strolled along as kids rushed by eager to escape school. Taylor's name was called out every so often, but no one around here would exert that much effort on Jaz. If she were as popular as Taylor was, then maybe she'd have more than three friends. Four if she counted Ryan.

'I was talking to Anna in History and she's keen to come to the firing range today,' Taylor said. 'Are you? I know Bags has The Ring open on a Thursday, so no excuses.' Taylor grabbed her hand and gave it a squeeze. 'Come on, you know you want to.'

'Why, have all your popular mates deserted you?' she laughed as she enjoyed his warm hand.

All too soon, Taylor let go of her hand to put it over his heart. 'Oww, Jasmine! It hurts me to hear you say that. You know you and Anna are at the top of the list.'

'I heard my name. I hope it wasn't spoken in vain!'

'It's Anna Banana. Hey beautiful, ready to knock some rust off your aim?' Taylor joked.

Anna's hair was swept up in a loose bun, her face framed by a few soft curls that had dropped free. She really was beautiful when she wasn't hiding behind a book or computer screen.

'Yep! You coming too, Jazzy?'

Jaz normally would have jumped at the chance but a part of her wanted to go to The Ring and see how Ryan was today. Yesterday had been so full of emotion and weirdness and she wanted to make sure things were still okay between them. But she didn't want to miss out on going to the range with Taylor. He was really making the effort to spend more time with them than with his more popular friends of late. She wondered if there was something behind it, or maybe he'd just finally realised what a hissy cat Minka and her friends could be. Whatever the reason, she didn't want it to slip by.

'Yeah, count me in. I have eight shots that need to hit a target!'

'That's my girls,' said Taylor, wrapping his arms around each of them.

Together they all walked out into the afternoon sunshine in their matching white school shirts and black ties, the girls in their red tartan skirts and Taylor, who still won the award for the best butt in the standard uniform black pants. Jaz felt invincible with her two best friends by her side, as if they could accomplish anything as long as they were together.

They walked through the school gates and towards the car park and Taylor's waiting Mustang.

Jaz threw her bag into the back of the car and turned at the sound of her name being called. Ryan jogged to them and paused beside her in his sandy-coloured cargo pants and a black singlet. He was still as sexy as hell but there was uncertainty in his eyes. He still wasn't a hundred percent himself.

'Hey, what's up?'

'I thought I'd walk or run with you to The Ring, if that's okay?' he asked.

Jaz opened her mouth but no words came. She turned around to Anna and Taylor, who were about to get in his car. Anna's smile was ridiculously overboard and Taylor had a frown that was bound to give him wrinkles. What was she to do? Maybe this was an opportunity for Taylor to get to know Ryan. She would like them to be mates, and besides they shared a common interest... guns.

'Can Ryan come with us?' she asked her friends. Taylor looked less than impressed, whereas Anna clapped excitedly.

'Yes, of course. Isn't that right, Taylor? More the merrier,' said Anna.

'Yeah, sure. Why don't you come?' he said blandly.

Jaz turned back to Ryan. 'We're going to the firing range. Do you want to come?'

'Really? Sure, thanks.' He slid into the back seat with Jaz, his long legs folded up behind Anna's front seat. 'Sweet ride, Taylor.'

'Thanks,' said Taylor as he put it in gear and took off with a smile on his face.

Anna was already trying to find Red FM on the radio as she chatted to Taylor. Ryan was watching the houses flick by out his window, deep in thought. Jaz touched his leg and he nearly jumped through the car roof.

'You okay?' she said quietly, so the front two couldn't hear.

He nodded and asked, 'Why do you say that?'

Jaz shrugged a shoulder. 'I don't know, you just seem a little preoccupied, that's all.' *And detached, not yourself and distant towards me at times,* she wanted to add but lost her nerve.

'Just deep in thought. Trying to sort out a problem.'

'Well, if there's anything I can do, I'm right here.'

He glanced back out the window, so Jaz slunk back into the seat and looked out her own window. Now she was deep in thought, thinking about him.

It wasn't until they got to the firing range and Derik was handing out weapons that he perked up, almost to his old cheerful self.

Taylor had gone first and fired all eight shots from his Browning 9-millimetre on target.

Ryan's face was a little gobsmacked.

'See, I told you he was brilliant,' Jaz beamed.

Taylor went a little pink from her praise, but she knew he was loving it.

Taylor handed the gun to Ryan. 'You ever used a gun before?' he asked.

'Once or twice,' said Ryan as he loaded the new clip with blind precision and fired off all shots quicker than Jaz could say 'wow'.

Taylor's eyes just about fell from his head as the target zoomed closer for inspection. Not only had Ryan hit the target's head but the shots were all that close they'd blown out a circle a bit bigger than a fifty cent piece.

'Holy shit. The man knows his stuff,' said Taylor still amazed.

Then that was the end of Anna and Jaz's existence. Finally Taylor had someone besides Derik he could actually share gun talk with, and someone he could compete with. They talked guns, ammo and everything in between, while Anna and Jaz found their own booth.

Fifteen minutes later while Anna was having another shot, Taylor tapped Jaz on the shoulder. Jaz shifted her earmuffs from her ears.

'You were right, he's okay.'

Jaz looked at him, dumbfounded. 'What, you're best buddies now? God, I will never understand boys!'

'Well, we *are* from Mars, isn't that what Anna reckons? Speaking of Anna, I think she needs my expertise.'

Taylor gave Jaz a wink and stepped around her to get to Anna, who was trying to correct her stance.

Jaz felt eyes upon her and glanced at Ryan. He looked like a bad-arse with a gun in his hands, enthralling to boot. It looked so natural, like it was a part of him. His movements with the gun were like that of a normal person with their mobile phone. She walked slowly towards him and took the gun he held out for her. She knew he wanted to see what she could do.

He hadn't even unloaded it, so with swift fingers she emptied the gun and slipped in the new clip. She felt nervous with him behind her; the pressure to do well was forefront in her mind. *Please don't miss, please don't miss.* Jaz breathed in and as she let out a slow even breath, she fired all the rounds.

After the last bullet was spent, she turned around to face Ryan. She emptied the gun before putting it down on the table, and took off her earmuffs. The target rattled behind her as it grew near but she didn't turn around. Instead, she watched Ryan's eyes, saw him glance to the target and then smile in approval. Had she just passed another test?

'Well?'

Ryan removed his own earmuffs. 'You've exceeded my expectations, yet again.'

She couldn't wipe off the stupid grin she knew was on her face. They stood staring at each other for a long moment before Ryan cleared his throat and said, 'Taylor, on the other hand, is better than half our operatives.'

'Yeah, that wouldn't surprise me. He loves this place and comes all the time to practise.'

'Hmm, it shows.'

'Are you thinking of recruiting him too?' Jaz asked jokingly.

'It's a thought, but we don't recruit often, because we can't cope with too many. We like to give you all one-on-one training with a qualified agent. But if you say no, then he's more than a possibility.'

Jaz was taken aback, unsure how she felt about that. Taylor as an agent? Especially if she said no – what the hell!

Ryan interrupted her thoughts with a question.

'Pardon?'

'I asked if you'd been here with your mum at all.'

'At the range?' Jaz asked and Ryan nodded. 'Ha, no. My mum doesn't get out much. She likes to stick to her little suburb and her job.'

'So... um... what was your mum's name? Natalie, was it?' he asked awkwardly.

'No, it's Natasha. Well, she goes by Tasha but I've heard Pax call her Nat a few times. I think it's a pet name.'

Ryan nodded slowly, and that weird feeling came over Jaz again. It was like Ryan had left the room, yet his body remained.

'You right?'

'Yeah, sorry. It's just, I have a bit of a problem and I was thinking maybe you can help me. But on the other hand I really don't want to involve you.' Ryan dropped his voice to a whisper.

'Ask me, Ryan. I don't mind.' Jaz cupped her mouth in a stage whisper. 'You want me to stake out at the club again?'

'No, it's a bit harder than that.' He eased her closer so he could speak into her ear. 'I need some information picked up tonight at ten but I'll be at the club on a shift, and you know how important it is for me to keep an eye out there.'

She nodded. 'How come you have to pick it up?'

'Because phones and emails are traceable. Jaz, we have spots where we go to pick up info all around the city. We can't just pick up a phone and call people. This is serious stuff.' His eyes darted around the room then back to her. 'Everyone else is away or busy, and I thought that maybe this would help you decide if you wanted to join.'

'Oh, right.' Another test. Another part of the life she could end up living. It was exciting and scary. 'Well, I can pick it up, no worries.'

He let out a deep breath and it tickled her ear. 'Jaz, this info is kept at one of our main pick-up points and you'd have to dress the part to go there and I'd be worried about your safety. It's not a risk free pick up.'

'Come on, Ryan. Don't you think I can look after myself? Did I not lay you out on your arse? Why are you being so cautious about this? I can do it.'

Ryan's jaw was flinching, hesitant. 'Jaz. The info is at a well-known brothel. I'd need you to dress up...' He left the sentence hanging as he glanced away.

'Dress up?' She frowned and then her mouth dropped open. 'Oh. Like a hooker?' Now Jaz got it. 'I see.' She shrugged. 'Well, I'm sure I could manage that part. I have a killer little black dress I could wear. Who do I need to see?'

Ryan glanced over her shoulder to check they weren't being overheard. 'The Madam who runs the place. Her name is Sasha. Look, are you sure you want to do this?'

Jaz nodded, but her racing heart was uncertain.

'Okay. If you're sure. Meet me at nine out the front of Ramblers before it opens and I'll go over it with you. It's just a simple pick-up. Just remember to come looking... the part. Can you get away?'

'Yep. Anna will be my alibi. But I'll have to tell her something convincing, like I'm sneaking off to the club to see you.' Ryan smiled and Jaz's heart raced even more. 'At least it's kind of true.'

'That's a good idea.' His face gave nothing away.

'Hey, Ryan, wanna have a tour of the new section? Derik can take us through,' said Taylor as he walked over.

Jaz turned around to see Anna standing by Taylor's side, her eyes questioning and glancing to Ryan. She knew that look from Anna: she was trying to read into the situation, and no doubt was reading far too much. Then Jaz realised she was standing only a foot from Ryan, but it would work well for her alibi tonight.

'Sure, sounds like a plan,' he told Taylor as he walked off leaving Anna and Jaz to take up the rear.

'Hey, you! Were you just having a little romantic pow-wow?' whispered Anna as she grabbed Jaz's arm.

'Um, well, he wants me to come see him at the club tonight,' said Jaz, laying the foundations for their plans. But Jaz couldn't help feeling that there was something there, a little spark, that was more than just work.

'Oh my God. You have to go. Oh, I wish I was you.'

'So, you don't mind if I use you as my alibi?'

'That's what friends are for. *But*, I want all the juicy details when you get back.'

Jaz felt the sickening wave of deceit that came from lying to her friend. She didn't enjoy it one bit.

'Did Taylor help you any?' asked Jaz quickly, to change the subject.

'Oh, yeah. All my shots are now hitting the target... but I just won't say where.' And it was as easy as that. Off Anna went, into depth about Taylor and his coolness.

Jaz followed behind Ryan and Taylor, trying to figure out how tonight would go. She was nervous, but she also couldn't help but feel excited too.

CHAPTER 21

JAZ PULLED OUT her clothes from her overnight bag and changed in Anna's bathroom. She hid her raunchy dress under a black jacket and carried a dangerously high pair of heels she'd borrowed from the back of her mum's walk-in-robe. They were sure to cramp her calves.

'Anna, can you do my make-up, please?' she asked.

A veil of strawberry blonde hair appeared around the corner. 'Really? You wanna go really glam?' she said walking into the bathroom. 'Ryan is totally worth it, and you'll want to look older because he *is* older.' Jaz nodded because she couldn't think of an answer to that. 'You look fabulous. Your hair up in that high ponytail is very sexy with those massive hoop earrings. How do you want the make-up?'

'Can you do dark and sexy? Put it all on.'

Anna smiled, showing all her teeth like Jaz had just given her the power to jump through time, and went to work. Ten minutes later, after putting on thick mascara, Anna stepped away and they admired her handiwork in the mirror.

'I am a legend. You look so hot, Jaz.'

Anna stated the truth. Jaz turned her head, amazed by the transformation. 'Wow. It doesn't even look like me.'

'You better get going or you'll miss your taxi. Now, if you kiss you must tell me. Got it?' Anna pulled her into a hug.

'Thanks, Anna. See you later.'

Jaz snuck out Anna's window, then pulled her short dress up to her waist so she could climb her way down the tree. Luckily she didn't have to wear stockings but it was a bit cool with not much on. On the ground she adjusted her dress, took off her jacket and hid it under a bush. When she glanced down all she could see was her breasts straining against the black material. My God, it was amazing what a push-up bra did. Anna would have freaked if she'd seen Jaz like this. Jaz was a little freaked herself.

Down the street, she could see the taxi sitting where she'd requested it to wait. 'Ramblers nightclub, please,' she said as she climbed in.

She put on her black pumps and opened her clutch purse to apply more lipstick. When the taxi pulled up outside the club, Jaz scooted forward and paid the guy. She would use another taxi to go to the pick-up point, which was a nice way of saying where she was going. As Jaz stepped out of the car with a shiver, she spied Ryan talking to a fellow bouncer mate who wore a matching black Ramblers' shirt.

His back was to her as she began to walk carefully towards them. The dangerously high heels threatened to topple her before she found her balance, but after a few steps she walked more smoothly and began to swing the hips. *Think sexy*, she told herself. *Just don't fall over!*

The other bouncer spotted her first, his eyes freezing on her as he paused mid-sentence. Ryan turned to see what had caught his attention, and she watched his jaw drop as she gave him a smile and a wave. The last ten metres seemed to take forever as she tried to concentrate on walking in the ankle-breakers. There were whistles and catcalls but Jaz only had eyes for Ryan. She was using him to keep her steady.

'Jaz?' He held out his hands to her and she was relieved to be able to grab onto something. His hands were strong and warm – but it was the look on his face that caused her insides to burn.

'Yes, it's me. Do I pass?' she asked.

Ryan turned back to his bouncer mate. 'Do you mind if I have a few minutes here? I'll be in in a sec, Peter.'

Peter gave him a wink, gave Jaz a final gawk and muttered how lucky Ryan was under his breath before heading inside the club.

'I'm speechless,' said Ryan as he stood back to take in her heels. His eyes continued up her legs, paused for a moment on her chest; he shook his head and then found her eyes again.

'What's the address?' she asked as she felt a blush creeping over her skin.

'Um yeah, right.' Ryan let go of her hands and pulled out a piece of paper. 'Go here, it's a green door. Go in and ask for Sasha.' Ryan spent ten minutes going over what she had to do and say. 'Then come back to the club and find me. Okay?'

'Sure, sounds easy enough.' If only her heart would stop pounding. If it kept up this pace she'd likely faint before too long, and what good would that do them?

'Good luck.' Ryan pulled her in for a hug. Jaz clutched her arms across his strong back, rested her head on his shoulder, and breathed. It was weird how safe she felt in his arms, how much it calmed her in the face of what she was about to do. But it was just a pick up, surely it couldn't be that hard?

She felt his hands move down her back to her waist and slowly he pulled her back a fraction. 'I'll get you a taxi and see you off before I go inside.' He raised her chin with his fingers so he could study her. 'Now is the time to speak up if you're not sure.'

Jaz smiled and brushed his hand away. 'I didn't tart myself up just to walk away, Ryan. I said I'd do it and I will. I'll see you back here soon.'

'I'll be waiting.'

They said no more but much passed between their eyes as she climbed into the next taxi. She could tell Ryan didn't want to let her go, he was worried but he also trusted her, and she wanted to do this for him, partly to prove herself. And she trusted him too.

The taxi driver didn't bat an eyelid when she gave him the address and when they arrived she pressed a fifty into his hand. 'Can you wait around, please? I won't be long.'

'Yeah, yeah,' he said pocketing the money.

Before she could lose her nerve, Jaz walked around the corner and straight towards the green door. It wasn't hidden, in fact it stood out on the quiet, well-lit street. She was half expecting a red light flashing at the top.

Holding her purse in a near death grip, she pushed open the door and headed inside without pausing. Get in and out quick, that's what Ryan had said.

The place smelled funky but Jaz wasn't going to stop and deliberate. She found herself in a small reception area and stepped to the dark desk.

A girl in what looked like a red satin slip smiled up at her. 'Can I help you?'

'I'm here to see Sasha.'

'She's in her office.' The girl flicked her platinum blonde hair and gestured to the door down the creepy-looking passageway lined with colourful doors. *Fantastic*, she thought.

With more confidence than she felt, Jaz strode towards Sasha's door. As she passed a bright pink door she heard a giggle and it caused her steps to falter. She told herself she should be relieved that that was all she'd heard. Quickly she lunged out the last steps and knocked on Sasha's door.

'Come in.'

A woman in her sixties dressed in a nice suit sat behind a desk, glasses sliding down her nose. Not at all what Jaz had imagined.

'Hi Sasha,' said Jaz, shutting the door before she spoke again. 'I was sent to pick up a message because my friend couldn't make it,' she said. She watched as Sasha's eyes went to her hand, spotting the 'sign' Ryan had told her to make with her thumb and little finger. With a nod her eyes went back to Jaz's face, then she opened her top drawer and pulled out a small wallet, one that you would hold a few cards in, and left her chair to come to Jaz's side.

'You're new, I see,' said Sasha, handing over the wallet. Jaz put it into her purse while trying to keep her shaking at bay. 'If you ever decide to change professions I could keep you very busy here.'

Jaz smiled weakly. 'I prefer what I'm doing, thanks.'

Sasha pushed up her glasses, her manicured eyebrows disappearing behind the frames. 'Give my best to him, won't you.' Then she sighed as if she'd just had a spoonful of chocolate mousse. She shuddered and licked her lips. 'He's just divine.'

Jaz nodded but couldn't find her voice as she launched herself at the door. Sasha followed her out. It was nearly over.

She had to endure the creepy walk back, her ears scared to hear anything. The front desk was soon in reach.

'Hey, who's this?' A deep voice sent shivers up Jaz's spine. Jaz turned to see a well-dressed man coming out of the closest door by the front counter. 'Sasha, have you been holding out on me?'

His green eyes leered and instantly she didn't trust him. She could tell he had money, and a wife.

'No, Michael, she's way out of your league.'

Michael stepped closer to Jaz, reaching out his hand to touch the skin on her arm. Jaz held herself firm; she couldn't give the game away. What if this guy was a spy for the bad side? Or worse, he'd want her for other things. Sasha glanced at Jaz and flicked her eyes to the door.

'Michael, have you come to settle?' Sasha drew his attention and Jaz didn't wait to be told twice. She left without saying a word. Sliding through the green door, she walked slowly to the corner. Once around it she fled to the safety of the taxi. *Stay calm, keep your act up until you're a block away in the taxi.* Jaz strung Ryan's words through her mind to keep her going.

'Back to Ramblers, please,' she told the driver, who put his newspaper on the passenger seat.

It was a twenty-minute ride back to the club and halfway there Jaz couldn't keep her purse closed any longer. She was dying to see what was inside the small wallet. She pulled it out, fought with her conscience a bit more, then carefully unfolded the paper.

Oh my God, she thought, putting her hand to her heart. It felt like it would explode from her chest.

She let out a rush of air, a whole lungful that she'd been holding.

The message was typed out in code.

Jaz had never felt so glad to see a bunch of numbers in her life. Part of her had been worried it would say, 'Your mission is to go and kill so and so…' As her heart rate went back to normal, Jaz folded the paper and put it back. She sank back into the seat and closed her eyes.

By the time she got back to the nightclub a queue had formed out the front. Feeling a little game after her big mission, she walked right up to Peter, who was slowly letting people in through the door. 'Hey, Peter, right?'

He smiled, nodded and waved her straight through. No ID check, no waiting in line. Jaz felt like royalty.

She took out the small wallet with the message and held it tightly in her hand. She had already worked out how she would transfer it to Ryan. The club was pumping with loud music and Jaz found it hard to walk through the crowd in her shoes. But they did give her extra height and she could see Ryan by the edge of the dancing crowd looking stern. Her heart fluttered from all the adrenaline, and from the relief of making it back to him.

Ryan spotted her quickly and smiled. Was that relief she saw wash over his face? With her plan still fresh in her mind, she went straight up to him and put her arms around him. 'Hey, you,' she said as her hands slipped into the back pockets of his jeans. She melted into his embrace.

'Jaz, I'm on duty,' he said but he didn't let her go. His hands held her and she could feel him nuzzle near her ear. Maybe she wasn't the only one relieved to have the pick- up over. 'Everything went okay?' he asked, pulling back and putting air between them. His eyes went back to searching around the club.

Jaz felt giddy from his lingering touch. 'Yep. How about you?'

'Not much happening tonight. Have you got—' he began to ask.

'No, you have,' she said with a smirk. 'Back pocket.'

He smiled as he realised. 'Clever. Thanks.' He didn't bother searching his jeans. 'You should probably head home now,' he added.

'I thought I might stay and dance up a storm. I didn't even have my ID checked.' She laughed and began to dance to the beat beside him, her hips swaying to the DJ's song.

'Jaz,' he almost growled and grabbed her arm, pulling her close. His lips brushed against her ear. 'You can*not* stay here dressed like that.'

She pulled away from him; his face was dark, unreadable.

'Scared I might get propositioned,' she teased. But he wasn't laughing.

'I still have to work and I can't be keeping an eye out for you too. Please, go home where I know you're safe. Please.'

'On one condition.'

'What's that?'

Jaz leaned in close. 'I need something to tell Anna.' She let her words hang in the air as she pressed her hand to his chest. His muscles underneath tightened from her touch. She was feeling all-powerful in the killer heels; certainly not herself. Was she drunk on the adrenaline? Had the danger sent her loopy?

Jaz glanced up to see his reaction but couldn't get past his lips. So perfect and smooth. She just had to taste them. Leaning in, she did just that.

Ryan's hand came up behind her head, increasing the pressure of the kiss. Jaz felt herself melt into him as she grabbed at his shirt. It was unlike anything she'd ever experienced. The noise of the club disappeared and all she could feel was the heat of his kiss. Their mouths opened, searching for more. His tongue brushed against hers and she shivered in his arms.

'I'm sorry,' Ryan said, pulling away abruptly, leaving them both catching their breath. Ryan avoided her gaze as he searched around the room. 'I really have to work, Jaz.' Now he glanced at her, his eyes resting on her lips, which felt slightly swollen. 'Go home, I'll catch up with you later.' He bent down but only to kiss the top of her head before disappearing into the crowd.

Jaz walked towards the exit but felt as if she were flying. Not even her aching feet worried her, or the pushing and shoving from the crowd. Some guys groped for her, begged her to dance, but she swayed past them on her cloud.

Somehow she found a taxi and ended up back on her street without even realising time was passing. 'Was any of that real?' she asked herself as she stepped out of the taxi. She touched her lips, remembered the taste of Ryan and shivered again but it wasn't cold outside. In a daze, she found her hidden jacket, took off her shoes and climbed up to Anna's room.

Anna was sitting in bed reading and put her book down as she climbed in. 'So, how did it go?' she asked as Jaz slumped onto her bed. 'You're back early?'

Jaz smiled. She couldn't find the words to tell Anna.

'Oh, I can *so* tell you got kissed. Damn girl, look at your face.' Anna flipped the doona cover back so Jaz could climb in. 'Okay, spill. I want all the details.' She all but threw her book from the bed in anticipation.

Jaz crawled under the sheet and leaned back against the pillows. Her mind kept replaying the kiss over and over as if proving to her it was real. 'Anna, I just had the best night of my life.'

CHAPTER 22

MR PEEL WAS talking through a problem on the board while Jaz doodled absent-mindedly on the corner of her page. Her phone vibrated on her lap, causing her to flinch out of her daydream state. The three-word message was from Anna: *Pax is back!* For the first time in four days Jaz cracked a smile.

She glanced at her page and saw the black inked 'R' she'd been doodling. With a sigh, she scrubbed it out with her pen until she couldn't see it. R was for rubbish and ridiculous, not Ryan. Or so she tried to tell herself.

Since the night of their kiss, Ryan had been gone. He'd disappeared, was dead for all she knew. He hadn't shown up at The Ring on Friday, nor over the weekend, or Monday. Jaz didn't want to admit how empty it seemed at The Ring without him, and if she admitted the truth she was worried about him. Had something happened at the club? Was the message a new mission? Did he meet with some bad guys? Or was he avoiding her because of the kiss? If only she had his number. She'd asked for it once and he'd said no. 'Best not to. Safer this way.'

But Pax was home, and finally The Ring might feel less vacant. A little voice in her head also said that maybe today Ryan would be there too.

Jaz texted Anna, *I wanna go now!* and received one word in reply. *Wait.*

She had one more class to sit through, damn it.

'Off with the fairies again, Jaz,' laughed Minka from in front of her.

Jaz smiled back sweetly. 'I'm just imagining Taylor wearing his sexy tie that matches my dress for the ball. Who are you going with, Minka?'

Minka swung back around to the front but Jaz caught the fall in her face. Helen, one of Minka's friends who was sitting beside her, turned to Jaz. 'She's going with a uni guy, he plays football for the Dockers.'

Helen pulled a 'so there' face and shifted back in her chair.

Like I care, thought Jaz. But trust Minka to find a replacement she thought was better.

*

'Jaz, can we slow... down... please,' said Anna breathlessly.

'Oh all right, but I'm already carrying your bag as well as mine. You need to get more exercise.'

Anna slowed to a walk and put her hands on her hips. 'The only exercise I want is with my tongue at the ball. I, unlike some people I know, haven't even had a kiss yet.'

Jaz smiled. 'Don't worry, you're not missing much. Wait till it's with someone you really like, then it's ten times better.' Jaz had only kissed a few guys but it was only on the dance floor and she didn't really know them. She'd figured kissing Taylor would be worth the wait and so much better. Would it be like kissing Ryan? Like fireworks and instant ecstasy? For some reason kissing Taylor seemed less of a goal now. She still liked Taylor but kissing Ryan, this hunky man who knew what he was doing, had corrupted her thoughts and messed with her mind.

'Come on, Anna, I can see The Ring, let's run the last bit.' Jaz picked up speed as she heard Anna groan but she was soon puffing alongside her.

They both ran into The Ring, eyes darting around the room looking for Pax. Jaz ditched their bags by the front desk as they headed towards the office.

'Is that a herd of elephants I hear?' said Pax, meeting them at the door.

'Pax,' they squealed and threw their arms around him, nearly bowling him over.

He kissed their cheeks and Jaz took a deep breath, smelling cinnamon, coffee and something different. It was like melted plastic and ink.

'So, where were you this time?' Anna asked. 'Were you overseas at some exotic location?'

'Were you in Bali? You like Bali,' said Jaz.

'Nope, you're both wrong.' He let them go, stepped back into his office and brought out two wrapped square parcels.

Jaz tore hers open and stared at a bright watercolour painting of a sunset. 'Wow, thanks, Pax. Did you do these?'

He nodded sheepishly.

'Oh, I get it,' said Anna. 'Bright colours, water and something about landscapes, that's what you said.'

'I was doing a course on painting watercolours. Do you like them?'

'Yes,' they both agreed.

'I'm going to hang mine in my change room, so I'll see it every day.' Jaz grabbed her school bag, her painting and headed off. As she changed, she studied the picture. In the corner on the tree trunk was a little squiggle that looked like a signature – only, it wasn't Pax's signature. Did he buy these ones because he didn't think his own were good enough? It didn't matter to her; it was the thought that counted.

Jaz joined Anna and Pax back in the office, where he had made coffee for them all, and served some apple slice from the bakery around the corner.

'Yum, I'm so hungry. Jaz had me run all the way here, can you believe it. I'm so exhausted,' sighed Anna before taking a huge bite from her slice.

Jaz laughed and Pax gave her a sly wink. Pax told them a little about his holiday; it was all a bit vague, and then Anna told him about their trips to the firing range. 'Oh, and Jaz has been busy with this guy Ryan too.'

Pax raised his eyebrow. 'A fella?'

Jaz shook her head. 'No, he's just a friend. Actually Pax, he said he knows you but I've never seen him at The Ring before. His name is Ryan Fletcher – does it sound familiar?'

Pax choked on his slice and coughed out a cloud of icing sugar across his lap. 'Sorry, got pastry stuck in my throat. Hmm, yeah, I think I remember him,' he managed between mouthfuls. 'So, who's taking whom to the ball? I seem to remember that was coming up?'

After their coffee and lots of talking about the ball, they went through the door to his house. Jaz and Anna had always looked after him, helping do his dishes or making him a few meals after school. Pax had never had a serious relationship, he reckoned he was married to The Ring and cherished his holidays too much to settle. And truthfully, they liked him being just theirs.

Anna headed out the back door with a full washing basket as Jaz opened windows to air out the place. She was making her way back into The Ring to grab their coffee cups and wash them when she saw Ryan enter.

Her heart lurched in her chest as she leaned on the desk and peered through the office window. He looked great in jeans and was wearing the black jacket he'd bought when he was with her. Jaz was about to go and say hi but froze when she saw Pax approach Ryan – and neither of them looked happy. Pax pointed to Ryan as she tried to read his lips.

What are you doing with Jaz? She thought that's what Pax was asking him. His face was dark as he repeated the question, and she saw Ryan say something like *recruiting her.* Then suddenly Pax took Ryan by his arm and dragged him closer towards the front door.

Damn, Pax was standing in front of Ryan's mouth but some harsh words were being said between the two.

Intrigue moved her from the office and towards them both. She walked slowly and silently, trying to see if she could catch what they were talking about. It was all so secretive, which made her all the more curious.

Pax was whispering. 'I helped her fake it all—'

'We'll talk later,' said Ryan, cutting Pax off as he spotted Jaz.

'Jaz,' said Pax in alarm as he saw her. But Jaz wasn't worried that they'd stopped talking with her around. What bothered her was that Ryan had walked off out the door, without so much as a hello or goodbye.

Damn you, she thought angrily, *you can't ignore me!*

Jaz ran outside after him. 'Ryan!' she yelled. 'Ryan, wait.'

He stopped but didn't turn around, so she had to run around to face him.

'What's wrong?' She threw up her hands as Ryan's eyes stayed on his feet. 'Have I done something to upset you? I'm sorry if I have,' she said. She couldn't bring herself to speak openly about the kiss. Not while he was like this.

Finally, his eyes rose to meet hers. He must have heard the pleading and hurt in her voice, because his eyes shone with empathy. Right there in that moment Jaz could tell he cared. His eyes always spoke the truth to her.

Ryan didn't answer her question, instead he lifted his hand to her face and traced his thumb along her cheek, catching a loose hair and brushing it aside.

Jaz could smell his scent on the warm breeze. Closing her eyes, she raised her hand and touched him. At once, he pulled away as if she'd zapped him.

'I have to go,' he said stepping back. 'I'll be in touch.' Then he crossed the road to his car without looking back.

Jaz watched him leave, her cheek still tingling from his touch and her mind more confused than ever.

After Ryan's car took off out of sight, Jaz wandered back into the gym and found Pax by the computer. He was shuffling papers looking like he was busy with work but Jaz didn't care. She sat on the edge of the desk and waited until he acknowledged her.

'Pax, what was that all about?'

'What was what about?' he said absentmindedly as he wobbled the computer mouse, flicking on the screen.

Pax was doing a great job of pretending nothing was up, so why the need to avoid her eyes? 'Pax, I'm not stupid, it's obvious something was going on between you two. How do you know Ryan?'

'I'm a friend of his family and there's a bit of stuff happening at the moment, nothing for you to worry about.'

'Is that why he's been acting weird lately?' Was it something to do with Ryan's parents? His sister? 'Is it bad?'

Pax put down the papers and sighed. 'You're not going to let this go, are you? Look, it's just a bit of miscommunication, Jaz. It will sort itself out in a few days. Just give Ryan some space, okay.'

'All right, if you're sure.' She wanted to tell Pax that she wasn't a kid anymore, that she didn't need to be protected from the world and its nasties. But she had a feeling he already understood that fact. Like any parent, he didn't like to think that she was growing up.

Jaz put her arms around Pax's shoulders and hugged him tightly. 'I'm glad you're home, I missed you. Do you feel like another cuppa?'

Pax patted Jaz's arm and smiled. 'I missed you too, and a cuppa would be great thanks, sweetie.'

Jaz kissed his forehead before taking the empty cups back to his house. So much was going on lately and school would be over at the end of the year. She sighed, and in that instant Jaz felt like her world was about to shift.

CHAPTER 23

'MIND IF I join you two?'

'Hey, Tay, you don't have to ask,' said Anna as Taylor sat beside her, his half-eaten lunch in his hand and his white school shirt half-untucked.

'To what do we owe this pleasure?' said Jaz as she swept her hair back from her face.

'Do I need a reason to visit my mates?'

Jaz and Anna glanced at each other, eyebrows raised.

'I know I don't normally have lunch with you two but I've just been feeling a bit out of place over there lately,' said Taylor nodding to his usual table where four guys and a couple of girls were mucking about. 'I don't know, maybe it's knowing that in another six months we'll be out in the big wide world and I just don't see myself staying in contact with them. You guys, on the other hand...'

'Aww, you're sweet,' said Anna, touching Taylor's arm.

'Why so glum, Jaz?' he asked.

'I'm not glum.' Jaz felt both sets of concerned eyes on her.

'Ah, hello? Yes you are. You've been sad the last few days and don't tell me it's got nothing to do with Ryan. I know you, you're thinking about him,' said Anna.

'Why, what's up with Ryan, are you two...?' Taylor's blue eyes probed for answers.

Jaz dropped her head on the table, narrowly missing her sandwich. 'No we are not going out, dating or anything of the sort. We are friends. Well, at least I thought we were,' she said sitting back up. 'But now something funny's going on and I haven't heard from him since he and Pax had that heated discussion.'

'I think you're reading too much into it, Jaz. What Pax said was probably right, it's just some family problem that's got him messed up.'

'I don't know, Anna. It's this feeling I have. And when I asked him if I'd done something wrong he never replied. Most people would say, "No, it's got nothing to do with you," but he didn't reassure me one bit. And Pax just about peed his pants when I sprung their conversation. If I didn't know better I'd say they were talking about me.' Jaz sighed. 'Oh, don't look at me like that. I know you think I'm nuts.'

Anna laughed as she reached her hand across to Jaz. 'Honey, you've always been nuts, but I still love you. Look, Ryan's a big boy who can take care of himself. I'm sure he's fine. He said he'd be in touch, just give him time.'

'Anna's right,' added Taylor. 'So, bring back that gorgeous smile of yours. Besides, I can't take you to the ball looking like your pet's just died, now, can I?'

Jaz shrugged and smiled just for them. A girl couldn't ask for better mates. 'Have you found a tie yet?' she asked Taylor. He was going to look so handsome in a suit and even better beside her.

'I picked up a blue tie and a silver one as well. I'll bring you home after school and you can pick the one that suits best.'

'Cool, sounds like a plan.'

Taylor glanced across at Anna just as she finished her apple. 'You wanna come with us?'

She shook her head and threw her core on her tray. 'Would love to but Ricky and I are going to the library to do some research on a project. And *no* it's not what you think.'

'What do you think it is that we're thinking?' asked Jaz cheekily.

'Piss off, you know what I mean. Come on, I'm going to class. You two coming?'

Jaz and Taylor got up to walk with Anna. Jaz was feeling better; well, she had her smile back, but still lurking in the back of her mind was Ryan. Part of her worried she'd never see him again, and that didn't sit well at all. And if she was going to be an agent she had to do it for herself, not just to be able to see Ryan… right? Maybe Ryan was annoyed she hadn't made up her mind yet. But she'd been thinking bloody hard about it. It was a pretty major career choice, scary and dangerous, but Jaz liked the idea of being able to help protect people. She'd like to be as amazing as Ryan. A secret super-agent.

'Jaz we're in this classroom,' said Anna from the doorway of their next class, the one Jaz had just walked straight past.

*

Jaz hung her head out the window of Taylor's Mustang and closed her eyes against the wind. A handful of black hair swirled out behind her.

'You remind me of our dog, but with less drool. He loved sticking his head out the window too,' said Taylor with a smirk.

Jaz put her head back inside. 'Smartarse. I was clearing my mind.'

'Did it help?'

'Nup,' she laughed.

Taylor tapped his fingers against the steering wheel in time to the music. 'You know, Jaz, something about you has changed. Nothing big, and nothing I can put my finger on, but you're different.'

'Is that in a good way or bad way?'

'Good… I think.'

'Gee, thanks… I think,' replied Jaz pushing Taylor's arm playfully. Maybe in a way she *was* different. Ryan had opened her eyes to a whole other world and she felt like she saw things in a new light. She also wasn't thinking about Taylor all the time. Like, a month ago she would have been delirious with excitement to be going home with him, but now there just seemed like more important things to think about.

'It's been a while since just you and I were here,' said Taylor as he pulled into his street.

A black car caught Jaz's attention, more so when it parked on the street opposite Taylor's house. She could have sworn the car and the guy in the driver's seat looked familiar but as Taylor drove into his three-bay garage she dismissed it as one of his neighbours busy talking on their mobile.

Taylor's home was a beautiful, big one-storey house with a tropical garden and pool out the back. It had probably been a year since her last visit to his place alone. She followed Taylor through the lounge room full of expensive artwork and sculptures. His dad collected guns, so his mother collected artwork – until she died four years ago from cancer. It had been a hard few years, but Taylor and his dad had their own rhythm going now.

They headed down the wide passageway to a door on the right, which led to his dad's big office and his prized gun collection.

'Come in here, I want to show you something,' he said taking her hand.

Taylor went past the floor-to-ceiling display cabinet to a bookshelf, pulled out a book and came back with a key. Then he opened a large vault that was hidden behind another bookcase on a hinge.

'This is Dad's new pride and joy.' Taylor put on some white gloves and threw a pair to Jaz. When he turned around, he was cradling an old, tiny gun.

'This is a .32-calibre revolver made by Henckell & Co and was found at Kate Kelly's house.' Taylor waited for the news to sink in.

'Soooo, as in Ned Kelly the famous bushranger?'

Taylor smiled with joy. 'You got it, and see this,' Taylor held the wooden stock closer. 'The initials KK are inscribed here, and also the insignia of the Royal Constabulary who hunted the Kelly Gang.'

Jaz took the old revolver with a sense of awe, whether from touching a part of Australia's history, or just being swept up in the magic of it all as Taylor spoke with such passion. 'It's beautiful, and no doubt very expensive?' Jaz asked.

'Yeah, but it's worth it. Just think what this revolver has been through and the stories it'd tell if it could. I reckon it belonged to Constable Alexander Fitzpatrick, apparently he claimed to have lost his gun during a struggle with the Kelly family.'

'Wow, Tay. You know so much about all this. Does your dad let you show it around?'

Taylor laughed and took back the revolver. 'That would be a no. He doesn't even know I know where he hides his keys. Adults underestimate their kids' abilities.'

'Typical. It's a weird feeling to hold so much history in your hands,' said Jaz taking her gloves off while Taylor locked up.

He put his arm around Jaz after hiding the key back in the book and led her towards his room. 'I knew you would appreciate it, Jaz. I can't wait to show Anna too.'

'She will probably know more about it than you do,' Jaz laughed as they entered Taylor's room. His double bed was against the far wall, the blue doona cover thrown back as if he'd just got out of bed. Jaz walked across the grey carpet and sat on it while he went to his walk-in-robe to find the ties. His floor was a lot like hers, covered in clothes.

'Your house cleaner on a vacation too?' she asked.

'Yeah, probably off sipping martinis with yours,' he laughed.

Jaz glanced over to his desk by his bed. His laptop sat open, alarm clock nearby and a photo frame, which she picked up. It was a photo of Jaz and Anna together, arms thrown around each other and pulling a finger at Taylor as he took the photo. He'd snapped it about four months ago after his photography class and she had forgotten all about it.

They looked so different, Jaz dark with blue eyes and Anna fair with green eyes and red hair.

'I love that photo of you two,' said Taylor, stepping back out of his wardrobe and throwing a bag at Jaz.

She put the photo back and dug into the bag, pulling out the ties. The blue one was the wrong shade for her dress but the silver one was perfect. 'This one will do,' she said showing him. 'Have you got your suit?'

He nodded and rolled his eyes. 'Yes, I went to get fitted and measured up last week. Dad actually came along to help, which was strange for him. He's been a bit funny lately.'

'Really, like how? Your dad is usually so easy, even considering he's a cop.'

'I know, right? I can't put my finger on it but he's a little more fatherly. If that makes sense? Asking me where I'm going and wanting regular text updates.'

Jaz laughed. 'Tay, he sounds like my mum. Something must be wrong. Your dad's the normally the cool one.'

'Exactly,' he said, throwing his arms up in protest.

Jaz brushed her finger down the silver tie. 'God, I'm so glad I got my dress without my mum. She was a little disappointed she wasn't there with me, but trying on a heap of dresses that she likes is not my idea of fun.'

'Has Anna got hers yet?' he asked, sitting next to her on the bed.

'Yeah, it's an emerald green strappy number. She did some major begging to get it but she assures me it was worth it.'

'Anna would look amazing in anything,' said Taylor before standing up. 'Well, I suppose I should get you back to The Ring. You probably have someone lined up to beat the living crap out of. Who is it today, Bags or Tick?' he laughed.

'One day I'd like to get you back there and teach you a few more moves. I reckon you've probably forgotten the ones I've already taught you.'

Jaz stood up just as Taylor picked her up and threw her over his shoulder. 'No I haven't and I even have a few of my own. You feel like a swim?'

'Taylor, you wouldn't dare!' she squealed, kicking her legs. 'I've got nothing to change into and my shirt's white!'

'Jaz, you're so not helping your cause,' he laughed.

Jaz didn't know whether to squirm free or to tickle him; either way she'd probably end up a heap on the floor. Taylor headed towards the kitchen to the glass doors that opened up to the pool area but at the last minute plonked her on the marble benchtop.

'I'll let you go this time, but next time I won't be so forgiving,' he joked. 'Wanna Coke for the ride home?' he asked.

'Sure, thanks, Tay.' Jaz watched Taylor open the stainless-steel fridge. How did she ever end up with such a cool friend, and a hottie at that? She was reminded again just how much more time they had been spending with him. She wasn't going to complain – it felt like old times when they always hung out before he got so popular and before his mum passed away – but she still wondered what was going on inside his head. She wasn't the only one who was a little different – Taylor was also changing. Could it be that they were just all growing up?

Taylor cracked her can and passed it over. 'Come on, let's get you back to The Ring before my car turns into a pumpkin.'

THE NEXT DAY at school had been a total bore. Not even Minka had the heart to annoy her. What was the world coming too? Taylor had sat with them again at lunchtime, and Minka hadn't even thrown daggers their way. Apparently her footballer boyfriend was giving her popularity a boost. Jaz still saw her glance longingly at Taylor, though; when she thought no one was looking. Jaz should know, that had been her for most of this year.

Jaz stood outside of school with Anna and Taylor, her earphones in her hands ready to put in.

'You're gonna love the surprise, Anna,' she said.

'I thought I was just going to fix something on your laptop?' she said turning to Taylor.

'Yes, that and I have something to show you,' he said.

Jaz was excited for Anna, who would love that tiny old gun and its history.

'I'll see you both tomorrow. Oh, and a word of warning: stay away from the pool.' Jaz squinted her eyes at Taylor and pointed her finger at him. 'And you behave.' Taylor laughed and gave her a scout's honour.

She watched her friends get into the Mustang and waved, before Taylor floored it down the street causing heads to turn. She was sure she could hear Anna squealing.

Jaz made it to the gym in her best time yet, even with her bag bouncing on her back and running in her commando boots. It probably helped that she'd listened to a selection of dance music with a fast beat.

'Hiya, Pax,' she said pulling out her earphones and giving him a kiss on the cheek. 'What's up? You look a little flustered.'

Pax rubbed his head, his eyes darting about anxiously. 'Just getting old, I guess.'

'Bah humbug, Pax. You'll never be too old. I'm gonna get changed. Any of the boys in yet?'

'Yeah, Niles is floating around somewhere. If you ask him to fight just go easy, he's a bit out of shape.'

Jaz laughed and nodded. It had been a while since she'd seen Niles around, but he did have a new girlfriend.

'Maybe his new girlfriend has requested some muscled arms,' she joked.

'Ha, maybe,' he said.

Jaz threw her bag on the floor in her change room. She took off her tie, and school shirt, stuffing them into her bag. That's when she noticed a magazine on the little bench. It was called *Reps* – short for *Real Endurance. Power. Strength.* – and a yellow sticky note was on the front.

You will need this to communicate with me. Ryan.

Jaz ran her finger over his penned words. Well, at least now she knew he was still alive. She flicked through the magazine. It was full of techniques, some kickboxing, nutrition and other exercises for great abs. What in the hell would she need this for? How was a magazine going to help her communicate with Ryan?

Jaz flipped open the magazine and shook it upside down, half-expecting another note to fall out. But none did. Well, this was puzzling. Maybe he thought she'd enjoy it. It was her sort of magazine and at least she could learn something from it, not like idle gossip of Hollywood stars, which accomplished nothing.

Oh well, Yoda Ryan must have some reason for it. Jaz rolled it up after re-reading his note, and put it in her bag. She finished changing and headed to her yoga mat, waiting and hoping for Ryan to appear and explain further. But long after she'd finished her yoga and a coffee with Pax, he was still a no show. Damn it. She'd forget what he looked like at this rate. A picture flashed up in her mind of Ryan with his shirt off, pounding the speedball. Then again, maybe not.

*

After dinner, Jaz plonked herself down on the couch next to Simon as her mum and Paul shared a bottle of wine in the chairs beside them.

Jaz let her head fall back and ran her arm along behind Simon. Her brother's legs were folded under him and the TV remote was guarded in his hands, as it always was when his favourite show was on. Jaz opened her eyes and found him looking at her. 'What?'

'Just wondering what's up with you lately,' he asked.

Jaz frowned, 'Nothing's up with me.'

'Um, I beg to differ. Normally you would be stealing the remote off me and changing the channel to one of your shows. You haven't picked on me in weeks and you sit in the back of the car now! Like, what's up with that? If I didn't know better I'd almost think aliens had invaded and taken over my sister's body.'

She shrugged and gave him a smile. 'Maybe they have,' she joked. 'What are you trying to say, Si? Want me to change back?'

'Hell no! As weird as you are, I don't mind this.'

Jaz put her arm around Simon and gave him a squeeze. He shook her off and pretended to be sick.

Jaz got up and ruffled Simon's hair. 'I'm going to my room. Night, bro.'

Simon looked confused again. 'Whatever.'

She walked over to her parents, gave them a hug, and ignored their shocked expression. 'I'm off to bed. Night, Dad. Night, Mum.'

'Night, sweetheart,' they both replied. Tasha held Jaz's hand before she could walk away. 'You feeling all right, Jasmine?'

'Yeah, just got a lot on my mind with the ball and I have some essays due.'

'Do you need a hand with any of them?' asked Paul, and Jaz smiled warmly. Paul wasn't her real dad, but he was the best dad she could have asked for. He helped her with her schoolwork and used to take her to things when her mum wouldn't, like the zoo, or into the city. She loved her mum, but at times she was such a recluse.

Jaz put her hand on Paul's shoulder as he adjusted his glasses. Paul was medium height and fair but he had a huge heart and the cutest smile to go with it. No wonder her mum fell for him. He wouldn't hurt a puppy, or a spider or any other creepy living thing.

'Thanks, I'll give you a holler if I get stuck.' She felt bad when she saw his eyes light up. It had been a while since she'd asked him for help or spent any quality time with them. Somehow, thinking about becoming an agent and learning about Chris's death had opened her eyes and made her realise how petty she'd been. She had a family who loved her, which was more than a lot of people had and she took it for granted. It was time she acted her age, especially as soon she'd no longer be a school kid.

Jaz headed up the staircase to her room. As soon as she turned on the light she saw Ryan's jumper on the end of her bed and thought of his spotless bedroom, which contrasted greatly with her messy space, which Simon had nicknamed Hiroshima.

Twenty minutes later she'd tidied her room and was amazed at how much flooring she could see. Her room really was big. She'd also had a shower and was curled up in Ryan's jumper, sitting at her desk with a blank page ready to start her essay. She picked up her mobile and messaged Anna.

Yes, she was procrastinating, but it wasn't due for another three days. Plenty of time.

You still up?
Yep, finishing history essay.
Don't wanna do mine 2?
Nup! :)
Bugger ⊠

Jaz was tapping her phone against her chin when it vibrated again. Had Anna changed her mind about the essay? But it wasn't from Anna.

16-9-4 / 34-19-1 / 4-4-6 / 18-10-2 / 26-15-8 / 31-5-3 Ryan

What the hell? How did Ryan get her number? He was a cunning man, she knew he'd have found a way. But, what was up with all the numbers? No doubt, this was another test for her. They looked like some sort of code.

She glanced at her phone and thought of Anna. She could figure this out in a flash, but Jaz couldn't get help. This was something she had to figure out on her own, especially if she was to make it in the secret agent world. Jaz got up and paced her room, which she could now do without tripping over clothes. She flopped onto her bed and studied her phone message. Could they correspond to the alphabet? That seemed like the logical place to start.

She went to her desk, got a pen and paper, and wrote out the alphabet. Then she put the numbers under the letters. She didn't have enough letters for the numbers, so she started at A and wrote the remaining numbers. No, it still didn't make sense. And were they all three-letter words in between the breaks? *16-9-4 / 34-19-1 /*

Jaz tried re-jigging the numbers under the letters to see if one format would start to make sense but by ten o'clock her brain was fried and her clean floor now littered with paper.

She turned off her light, crawled into bed and glanced at the text once more. The only thing that made sense was the last bit, and that was Ryan's name at the end.

'Couldn't you at least have given me a clue!' Jaz sighed, threw her phone on her bedside table, rolled over and snuggled her black pillow. Maybe she'd have more luck in the morning but right now her brain hurt.

CHAPTER 25

'DID YOU FINISH your essay?' Jaz asked Anna at school the next day.

'Sure did. Did you even start yours?' Jaz groaned in reply and Anna laughed. 'I didn't think so.'

'Hey, I tried. What are you doing for your free period?'

Anna waved the load of books in her arms under Jaz's nose. 'Off to the library to swap books and start my next assignment. I suppose you're off to shoot some hoops?'

'Actually I was thinking of going to the library too.'

'Are you for real?'

Jaz nodded. She was hoping to find some books on codes or something to point her in the right direction. Who knew if Ryan's message had a time limit on it.

'Yep, so which way is it?' she joked as she took some of Anna's books.

They walked down the corridor and through a covered walkway that joined the separate library building. And into the silence.

'Come on, I use a desk down here, it's out of the way and quiet,' said Anna.

'How could it be any quieter than this?' asked Jaz. She followed Anna past the shelves of books towards the back. Jaz found the smell unique and couldn't help but run her finger along the spines of the books. She liked to read and had a collection of her own but Anna loved all the non-fiction, factual stuff she could learn from, whereas Jaz enjoyed escaping into a book, where the main characters overcame challenges and it all ended happy ever after.

'Here, I'll just go and return these ones, we can sit here.' Anna took the books from Jaz and nodded to the small grey table against the wall under a window.

Jaz threw her bag on the table, got out her phone and sat down.

16-9-4 / 34-19-1 / 4-4-6 / 18-10-2 / 26-15-8 / 31-5-3 Ryan

Last night's headache returned as she looked at the message. All of a sudden it was the last thing she felt like thinking about. Numbers... she hated numbers, hence maths was her worst subject. She'd rather poke her eye out with a stick than do maths. With a sigh, she shifted her bag closer and started looking for a pen and paper. She would make herself persist! As she looked inside her bag, she saw the magazine from Ryan and pulled it out. The moment she touched it she realised it was the key. She'd read his message enough times to remember it.

You will need this to communicate with me.

The magazine was what she'd needed all along.

With a forehead slap and renewed enthusiasm, she got out a notepad and pen and wrote out the coded text from Ryan. She saw that the first set in the group of three could get as high as 34, the second number in the set not as high and the third numbers were the lowest.

Jaz opened the magazine and started to turn the next page, her finger about to cover the page number when it dawned on her. She flicked to the end of the book: forty pages in this magazine. She was onto something, she could feel it.

The first number was 16, so she turned to that page. Next was 9, so she counted down nine lines in the text. Then a 4. She counted in four words.

Meet

She tried the next lot of numbers in the bracket.

Me

'Well, look at you working hard... oh, you're reading a magazine. And here I was thinking you were actually doing real work,' laughed Anna.

Jaz smiled and shrugged. 'What can I say, I got distracted.'

Anna rolled her eyes before sitting down with a new pile of books and getting out her notepad and pen.

Jaz quickly got back to the next set of numbers.

Outside

Meet me outside. Yes, she was sure this was right. But it seemed so simple.

She found the other three words and read it all together.

Meet me outside school twelve tomorrow.

Holy cow, she'd done it. Twelve tomorrow, that was today. Jaz checked her watch: fifteen minutes to twelve. She was cutting it a bit fine.

What could she say to Anna? If she went now she wouldn't be here for lunch and there'd be too many questions to answer. Jaz looked at her phone. 'Oh, I got a text from Ryan; he wants to take me out for lunch and talk.' The lie slipped like warm butter from her tongue.

Anna's eyes grew large. 'What are you waiting for; you've been dying to talk to him for ages. Go see what he wants.'

Jaz gave Anna a funny look. 'You're actually agreeing to me sneaking out of school?'

'What can I say, it's romantic.'

'OMG, Anna, I worry about you,' Jaz laughed as she threw all her stuff back in her bag, relieved the lie was easy. Well, there was some truth in there, plus she knew how Anna would read into it.

'Okay, I'll catch ya later.'

'Yes, I want to hear all about it,' whispered Anna as she waved her goodbye.

Jaz had to contain herself as she almost skipped out of the library. So not a good look and it would draw attention to herself.

She carefully walked the corridors, ducking under the classroom widows as she headed along her normal escape route. The doors at the front of school were always monitored, so she'd figured this way out her first year here. She crawled past the teachers' lounge and through their exit door to the balcony. After a quick scan for witnesses, she made her move onto the roof and across to the wall. She jumped down between the two pines, pulled her hoodie out from her bag, and put it on before stepping out.

As she looked up, she saw Ryan watching her from further up the road, expecting her to come from the front of school. He was leaning against his car wearing jeans and a black singlet, smoking a cigarette. She walked up to him casually.

'I didn't know you smoked.'

Ryan shrugged as a smile tugged at his lips. 'Not really, it's more for camouflage purposes. You can get away with standing in some places if you're smoking. People tend to think that's the norm.'

'Hah, I've never thought about it before but I guess you're right, you just assume they've stopped for a smoke.' Jaz stood opposite Ryan as he put out his cigarette. She realised just how much she'd missed him, from his mysterious eyes to his cropped hair.

'Wanna jump in before you get busted?'

Jaz smiled and headed for the passenger door.

'So, you figured out the code?' he asked as he drove away from Saint Christian's.

'Yep, eventually, and I didn't even ask Anna for help. I just needed to put the two bits together and when I finally figured that out, it was easy.'

'It's a simple code but effective as only you and I have the magazine and if we thought it was compromised we would just need to destroy the magazine and change it to something else.'

'Cool. But...'

Ryan glanced across the car at Jaz, his eyebrow raised again. 'But?'

'How did you get my number? Do you have secret satellite stuff or programs that hack into phone data bases?' Jaz asked while Ryan laughed. 'What?'

Ryan smiled. 'Jaz, I asked Taylor for it.'

'Oh.' Then Jaz felt like a twit and laughed at herself.

They had pulled up outside a park with rolling green lawns and kids play swings, which were empty. Silence filled the car after Ryan turned it off.

Where to start and what to ask? 'What's this about?' Jaz asked fiddling with the hem on her skirt. 'I've had this feeling that you've been avoiding me.' She made herself look him in the eye, no matter how scared she was of his reply.

Ryan cleared his throat. 'In a way I have. I'm sorry, Jaz, but I just had to sort a few things out before I could talk to you about them.'

'Well, I'm here and I'm listening. What's been going on, Ryan? You've been so up and down. And what's with you and Pax?'

His eyes were a conflict of emotions, and she was struggling to read them.

'I've been talking to my boss about you. MTG Agencies was started by Louis Montenegro many years ago. He was very rich and connected. He put his plan – of running a secret agency that would work to keep drug dealers, terrorists and general bad people out of our country – to the government, and MTG Agencies was born. They have a base in most states and overseas, so you can see how big it has become. Louis has since passed on but his family has continued what he started. His son, Louis Jnr, has just stepped aside to let his own son, James, take over some of the reins. That's who I've been talking with. James is in Perth for a few weeks.'

Jaz nodded slowly. 'And what has Pax got to do with all this?'

'Well, Pax wasn't too happy knowing you and I had met. See, Pax knows all about me and when I told him I wanted to recruit you he wasn't impressed.'

'How come Pax knows about you? How can he…' Jaz saw the look on Ryan's face and the penny dropped. 'Oh. Pax is one of you?' Ryan confirmed it with a nod. 'No way. Really?'

'Yes, really. Pax has been involved with MTG Agencies way longer than I have.'

Jaz rubbed her temple as she tried to understand. 'All this time Pax has been an agent? Has he been out…' Jaz couldn't bring herself to say *killing people*. Not Pax, her big cuddly, cinnamon-smelling adopted grandad.

Ryan laughed. 'No, Jaz. Pax is more an office type. He gets us documents, new IDs, alibis and anything computer-related. He can make a whole person appear on the net under a fake name and make it believable. It comes in handy when you're trying to infiltrate a gang or when we need an alias to fly to other countries.'

'So, Pax is like the computer geek of agents?' She let out her breath. 'It all begins to make sense. How Anna was able to print us those fake IDs using stuff she found at Pax's place.'

Ryan signed. 'Yes, Anna is a bit too clever for her own good. Maybe she'd like to work with Pax one day. What do you think?'

'I think you better stop threatening to poach all my friends into your secret stuff,' she said gruffly.

'Fair enough.'

They sat in silence for a while. Jaz had so many questions but wasn't sure which one to ask first. 'Every time Pax has taken off, he's been off doing stuff for you guys?'

Ryan nodded.

'Is he ever in danger?'

'No, not usually. Most of the time he will make up documents and leave them at our drop points for us to collect.'

'That's good to know.' Jaz picked at her fingernails. 'But you're always in danger, aren't you?'

'Sometimes, yes. At the moment it's not so bad, but sometimes if we get a lead on a drug cartel I go in undercover to try to infiltrate and it can go wrong.'

'Like with Chris?'

Ryan swallowed hard. No answer was necessary.

Jaz wondered what things Ryan had to do to get inside these gangs. To prove he was one of them. Did he use the drugs? Did he kill people? She had no idea what it would be like. She only had movies to go off. She had always thought movies were make-believe but now wondered just how much of it was a variation of the truth.

'So, Pax wasn't happy that you'd asked me to join?'

'No. Of course he wasn't. In his eyes, you're his little granddaughter. To him it's like I just handed over a gun to a ten-year-old. I can see where he's coming from, I'd hate for someone to have recruited my sister. But I wouldn't be doing my job if I hadn't recognised the potential you have. I'm trying to think of all the people you can save, Jaz. To me, that's the bigger picture.'

'It sounds like a noble job, an important job. But it comes with high risk. I just don't know if I can do it.' Jaz wrung her hands. She wanted to join, to be like Ryan, but would she be digging her own grave? 'Have many agents died?'

Ryan rubbed his hands down his jeans. 'Jaz, I won't lie to you. There have been a few, like Chris. But if you knew or could see all the people he had saved, you'd be amazed. And Chris knew what he was doing. He loved that he could get the bad guys off the streets.' Over the road in the park,

Ryan was watching a mother with her little girl running around. 'He'd saved a boat load of girls, younger than you, from being forced into prostitution. They would have been treated badly but he saved them and that's what kept him going. It's what keeps me going. I'm looking after my country and its people. There is no greater job, in my eyes.'

Jaz was watching Ryan as he spoke, the passion and fight in his eyes was alluring. Right then, she would have followed him to the ends of the earth.

'What made you say yes?' she asked.

He pressed his lips together before taking a breath. 'Back in school my best mate bought some drugs to try out, and it ended up killing him. So, I jumped at the chance to stop these people who were trying to sell to kids. I guess I want to make the world a safer place.'

Jaz tried to imagine losing Tay or Anna the same way and she knew she'd be just like Ryan. She'd have said yes to joining already.

'Come on, I better get you back to school.' He started his car and drove away from the park.

Outside the school walls, Ryan stopped. 'I didn't really thank you for getting my message for me. You were amazing.' He turned to smile at her. 'You'd be brilliant on our team.'

Jaz wanted to bring up their kiss. She hadn't been able to stop thinking about it, but what did it mean to Ryan? Had he wished it had never happened?

'About that night in the club…' she said slowly.

'It's okay, Jaz. It's just the adrenaline rush, I understand. It happens in our job.'

Damn it, no you don't, she wanted to say. Jaz was sure it was more than that. She knew it wasn't just adrenaline. If anything, the adrenaline had merely given her the courage to do what she'd been thinking about for a while now. Did Ryan's reply mean he had forgotten it already?

'Oh, okay,' she mumbled as she grappled the door handle. 'See you later, I guess.' With her parting words, she shut the door and watched him leave. Why did it feel like he'd driven away with her heart squished in the door?

CHAPTER 26

OKAY, SO TECHNICALLY, getting out of the school was easier than getting
back in. She'd had to convince the guard at the front doors that her mum
had just dropped her off after a dentist's appointment. Jaz even went to the
extent of showing him her teeth. You gotta do what you gotta do.

Nonetheless he'd let her go and now she was in her last class of the
day. They were supposed to be reading the next chapter of text in Human
Biology but Jaz had no interest in it. Her book sat open to the right page
but inside it was the magazine Ryan had given her. She had his number but
she didn't know really what to text him and in the end thought the code
would work best.

She'd gone about finding the words through the magazine, which was
a little harder than she thought. At first she wanted to say *I want to talk
more* but she'd just about read the whole magazine without finding the
word *talk*. She found *information* on the third page and decided to use
that instead.

18-4-3 / 28-11-7 / 22-4-5 / 3-8-2

I need more information

The siren went and Jaz sent the text and packed up. She met up with
Anna just outside the main doors.

'Hey, how did the lunch go? What can you report?'

Jaz put on a smile and tried to hide her anxiousness at wanting to
hear from Ryan. 'Yeah, it was good. Had a chat and he told me much the
same as Pax did. Just a few family problems at the moment, but we're still
friends. What are you doing now?'

'Whoa up, just friends?' Anna queried as she studied Jaz through slit eyes. 'You're changing the subject, are you trying to hide some juicy goss? Did you kiss again?'

'Of course not. Actually, I get the impression he doesn't want to kiss me ever again. In fact, I think he wants to pretend the first one didn't happen.' Jaz found the words hard to admit.

'Oh, no. Really? That sucks,' said Anna with a frown. 'But I do think you like him more than Taylor, am I right?' she said pointing her finger.

Jaz opened her mouth but no reply came. Anna was right: she did like Ryan. It was different to how she felt about Taylor. She would always love Taylor, they'd been best friends for ages, but did she want to date him? Not anymore. But Ryan – well, he was a whole different ball game.

'I mean, what's not to like about Ryan, hunky saviour and all,' Anna added.

'Yeah, he is pretty cool.' If only Anna really knew what Ryan was capable of.

'That's an understatement. Anyway, are you off to The Ring? Mum's picking me up to take me to dance lessons. Dance lessons! Can you believe it? I mean how hard can it be, don't you just wrap your arms around a guy and shuffle from side-to-side?'

Jaz laughed as Anna did a dorkie side-step move, her hair flicking about around her shoulders. 'Maybe your mum's right; dance lessons might be good for you.'

Anna hit Jaz in the arm. 'Bugger off.' A horn sounded from the parking area. 'Oh, that's Mum. Better go, don't wanna be late – I might find some hunky dance teacher.'

'Good luck with that,' Jaz laughed as she waved goodbye.

When she turned onto the main road, Jaz started towards Ryan's house. She had a vague memory of which area to go to and was sure she'd find it when she got to the familiar streets. She pulled her hoodie out of her bag and put it on as the clouds came over, threatening rain.

Her legs were covered in goose pimples but she began to run and knew she'd warm up soon enough. She just hoped Ryan was at home.

An hour later she'd found his place, the only one in the street with a large fence hiding the whole yard and house. Jaz could remember waiting for the big roller-door to open the night of the attack.

A few showers had passed overhead and Jaz was feeling a little cold and damp. What was worse was the sight of another dark cloud bearing rain headed her way. After a quick glance up the street Jaz scaled the Colorbond fence and fell into the garden on the other side. Luckily there were no rose bushes, instead she landed on a daisy bush and was now pulling yellow petals from her hair. *Crap.*

With quiet steps, she went to his side door and knocked on it. No answer. She turned and looked into his empty garage. No car. Bummer, she'd have to wait. Should she call him now? She'd decided against that as she had a feeling he might not want to see her again. Jaz sat down on the cement, circled her arms around her cold knees and rested her head against them. Her hair was wet around her face from where her hoodie didn't cover, and she tucked a strand back behind her ear as her mind began firing off questions.

What was she going to ask him? *Did you not like the kiss?* No, she wanted to ask him about the Agency, not the kiss. Would she meet this James guy? The sound of a car and the roller-door screeching relieved her from her inner torment as she stood up and waited.

A few minutes later Ryan walked up to the door carrying a big paper bag.

'Jaz!' he said, spotting her over the top of his groceries.

Jaz felt like laughing; for some reason she'd never pictured Ryan shopping for groceries. He seemed too macho for such a menial job.

'Hi.'

'Don't tell me you remembered how to get here, after being here only once, in the dark, after an assault?' He shook his head in disbelief.

Jaz shrugged it off. 'I like to know where I'm going. I hope you don't mind, I just needed to talk… you know.'

'So you're stalking me this time?' he teased.

'Maybe,' she admitted, her belly doing a little summersault due to his playfulness. So loved the banter between them, almost borderline flirting in her book.

His eyes melted with warmth as he smiled. 'I know. I got your text.

Nice one, by the way.' Ryan struggled to get his keys from his pocket without spilling his groceries.

'You need a hand?' asked Jaz.

Ryan held out his keys. 'Sure, it's the square key. Thanks, Jaz.'

She opened the door and let Ryan through before following him to the kitchen. He quickly put away his shopping under her watchful gaze then folded up the paper bag and stored it in his pantry, before touching Jaz's arm lightly. 'Come and sit, we'll talk.'

He led her to the couch before heading off to the direction of his room.

'Here, you look cold. Put this on, at least it's dry,' he said throwing her a soft woollen black coat. In his other hand he held a brown folder and placed it on the table.

Jaz pulled off her wet hoodie, struggling with numb fingers, then wrapped herself in Ryan's coat. Her shivering stopped at once. 'Thanks.' She eyed the folder, wondering what was in it, but remained silent.

'You didn't bring my other jumper back, by any chance?'

'Sorry, I haven't washed it yet,' she said with a sly grin.

'I bet,' he said sarcastically.

Ryan sat down a bit closer to Jaz, their legs just about touching and then reached for the brown folder.

'What's in that?' she asked, the curiosity getting the better of her.

'This is something I talked about with James. *If* you decide to join us, this would be something we would like you to be involved with.'

Jaz looked into her lap, her hands clasped together tightly. 'Can I see it or do I have to pledge my loyalty first?'

He looked like he was going to touch her hand but changed his mind. 'I can tell you about it.'

'Well, I'm listening, so lay it all on,' she said to hide the growing heat in her cheeks. Did he realise just how much she wanted him to reach out and touch her, even to hold her and whisper that everything would be all right? But their relationship wasn't like that. With a sigh she added, 'What have you got?'

Ryan fiddled with the folder. 'We're after information about a guy we think is involved with a company that we believe is a front for drug running. This guy has a son around your age. We'd need you to strike up a friendship with him and learn as much as possible about his father.'

'What kind of friendship?' she asked.

Ryan looked at the floor. 'Whatever one gets you the most information.'

'Oh.'

'Jaz, you wouldn't have to do anything you weren't comfortable with. You don't have to endanger yourself. We wouldn't expect you to…' Ryan trailed away.

Jaz laughed. 'I've never seen you so lost for words, Ryan.' She wanted to touch his face where the red blush crawled up his cheeks.

'You know what I mean, Jaz.' His eyes caught hers.

Ryan reached over towards her hair. Jaz waited to feel the pressure of his hand against her head and was disappointed when he pulled it away with a yellow petal between his fingers. He raised his eyebrow curiously.

'Your fence is high.'

He smiled and this time reached for her hand and held it tightly as the warmth spread through her fingers. 'I know it's a lot to take in. But we'd still love to have you at the agency. I can see you'll make one of our best agents, but I can't force you. It has to be your choice. James said to bring you into the agency. He's keen to meet this young firecracker I found.' He winked.

'Will I still see much of you if I don't join?' she asked quietly.

She felt his thumb rub against her hand and it sent tiny shivers all over her skin, and it wasn't from being cold.

'I'd try to drop into The Ring and say hi when I'm around. Maybe even to try to convince you to join still. I'd like to keep sparring with you, and besides, you're still one up, as I seem to recall,' he said. He pulled his hand away and cleared his throat. 'You do remember that everything we say is not to be repeated.'

'Yeah I know,' she sighed. 'But what about Pax? Can I talk to him about this stuff? Will he talk me out of joining?'

Ryan scratched his head. 'I don't know, Jaz. You can talk with Pax, but right now I'm not his favourite person. He loves you and doesn't want you in harm's way.' He shook his head, frowning. 'Maybe you shouldn't join us. It's all a bit of a worry and I don't really know what's best for you, Jaz. I think only you can decide that.'

Damn, why is nothing ever easy? Jaz bit her bottom lip as the thoughts ran through her head.

'I have a work case on the weekend, so we'd like your answer before then if possible. The board are chasing an answer – they don't like people running around with too much detail, if you know what I mean. And they want to find someone for this job,' he said lifting the folder. 'We have some young guys who could do it.'

Jaz had the feeling they thought she would be better for it, though. Maybe a girl would raise fewer alarm bells, and she could gain trust and get into his house faster under the guise of a girlfriend.

'I've gone over more with you than I probably should have,' he added as he glanced away. 'But I want you to know what you could be getting yourself into.'

'Yeah, that's cool. I understand. So, this case – are you leaving?' *Will I see you again?* is what she really wanted to know.

'Yes, Saturday will be my last day.' His eyes watched her and for a moment, he looked sad. 'Don't you have your ball on?'

'That we do. Gonna swing by?' she asked, almost hopeful. Going to the ball didn't seem as exciting if she couldn't see Ryan.

'I can do that; my flight leaves around midnight.'

'Flight? To where?' Ryan gave her a funny look. 'Yeah I know, you could tell me but then you'd have to kill me.' Jaz glanced at the folder again. 'When can I meet James?'

'I could set that up for you tomorrow, if you like?'

Ryan's eyes were so deep with warmth she felt like she would get lost in them. 'Thanks, I'd like that a lot. At the moment it just doesn't seem real.'

'I get that. You only have me to go by, and Pax, I guess, but it *is* all hard to believe. How about I swing by and pick you up after school?'

'Cheers, I'd like that.' Jaz smiled weakly at him. He would make sure she was okay. 'Ryan, I…' She reached for his hand, wanting to tell him just how much he'd come to mean to her. She didn't quite understand it much yet herself but just being near him caused her heart to pound. He made her feel safe and adored at the same time. Her fingers slid over his wrist, causing a tingling sensation throughout her body. 'I'm so glad you came to The Ring that day. I—'

Someone knocked at the door.

'You expecting company?' Jaz asked curiously, drawing her hand back quickly. A woman perhaps? Oh, why did that thought make her stomach turn?

Ryan frowned. 'No.' He went to his door and opened it.

'Steph, what are you doing here?' Jaz heard him say excitedly. She leaned back on the couch to see who he was talking to. Ryan was hugging a tall, blonde girl who looked amazing in skinny jeans, high heels and a fancy short leather jacket. She was closer to his age, and wow, she was beautiful – and she was hugging Ryan with gusto. How could Jaz ever compete with that? She felt dizzy.

Jaz suddenly she felt like she shouldn't be there, so she quickly stood up and slipped off Ryan's jacket, folding it neatly over the chair, and picked up her wet hoodie. They were coming into the lounge, happy laughter and mocking tones filling the air, giving the impression they knew each other well.

Jaz stood and waited like a wet sock, wanting to be any place but here as Ryan entered with his arm around the girl. Jaz wondered if maybe she should have hidden. She felt like a twit, standing half-wet in her school clothes.

'Sorry, Ryan. I didn't know you had company,' said the girl.

It wasn't said in a nasty way that Minka might have used, instead the girl sounded interested and apologetic.

'It's okay, Steph, this is Jaz. She's from The Ring where I've been working out.'

'Hi.' Jaz smiled and waved, but she really wanted to run off like a frightened rabbit.

Steph ran her deep brown eyes over her uniform, then raised an eyebrow to Ryan, which he didn't see.

Jaz glanced to Ryan, hoping he'd tell her who this woman was. He must have caught her questioning look because he cleared his throat and added, 'Jaz, this is my little sister I was telling you about,' he said nodding to Steph.

Oh, thank God.

His little sister was still a few years older than Jaz. 'I can see the similarities now.' Now that she'd stopped her overactive mind and took the time to look at Steph and not think of her as the competition. 'You have the same smile and eyes.' Well, they came from great breeding stock; what a gorgeous family. 'Nice to meet you, Steph.'

'You too, Jasmine. I don't get to meet many of Ryan's friends.' She said nudging Ryan in the ribs. 'He keeps to himself a lot,' she said. 'So, you work at this gym place?'

'Yeah, I keep it going when the boss is away. It's a second home for me and I like to train.'

'And kick my butt. Seriously, sis, you do not want to meet Jaz in a dark alley. Don't let her innocent face trick you, she can hold her own with the best of them.' Steph raised her eyebrows at Ryan's praising words. She glanced between them as Jaz felt heat rising in her cheeks.

Jaz realised she was wringing her hoodie in her nervous hands; soon she'd end up leaving a pile of water on Ryan's carpet. 'Um, well, you'll wanna catch up and I better get back to The Ring before Pax thinks I was run over. Catch ya later.'

Steph raised her hand, 'Bye, Jaz.' Then started to take her jacket off.

Ryan moved to walk her to the door, but Jaz stopped him by holding up her hand. It nearly met his chest. She was glad she hadn't touched him, she was scared of how her body would react and that Steph would notice. Girls noticed things like that better than the guys.

'I know my way out, Ryan.'

She'd taken a few steps when Ryan grabbed her hand. 'Hey, Jaz? We'll talk later,' he said, shooting her a look that said he hadn't forgotten she was trying to tell him something before Steph arrived. 'Okay?'

Jaz shrugged and pulled away. She was at the door when he called out her name again.

Pausing, she glanced back to see him smiling.

'Maybe take the gate this time,' he laughed. 'There's a release button on the side of it.'

Jaz felt her cheeks glow. 'Sure.'

She opened the door just as she heard Steph's quiet voice. 'Ryan, why do you have a schoolgirl in your house? I mean, she's gorgeous and I've been waiting for you to introduce me to someone special, but did you not notice the uniform?'

'She's a friend, Steph, and she's nearly eighteen.'

'Friends, really?'

Jaz was itching to hear his reply but she figured he'd be listening for the door, so Jaz shut it then placed her ear against it in the mere hope of still hearing something. Nup, just the sound of solid wood. *Damn.*

She picked up her school bag, which she'd left by his door, and made her way to the front gate all the while thinking about Steph's words. She'd actually thought Ryan and Jaz were... well, maybe... together. Jaz couldn't help the grin that spread across her face, and her steps were light as her mind ran with thoughts. Steph had thought she was pretty, which was weird considering Jaz would never match up to Steph in a million years. If anything, she resembled a drowned rat. Oh, how she wished she could have heard Ryan's reply. Could they ever be more?

Jaz was a few blocks away when she realised it was spitting. For a moment she thought back to the night she was attacked. She wouldn't let it make her cower in fear, instead she used that night as a lesson. If it happened again she'd be better prepared.

Her mind skipped to Ryan: the warmth of his eyes, his concern for her, how amazing it felt when he held her hand, and then there was the meeting with James at the Agency. Life certainly was interesting now. The raindrops didn't worry her. Instead she started running to warm up, with her mouth open to taste the rain.

CHAPTER 27

ANNA THREW HER bag down on the spare chair at their lunch table.

'Hey, Taylor might want to sit there,' Jaz said. 'Bad morning?'

'Oh, yeah,' said Anna shifting her bag to under the table. She sat opposite Jaz and plonked her head on the table. 'You won't believe it; I've been stuck with Angelica as a class partner!' She started banging her head repetitively.

'Bahhaha, that's hilarious... I mean, that's terrible. Can't you swap?'

Anna lifted her head and frowned at Jaz. 'Yes, it *is* terrible and no I'm *not* allowed to swap. Stupid cow of a teacher.'

'I thought Miss Swanson was your favourite?'

'Yeah, well, she's just burnt all her bridges. No more nice Anna! Anyway, how was your morning?' asked Anna with a dramatic sigh.

'The usual – total bore. Hey, how was your dance lesson? Did you have a cute partner?' Jaz asked. 'You did, didn't you?'

Anna smiled sheepishly. 'I wish! I had some little old lady. But on the plus side, she knew how to move.'

Jaz burst out laughing and just about spat her egg sandwich over the table. She was still brushing off the crumbs around her mouth when Taylor sat down.

'Did I miss a good joke?' he asked, adjusting his sunnies on his head. No one else got away with wearing sunnies at school. Taylor was one of the gifted few who had the teachers on side.

Jaz was about to explain when Anna kicked her under the table. 'Um...

yeah, funny joke about a little old lady but I think you've already heard it,' Jaz said under Anna's glaring gaze.

'So, tomorrow night's the big one! I hope you dust off your dancing shoes, Jaz, you'll have to keep up with me,' said Taylor moving his arms and shoulders in a smooth roll from one side to the other.

'Oh, please, no boy-band moves,' she laughed.

'Why, would you rather the Funky Chicken?' Taylor started flapping his wings and sticking out his chin. Jaz and Anna were practically falling off their chairs in fits of laughter. 'How about the Sprinkler?'

'I'm sooo glad he's your partner,' said Anna after her chuckles died down.

Taylor turned to Anna. 'Oh, no. Don't you worry, I'll be finding you for a dance too, Anna Banana! You can't escape me and my cool moves,' he joked.

Anna rolled her eyes and turned to Jaz. 'You should have invited Ryan to the dance and ditched MC Hammer over here,' she said.

'Well, actually, he said he's going to drop by before he flies out tomorrow.'

'Really, where's he going?' asked Taylor.

Jaz shrugged. *If only I knew!* 'I don't know, he's gotta start work again. But it's nice that he's going to come say goodbye.'

'Yeah, real sweet of him,' added Anna in a dreamy voice.

Jaz picked up her napkin and threw it at her.

'What's happening after school? You girls free?' Taylor asked.

'Not me, I might go to The Ring,' said Jaz, hoping Anna hadn't planned to go also. Her meeting with James, the head boss bloke at MTG Agency, was today, and The Ring was her alibi.

'You wanna come home with me then, Anna, and watch a movie?' asked Taylor.

Anna smiled and tucked her hair behind her ear. 'I was going to go and see Pax, but a movie sounds great.'

Jaz breathed a sigh of relief that her lie was safe.

'Besides, you do have the best theatre room around. Do I get to pick the movie?' asked Anna.

Taylor squirmed in his seat, reluctant to answer. 'I guess so,' he said unsurely. 'Please, don't let it be too chick-flicky!'

Anna smiled and pushed his arm gently. 'All right, I'll try to pick a good one.'

For a moment Jaz wished she could join them. But she had bigger fish to fry. She was going to see what her possible future could be like.

*

A tingle spread its way through Jaz's body when she saw Ryan standing against his car, waiting for her after school.

'Oh, lucky you. I guess you've got a ride to The Ring,' teased Anna. 'Don't do anything I wouldn't do!'

'Right back at ya,' she smiled. 'Catch you both later!'

'Hey, you,' said Jaz as she walked towards Ryan.

'Hey, yourself,' he replied, with a smile and wave to Anna and Taylor. 'It's good to see Taylor doesn't glare at me anymore,' he added as he opened her door for her.

'Oh, are you kidding, he thinks you're God's gift after the time at the range. If you weren't a guy I think he'd want to date you!' she said teasingly before jumping in his car.

She stowed her bag near her feet and waited as Ryan got in. Today he was wearing baggy jeans and a grey-and-white hoodie.

'Hey, I like that jumper.'

Ryan paused, with his hands on the keys, to give her a dirty look.

'What? I was just saying. If it goes missing, don't blame me,' she smiled as he shook his head.

The afternoon sunshine was warm through the car windows, but it did nothing to calm her nerves as they drove closer to the city centre.

'You okay there, Jaz? You seem a bit nervous.'

'What gave you that impression?' said Jaz, taking her finger out of her mouth and away from her chomping teeth. 'I can't help it; it's just all so bizarre.'

'We don't have to do this if you don't want to. Just say the word, Jaz, and I'll take you home.'

One look at the concern on Ryan's face filled her with an unknown strength.

'No, I need to know more.'

'Don't worry, you'll be fine, James is great.'

Jaz breathed in deeply as she watched the cars pass by. Before long, they had parked in an underground car park and were heading to a set of doors. Jaz was a little disappointed when they opened to reveal an ordinary elevator, no secret codes or eye-scan stuff. Similarly, soon the doors parted and they stepped into a regular foyer and walked towards the right, down a corridor to a desk, *MTG Agencies* in bold print on the wall behind it. The receptionist saw Ryan and nodded him through to a door that clicked open as they approached.

'You know her well?' Jaz asked curiously.

Ryan smiled as he put his hand on her back to direct her down the corridor. 'Tina has been here for as long as I have, she knows the deal.'

Ryan stopped outside a door on which sat a panel label: *James Montenegro*. A hundred butterflies fluttered and took flight in her belly, and she felt like throwing herself against Ryan and hiding away in his arms. But that would be a show of weakness, and he had praised her for her strength. So, she would show him her strong backbone.

Ryan knocked twice then opened the door, poking his head in.

'Hey, James, we're here.'

'Bring her in,' she heard him say in a smooth, warm voice.

She reached forward, her fingers just grazing Ryan's strong back. The touch was enough to stand her straight and give her courage to stride into the room.

In the large office were shelves and a desk with a flash-looking computer. Slowly she dragged her eyes towards the towering figure in the middle of the room and ran them up his body: tall, lean, dressed in a simple grey suit. Then she got to his face. He was blond but she could see the edges tinged with grey, his face clean-shaven, and his eyes were blue just like hers.

'James, this is Jasmine—'

'Jaz,' she cut in.

'Jaz, this is James,' Ryan finished. 'I'll leave you two to talk.'

Jaz's eyes flew to Ryan's, pleading for him not to leave her.

Sensing her discomfort he said, 'I'll be just outside the door.'

She nodded and watched him exit before turning back to James.

'Hello,' she said awkwardly.

'Hi, Jaz. Please take a seat.'

She did as he asked.

Instead of sitting behind his desk, he sat in a chair next to her and focused all his attention on her. It was a little unnerving but she figured she was doing the same to him.

'So, you're the boss.' Of all the things she wanted to say and ask, she came out with that first. *Damn it, where is your head?* she silently berated herself.

'Yes, like my father and his father before him. A real family affair. I was actually an agent like Ryan, so was my sister. But when my dad got sick I left the field work and came to run the office side of things.' James glanced away and Jaz felt a sadness wash over him.

'So, there are a few girls who do this job?'

'Oh yes, Jaz. Some of them are our best agents. My sister was one of them.' He paused, then added quietly, 'She died, but it wasn't on duty.'

'Oh, I'm sorry.'

James smiled. 'Don't get me wrong, this can be a dangerous job, but so is being in Afghanistan with the army or surfing with sharks.'

'I hear you.' Jaz liked James already. He was easy to talk to and not full of self-importance. The fact that he sat beside her and not behind the desk reassured her that he was easygoing.

James glanced at his watch and then apologised. 'I'm sorry, Jaz. I don't have much time, because I have an interview. I would love to spend more time talking with you but I don't want to pressure you either. You under-stand that in this business we have to keep up appearances, so if you do decide to join us we will have a cover job organised.'

'Much like Ryan's?'

'Yes. He mentioned the job we could use you for?' She nodded. 'Again, we don't want to pressure you. But Ryan believes you will be a great asset to us and he's already told me what you did for him. You will be paid well for this job. Also, you know our guru guy Pax?'

'Oh yes.' Jaz laughed. 'It makes so much sense now. He was always disappearing on us.'

He nodded. 'So, you've seen our building. There's not much here, we try to keep a paperless trail. The basement is where the guys train sometimes, but generally we try to keep everyone going about their normal lives. We prefer one-on-one training. Secrecy is the key here, Jaz. We don't want to draw unwanted attention, so we keep everything low-key. If people come through this building it has to be and look like what it is, therefore we don't have official training rooms. Training is done out on the streets.'

As he stood up, so did Jaz. He held out his hand, so she shook it. 'Thanks for coming by. Any questions you have, you know you can ask Ryan. He's one of our best. He wouldn't have brought you to us unless he thought you were something special.'

'Thanks.' She didn't know what else to say.

Jaz headed for the door as James followed.

'Bye,' she said turning the knob. Ryan was waiting for her on the other side, just like he said, and instantly she felt relieved and safe.

'Bye, Jaz.' James watched her leave before calling in a boy who was also sitting by the door. He looked no older than Jaz.

'Who was that guy?' Jaz asked Ryan as they headed to the elevator.

'A new recruit. He said yes to joining; now he's off to his interview.'

'Really? So, if I said yes I'd still have to do an interview too?' she asked as they rode the elevator down. Ryan nodded. 'Would it be with James?'

'Yes, and maybe the group commander. I could sit in too if you wanted.'

Yeah, she would want that. Jaz realised her thoughts were leaning towards accepting. She knew deep down she wanted to, but on the surface, she was scared. Scared to say goodbye to the simple schoolgirl and hello to an agent who was trained to kill if needed. But what else was she going to do with her life? The Ring? Not now, not when she knew about stuff like this. Meeting Ryan had changed her, that's for sure.

They had the quietest trip back, and she didn't even realise that it was over until Ryan pulled up outside The Ring.

'I'll see you tomorrow before I leave, okay,' said Ryan. His eyes again held her in a spell.

'Cool, I'll see you at ten. You can have my answer then.' She gave him the address for the ball and climbed out, then watched him drive off, all the while wondering what she'd be thinking about if Ryan had never stepped foot into The Ring.

Turning around, she went to find Pax. She couldn't give Ryan her answer until she'd spoken to Pax. She couldn't talk to Anna or even her mum about her future but she could speak openly with Pax. His opinion counted.

Bags was down the back, busy giving a lesson to a woman in her thirties. Her jabs were sloppy, but his deep voiced cheered her with each punch. Jaz just hoped Bags didn't push his client too hard or else she might not come back.

Jaz walked into Pax's office and found him sitting at his computer. He looked up as she shut the door, then sighed heavily and leaned back in his chair. 'I guessed this was coming.'

Jaz sat on the desk in front of him. 'Do you hate Ryan?' she asked. 'For telling me about this stuff?' she said waving her hand. She couldn't bring herself to mention the Agency out loud to Pax just yet.

Pax leaned forward and held her hand. 'Jaz, I don't hate Ryan. He's a terrific guy and one I'd want around in a tricky situation. What I don't like is that he found you. You are my little angel. You and Anna are both my girls, have been since day dot. It was a rude shock to come back to find you had been dragged into my world. It's not an easy life. Ryan is living proof of that; he's still coming to terms with Chris's death, and I would hate for you to go through that.'

'I know you would, Pax. But people die all the time in accidents or through illness. At least Chris was doing something he believed in.' Jaz squeezed his hand. 'I don't like that I'd have to lie to everyone I love, just as you have done to us. I can't imagine that it's easy.' The sadness in Pax's eyes agreed. 'But I can't see myself doing anything else worthwhile. You know I hate the rich, blasé life. You know I've always wanted to do something meaningful. Pax, what's more meaningful than trying to save lives?'

Pax sniffed and cleared his throat. 'You don't have to tell me, Jaz. It's what I try to do too.' He smiled up at her. 'You have grown up so much, I guess it scares me. You are no longer my little angel.'

'Pax, I will always be your little angel.' Jaz leaned across and hugged him, and they stayed like that for a long time.

'How did you come to work for them?' Jaz eventually leaned back so she could memorise Pax's features, from his wrinkles to his soft, kind eyes.

'I was approached by James's father, Louis Jnr. Apparently, they had been watching me from an early age when I started winning some prizes for my computer work. I was a computer nerd, so to be offered something like this, something where I could help and save people without having to leave my comfort zone – it was a once in a lifetime chance.'

Jaz took a deep breath, the next question burning to be asked. 'Have you ever killed anyone?'

'No. Not directly. But I have helped get the job done. Jaz, our job isn't to kill people, it's to make them do the time for their crimes. But sometimes you get caught in the crossfire and it's either them or you. That's what Ryan has to deal with, and I guess maybe you too if you decide to join. That's the part I'm struggling with.'

'Me taking someone's life?' Jaz hadn't really thought about that much. *God, could I even do it?* When she was attacked by those guys… if they'd started to really hurt her, or rape her, if she had a gun would she have used it? 'Hopefully it wouldn't come to that for me.' Maybe she could leave the hard-core gang infiltration to Ryan and the rest. At least for the first few years.

'Does this mean you want to do it?' he asked softly.

'Yes, I do, but not if you're dead against it, Pax. Coming here is my home and I don't want it to be strained. I want your blessing and your support.' Jaz glanced around the office. 'I like knowing I can come here with you and for this not to be a lie. I know too much already, Pax, and I can't turn a blind eye to what's going on. Not if I can help save someone. I know I can do this if you're with me. You are one less person I have to lie to. Keeping this from Anna and my family will be hard enough.'

'I know, Jaz. I know. Just take tonight to really think on it. Please? For me?'

'Okay.'

After a few silent minutes, Jaz pulled out her wallet and handed over her fake ID to Pax.

'What is this? Where did you get it?' His eyes grew wide as he questioned her.

'Anna takes after you more than she realises. You should really hide your stuff better. Anna is smart and she'll work out sooner or later that you're up to something.'

Pax paled slightly. 'I hope it's later. My God, she's good.' He handed back the card.

'I know. She would be great working alongside you,' she said with a smile. Although Pax didn't return it one bit. In fact, he looked a little green.

'For my sake, I hope you're joking, Jaz. My poor heart couldn't take much more today.'

'Well, rest easy. I'm going to go for a workout. I need to clear my head.'

Jaz hugged Pax, and he gripped her back tighter than ever. 'I love you, kiddo.'

'I love you too, Pax.'

Jaz headed out to the change rooms to put on her workout gear. She felt so different. No longer naive and young. And as she worked out on the mat she felt like she had a purpose. That finally her life meant something.

CHAPTER 28

'OH MY GOD!' said Anna as she walked into Jaz's room. 'What the hell happened here? Did your mum hire another cleaner?'

'Ha ha, very funny. You know, my mum said the exact same thing. She even checked my temperature.'

'I'm not bloody surprised. Wow, you have a nice room, I'd never noticed before,' laughed Anna as she walked across the clean carpet to the window, where the curtains were drawn open, letting in the dying afternoon light.

Anna spun around and squealed. 'Can you believe it, the ball's tonight! I might finally get to second base!'

'Anna, you're beautiful, you could have been kissed long ago if you'd leave your computer desk,' Jaz laughed.

Anna frowned. 'I don't know how to take that, Jaz. It's like a backhanded compliment.' She glanced at her watch. 'Only a few hours to go. Do you wanna see my dress?'

'Oh, I'd love to,' said Tasha coming into Jaz's room. 'I've got the camera fully charged too.'

'Mum,' groaned Jaz. 'Can we not do the overexcited-parent thing?'

Tasha ignored Jaz's comment and walked straight over to Anna's dress that lay on the bed in its black cover bag. 'Come on, darling. Humour your old mother. I never got to go to a ball.'

'Really? How come, Mrs T?' asked Anna.

Tasha tucked a blonde strand behind her ear, as her face dropped, deep in thought. 'I was always doing more important things... or so my family

told me. But all I wanted to do was be like the other kids and go to a ball.'
Tasha opened the black bag, peeked in at Anna's dress, and smiled wistfully.

Jaz glanced at her mum, shocked at her words. 'Your parents wouldn't let you go?'

'I wasn't at a school by then; I left after year eleven, so I missed out.' Tasha smiled and turned away.

'Oh, that's a shame, Mrs T. But now you can experience it through us,' said Anna brightly. 'Besides, my mum will be here any minute and all hell will break loose.'

Tasha laughed and hugged Anna. 'Don't worry, I've got a bottle of wine chilling to keep us occupied while you get ready. We will cry into our wine at how quickly our girls have grown up. Oh, don't look at me like that, Jasmine,' said Tasha, giving Jaz's cheek a squeeze. 'Fine, I'll leave you both alone.'

Jaz and Anna watched her leave, shutting the door behind her, before breaking out into giggles.

'I'm so nervous, Jaz. I can't believe I've got a date.'

'I can't even believe we're going,' laughed Jaz. She could hardly fathom that she was succumbing to this, being like everyone else, what they expected. Well, actually, maybe this was the opposite of succumbing: after all, no one would have expected Jaz to go to the ball, let alone wear a dress without boots.

She opened her cupboard and pulled out a silver high heel. 'Look what Mum bought me,' she said, hanging onto it by the heel.

'Bloody hell, my mum wouldn't let me get anything that high. Your mum is so cool. Mine is from the fricken dark ages.'

'She can't be that bad, you said your dress is great. Come on, let's start getting ready. Mum's got the hairdresser here in half an hour.'

'I bags first shower,' said Anna, grabbing her bag and heading for the bathroom.

*

An hour and a half later, the paparazzi had descended.

'Okay, now just one more against this door, I think the cream will show up your dresses better.'

'God, Mum, you've taken, like, a hundred already!' Jaz complained as they shuffled across to the large front doors.

'Say cheese,' said Tasha, slightly tipsy.

'No.' Jaz smiled back with her arms crossed.

Tasha sighed and put down her camera. 'Okay, you win. I'll stop with the pictures. But you both look so beautiful.'

Anna's mum was still clicking away, her red hair over her shoulder and halfway down her back. Anna was trying to cover the camera with her hand. 'Enough, Mum.'

The front bell sounded, sending the women in the room into a frenzy with their cameras again as Jaz opened the door for the boys.

The plans had already been set for Taylor to pick up Ricky and drive them all to the ball. Both guys walked in smelling of aftershave and hair gel. Ricky was wearing a white suit and a green tie, and Taylor looked smashing in his black tux and silver tie. Jaz noted that Ricky was quite cute with his normal mop of hazel hair sculpted and trimmed, but she felt uncomfortable seeing the way Taylor's eyes popped from his head as he looked from her to Anna.

'Holy cow, you girls look fabulous.' Taylor's mouth was still open like he wanted to say more but couldn't remember how to speak.

Anna did look stunning. The emerald green brought out her eyes. Thin straps held up a fitted bodice and skirt, and they'd both had their hair done up on top of their heads with soft cascading curls.

'Well, let's get this show on the road,' said Jaz trying to shepherd everyone to the car. Taylor took Jaz's arm and had to look up to talk. 'You are so tall, Jaz.'

'I know, check out the weapons.' She hiked up her dress to her knees and showed him the elegant silver shoes.

'Jasmine, please don't be doing that all night,' scoffed her mother. With a sigh, Jaz dropped the material back in place and headed to the car. They hugged their mums goodbye and sat in the back of the Mustang. Some people were going in stretch Hummers but they all agreed the Mustang would do them.

'Oh my God, I think my mum is wiping away tears,' said Anna watching out the window.

'Don't worry, they will forget all about it by the time they get to the third bottle.' Jaz leaned closer to Anna. 'I'm so nervous.'

'Me too.'

They both laughed and for a moment Jaz forgot about her nerves, until they drove through Dalkeith and arrived at their destination. Tawarri was a function centre right on the edge of the Swan River. Green grass and the shimmering water painted a perfect picture.

The guys opened their doors and helped the girls out, as cold air swirled around Anna's naked skin as she clung to Taylor's arm. 'Wow, how perfect,' said sighed.

A *doof-doof* noise pumped from a pink Hummer that pulled right up to the door of the function centre. The four of them paused and watched Minka and her friends exit with their dates. Jaz and Anna stifled laughs as Minka strolled through the doors and onto the red carpet like she was royalty.

Dressed in a strapless gold gown, no doubt worth more than a small fortune and probably designed by someone who Jaz had never heard of, Minka posed for photographs.

'Taylor!' she said when she caught sight of him. 'You look great.' She smiled as she dragged her very tall date over.

'Yes, he does,' said Jaz running her hand over Taylor's silver tie. She loved rubbing it in, and besides, when she became an agent, this part of her life would cease to exist. No more pain-in-her-arse Minka and cronies; instead, she would have real-life criminals and issues to deal with. Jaz almost wished her last year at school was over, but not before she could lord it over Minka just a little more tonight.

'Hi, Minka, great night isn't it,' smiled Jaz, clinging to Taylor as Minka's eyes exploded with envy. 'Have you finished with your photos? We'd like to get to the dance floor.' She tried to keep her voice sweet and innocent, just like Minka used whenever Taylor was around. Jaz side-stepped Minka, taking Taylor with her as they lined up for their photos. Minka grabbed her footballer date and took off towards the drinks table.

'That is so cool,' said Anna as they looked up at hundreds of tiny lights edged with white silk and chiffon drapes.

'Yeah, it's not bad. Worth coming,' said Jaz as Anna rolled her eyes and pushed her playfully.

'Come on, Ricky, let's check it out.' Anna grabbed her date's hand and headed off into the middle of the room with gusto.

'Anna looks amazing,' said Taylor over Jaz's right shoulder before he took her hand. 'Shall we follow?'

Jaz nodded, feeling like Cinderella as the crowed parted around them. She felt like all eyes were on her. She could only guess what they'd be saying. *Why is she with him?* But Taylor squeezed her hand and whispered, 'I think I've got the hottest date here, look how jealous they all are.' And all of a sudden Jaz didn't care what anyone thought.

Time sped by quickly as they danced the night away. Taylor tried to teach Jaz his Funky Chicken and Sprinkler moves, and then the next song was a slow one. She smiled as Taylor rolled his eyes and motioned her closer.

'Come on, partner,' he said as he put his hands on her hips. Jaz followed suit and put hers on his chest as they side-stepped slowly, looking around to see if Anna was putting her dance lessons to good use with Ricky.

Ricky was doing an awkward side-step with his arms around Anna. Then, in the next second, they were lip-to-lip and trying out some major tongue hockey. As first kisses go, it looked kind of sloppy but Jaz cheered internally for Anna and turned back to Taylor to mention it.

But before she could move her lips, Taylor was kissing her. She felt his hands tighten around her back, pulling her closer and deepening the kiss.

Jaz went with the flow as her mind ran through a hundred thoughts, none of which she could catch long enough to understand. She pulled back for air and searched his eyes for an explanation. Taylor's eyes darted to the left and back again. Jaz followed the path of his gaze and two things occurred to her in that moment. One, that kissing Taylor wasn't what she thought it would be. She'd been dreaming of this moment and now that it had happened it wasn't as earth-shattering as she had expected. The kiss was perfectly fine, but Jaz had been waiting for a tingle that didn't come. If anything, if she was truthful with herself, it felt all wrong. Kissing Ryan had been right.

The second thing was Anna. Why had Taylor glanced at Anna? Jaz felt tiny jigsaw pieces fitting themselves into place. Taylor joining them for lunch, being around more often, the photo by his bed, and asking Anna back for a movie. Taylor liked Anna? She questioned herself and then decided her gut instinct was right.

'Why did you kiss me?' she asked Taylor as she fiddled with his lapel.

He shrugged and smiled sheepishly. 'It's our ball, I just thought...'

'Yeah, no.' Then she found herself saying words she never thought would come out of her mouth. 'You're my best friend, Tay, and... I'd like it to stay like that.' She watched him sigh with relief. 'Besides, that just wasn't quite right, hey,' she laughed.

Taylor smiled and Jaz couldn't understand why she didn't want Taylor anymore; he was so cute.

'Hmm, it so wasn't right,' he laughed as the tension eased out of his shoulders.

Jaz was relieved. She was going to need Anna and Taylor, her best friends. Her life as an operative would be complicated but she was sure she could handle it with her friends by her side, even if they didn't know what was going on. Maybe one day she could share it with them, but for now she wanted to follow the rules and not disappoint Ryan.

Jaz took Taylor's arm and checked his watch. Five minutes to ten, nearly time to meet Ryan.

She saw Anna standing on her own. Ricky must have gone for drinks so she grabbed Taylor's hand, dragging him towards her.

'Hey, Anna. Can you dance with Tay? I'm gonna go wait for Ryan.' She watched a flush appear on Taylor's cheeks. Yeah, she was sure he had it bad for Anna.

'Cool, no worries. Say goodbye for me,' Anna said before grabbing Taylor's arm. 'Come on, cowboy, show me your moves,' she laughed.

Jaz headed to the foyer and out the doors. City lights reflected off the smooth water from the river no more than twenty metres away. In her line of sight was a silhouette against the silvery water, an outline she knew so well: the cropped hair, the strong determined shoulders, the imposing height. Ryan was here early. As she walked towards him her chest constricted, causing her breaths to shorten as the cool air touched her lungs.

Reaching out, she touched his elbow. 'Ryan?'

He turned, the path lights illuminating his face enough for her to see those wonderful gold flecks in his eyes.

'Jaz, you look…' He held up his hand and touched a strand of her hair tenderly. 'Amazing.'

Had someone cut off the air? Jaz was struggling to breathe and suddenly felt light-headed.

Ryan's eyes drank her in from top to bottom. 'Are you wearing your boots too?' he asked curiously.

Jaz did what her mum had specifically asked her not to, and hoicked her dress up to show off her shoes.

Ryan cleared his throat. 'Very sexy.' He gave her a wink. 'Don't be afraid to use them if you're ever attacked. They're quite dangerous.'

'Hey, you don't have to tell me that. I nearly broke my ankle earlier. Boots are much safer,' she laughed as a wave of chills shook her body.

Without a word, Ryan shrugged off his jacket and wrapped it around her shoulders, the warmth spreading through her quickly. Jaz breathed in the leather and heady scent of Ryan, and that feeling of safety returned.

'Thanks. I do like this jacket.'

Her shoes made her taller, but not enough to see eye-to-eye with Ryan, but still she caught his raised eyebrow and glare.

'Yeah, well, I like it too,' he said nudging her shoulder.

'So, how long will you be gone?' she asked. Her shoulder rested against his arm as they looked out over the water.

His voice was deep and caused little tremors through her body. 'It could be a week, it could be a month.'

Oh.

Jaz was lost for words as she resisted the urge to wrap herself around Ryan so he couldn't leave. She knew without a doubt that where he was going and what he was doing could be dangerous, even life-threatening. Not seeing him for a day sent her mad, how would she cope with months?

'Have you made your decision?' he asked softly.

Jaz nodded as she felt the vein in her neck pulse. 'Yes, I've decided to join.' She had made her decision, but saying the words out loud was the scariest thing. 'But I want to finish school, otherwise Mum would get suss.'

'I understand, but if you're interested in that operation I told you about, you can do it while you're still at school. I'm just saying. In the meantime we'll work with you to come up with a cover job after school's over. And until then you can still do some training on weekends or afternoons, if you like.'

'What, like what we did in the city that time, following that man?'

'Yeah, bits like that. They may even use you to retrieve messages or deliver them, maybe keep track on someone. Just little bits that can be a real help, you know.'

She nodded and looped her arm through his, just to touch him and feel his warmth.

The water was lapping gently against the side of the riverbed, almost musically.

'What happens now?' Jaz asked, trying to swallow the lump in her throat. She was fixated on the moon reflection shimmering on the water, so much so her eyes began to well with tears. Well, that's what she put it down to. Not the whole freaking-out session going on in her mind.

'You'll go through the interview stage next. And they will probably brief you on this kid they want you to befriend. I would usually do it but I'll be away for a while.'

She felt Ryan watching her, his hand gripping her shoulder.

'Oh, Jaz,' he said with such emotion that she felt a tear fall from her grasp. He wiped the tear away with his thumb before pulling her into a tight hug. She was trying not to go all soppy but she couldn't help it. Her life was about to change. She'd reached that fork in the road and had chosen a path. She was about to put her life in some sort of danger while hiding it from all the people she loved.

Jaz clung to Ryan's chest as her tears soaked through his shirt. His heartbeat was like a percussion concert as she listened to it thrashing out a fast rhythm much like her own.

Ryan was rocking her gently in his arms, rubbing her back.

'It's okay, Jaz, I know exactly how you feel.'

She looked up into his chocolate eyes and felt herself drowning in them.

Jaz wiped away the last of the tears, hoping her make-up wasn't ruined. 'I must look a mess,' she sighed.

Ryan shook his head gently, raised her chin and bent to kiss her forehead, but Jaz rose up to meet him and their lips met. The ground shook beneath her feet as her lips tingled against his softness. Ryan pulled back, but she could read the desire in his eyes. She wasn't the only one feeling something between them, that underlying current he'd kept at bay. Not letting him pull away, she slid her hand up to his neck.

'What if you don't come back?' she whispered as she searched his eyes for an answer. So what if she wasn't yet eighteen, she understood enough to know how important this moment was for both of them, ages be damned.

Ryan was trying to deny it, but Jaz could read the conflict in his eyes; always his eyes giving him away as much as he held himself back. So, she arched up and met his lips again. He gave in for the briefest moment, before pulling away with a growl at his lack of self-control. But he didn't let her out of his arms.

Jaz was floating across the water, dancing like the city lights, as she experienced what a real kiss felt like. When had her heart given up on Taylor and found Ryan? And why did this seem so much more powerful than anything she thought she'd felt for Taylor?

Ryan held her face in his hands and gazed at her with such desire that her breath caught. 'Ryan, I— ' He didn't let her get the words out, instead he covered her mouth with his own. This time he didn't hold back. This time he kissed her like it was his last moment on earth. The kiss deepened. Hungrily they explored, tasted and teased. Clinging on to each other tightly, hearts clashing together. Her hands reached for his chest, which was hard and ripped. She didn't want this moment to end. Her heart felt like it was going to burst and her body was burning with desire.

Eventually he pulled away. 'Oh, Jaz…' He didn't finish but Jaz could hear the regret in his voice and guess what he was going to say. He kissed her gently one last time. 'That shouldn't have happened. Now that you are one of us, it really can't happen again.' He fought so hard to stay strong, to do what was right, and all that did was make her admire him even more. He tucked her back under his arm and they stayed like that, watching the lights on the river in silence. So many unsaid words hung in the night air. Neither wanted to ruin this perfect moment or the few minutes they had left together.

Jaz didn't know what life was about to throw at her. The world was huge, and this job could possibly take her all over. Would she be good enough? As she rested her head against Ryan's shoulder she knew she would cope. She was determined to be brilliant and to stay alive. She had Pax in her corner and the best friends a girl could have. And she had Ryan watching her back. As scared as she was, she would face it head on, for she was the new recruit and there was no way she'd let Ryan down.

THE MISSION

From bestselling author Fiona Palmer comes the second in a young adult / new adult crossover series about sexy spies, a super secret agency and the work they do to save the world.

Recruited into the secretive, shrouded MTG Agency, Jaz dives head-first into her training, regretting nothing about her decision to help save the world at the age of 17. Now she's ready and anxious for her first mission — to prove she has what it takes... and to start making a difference.

The only thing that stands in her way is Ryan, the dangerous and sexy agent who first recruited her, and is now guiding her. He doesn't want Jaz to sink too deeply too quickly into his world of secrets and lies, but his inability to trust her to know her own mind only makes Jaz furious.

When a job comes along that only Jaz can do, Ryan has to let go, and Jaz soon learns that she can swim with sharks, but she'll come away with scars.

The Mission is the second in the MTG Agency series.

www.ingramcontent.com/pod-product-compliance
Lightning Source LLC
Chambersburg PA
CBHW030647110726
47901CB00002B/604